SILENT TIDE

A DCI BOYD THRILLER

ALEX SCARROW

GrrBooks

For Debbie Scarrow, whose wisdom, love and support keeps me sane

1

I t's funny how flesh in the moonlight looks like puff
pastry. Blood, of course, looks like ink. He stared at the
abattoir in the cockpit, watching the blood slosh around
as the sea gently played with the boat.

It was interesting – how much of it there was in the human
body. And, contained like it was in this small area, unable to
run-off or soak away into anything, there was so much of it. A
small dark pond.

He stared at his handiwork.

If the killing had been hard, the sawing had been *brutal*. His
arms ached from the labour. With a hacksaw, the job would
have been a whole lot easier.

But with just a kitchen knife to hand, it had taken all night.

THREE MONTHS LATER

2

Magpie didn't look like your typical migrant boat. They were usually beaten-up old small fishing boats or – far worse – unseaworthy inflatables. This was a yacht; although, to be fair, it *did* appear to be somewhat beaten up. It was wallowing low in the water and a sail trailed behind it, like a bride's wedding train. To Duncan's eye, it looked as if it had been drifting in the Channel for some time, gradually taking on water.

The vessel had been called in by a Danish tanker heading north-east up the Channel. The tanker crew had tried raising it on short-wave and got nothing. They said that they hadn't spotted anyone on the boat waving for help, so assumed it had been abandoned.

Still, it had taken *four hours* for the crew to finally call it in due to a shift change on the bridge.

Bloody idiots.

It had only taken the RNLI *Shannon*, scrambled out of Hastings, eighteen minutes to get there.

Duncan Cudmore was standing at the prow as his helmsman, Ryan, nudged them carefully forward through the last dozen yards of choppy water. The yacht's aft was higher than her bow, the foredeck only inches above sea level and spending almost as much time under it as above it.

It was a woeful sight.

He tried his loudhailer again. '*Magpie* – this is the RNLI *Shannon*. Is there anyone aboard? If so, please make yourselves known!'

There was no response. He raised a hand, and Ryan reverse-throttled the boat for a couple of seconds to slow their drifting approach. He was good with *Shannon*, handled her beautifully.

The last few feet between the vessels closed, and Duncan swung a leg over the rail and stepped cautiously onto the swamped foredeck of the yacht.

He had an uneasy feeling about this call-out. In the last year migrant-boat encounters had become more hazardous. The freezing, terrified wretches on board were prone to scramble en masse onto any intercepting vessel, sometimes even jumping into the Channel to get to them.

The cold shock of the water could be deadly. Far too often it was.

The boats they usually encountered tended to be overburdened rubber dinghies with outboards that had crapped out or run out of fuel. It was almost as if the traffickers *wanted* their clientele to die. He supposed dead clients couldn't ring back home and warn their loved ones not to make the same mistake.

Duncan was pretty sure no one was aboard. The yacht looked as though it had been drifting for days. Possibly weeks. He made his way carefully up the gentle incline towards the aft, listening out for any faint cries for help from within.

But it was quiet, save for the clanking of halyards and the lazy sea slapping the boat's raised backside.

'Anyone aboard?' he shouted.

No answer.

Good. That was good news. If anyone was on board they'd

surely be in an appalling condition. Whoever had been on this boat must have assumed the yacht was going to sink and had bailed. He suspected it had hit some debris floating in the Channel. It happened from time to time; there were enough container ships going up and down it that floating debris – slipped freight – was a thing to be mindful of.

The sea rocked the boat gently and the boom swung lazily away from Duncan, dragging the tattered sail with it. As the boom swung, the canvas pulled clear of the cockpit, revealing the contents.

The stench was overwhelming.

Duncan stared down into the sloshing mixture of blood and seawater below.

3

William Boyd – Boyd to his friends – simply wasn't used to seeing this much open sky in one helping. He was more used to glimpses, between facing rows of townhouses or city-centre blocks, tinged either a mean-spirited grey or a sickly light-polluted sodium orange.

This was horizon-to-horizon sky. All-you-can-eat.

The low clouds surged above him like angry grey whales across a Tupperware-white sky. The wind was stiff up here, cold, rattling his anorak against him.

He stood on the brow of East Hill looking down onto the old part of Hastings. So picturesque – all the obligatory clichés of a small fishing town: boats drawn up on the shingle beach, tall dark wooden net huts. And gulls.

Hundreds of the vicious little bastards.

Since moving down from London, gulls had become his nemesis. At least London pigeons, dirty scavengers though they were, didn't have the same arsey stare-you-down attitude that these buggers did.

These were chavs with wings.

Gulls aside, the view was pretty. It hit all the right notes. A picture-perfect rendition of a Sussex seaside town – well, this end of it anyway. The far end of Hastings, the 'modern bit', was less so.

Boyd sucked in a deep breath of the bracingly cold morning air, tasting sea salt instead of the usual car exhaust or the Tube stew of body odour and Lynx.

Today was his first day back at work.

After nearly two years spent hiding at home, watching the world outside struggle with Covid while he wrestled with his own personal battle, he was going back into an environment where he'd be referred to as 'guv'.

Two years of compassionate leave. The Met had been generous giving him the headspace and that amount of time to recover. And then, after all that, they'd granted his request to transfer to another force entirely.

His gaze was drawn by movement to his left, down on the small shingle cove directly beneath him. He could see a yacht tethered to a jetty and beside it a CSI van. Two people in their forensic bunny suits were attempting to assemble a protective canopy over the rear end of the boat.

CSI meant serious crime. The backdrop to his life may have changed but the work looked as though it would remain the same.

Murder – the gift that keeps on giving.

Boyd thought that would make a handy T-shirt slogan for all the boys and girls of CID. Maybe he'd print one up and put it into next year's Secret Santa gift pool.

He checked his watch. It was gone eight.

Time to get back to being a copper, Boyd. You ready for this?

'Am I fuck,' he muttered.

4

The police station on Bohemia Road was like many other stations he'd seen in his nineteen years on the force – a three-storey red-brick and tinted-glass sandwich with a forecourt packed with patrol cars, dog vans and arrest wagons.

The station, District HQ for Sussex Police, was at the west end of Hastings – the 'modern' bit – at the point where the town seamlessly and inexplicably became St Leonards. It was flanked by a Travelodge on one side and the magistrates' court on the other.

Boyd had decided to walk to work this morning, since there were some promising threads of blue in the sky and he wanted to get a feel for whether the daily commute was going to be walkable. He'd put on a stone and a half over the last twenty-four months – most of it around his middle. He was damned if it was going to take him twenty-four months to lose it.

He entered the station's reception and walked up to the Perspex-shielded front desk.

'DCI Boyd, starting here today.' He flashed his warrant card next to his face.

The desk sergeant looked up and frowned at the picture on the ID card. Boyd was clean-shaven in that, nearly a couple of stone lighter and about five years younger. The face beside the ID was framed with a scruffy dark beard and wilful dark brown hair that refused to stay down. The sergeant took an insultingly long time to reconcile the slim face in the photograph with the flabby stranger glaring down at him.

'Morning, sir,' he finally conceded.

He pressed the buzzer and a light went on above the security door next to the counter. Boyd stepped through.

'Ah, you must be Boyd!'

Detective Superintendent Iain Sutherland stood up behind his desk and waved him inside. His office was a small glass-walled cubicle at one end of the CID's open-plan floor. It reminded Boyd of the obligatory aquarium in a dentist's waiting room.

Boyd closed the door behind him, muting the office hubbub outside.

Sutherland was short and plump. He had narrow shoulders that were doing a damned fine job of keeping his perfectly round head from rolling off. He had a tuft of white hair on his chin and a toothbrush of white bristles across his upper lip: a goatee, sort of – but, honestly, blink and you'd miss it.

'I'm really sorry we can't give you a proper welcome aboard. Things just got very busy this morning.'

'The yacht?' said Boyd.

'Yes. You've seen it, then?'

'From the cliff top.'

'It was pulled in last night.'

Boyd reached for the back of the one visitor's seat, but

Sutherland came round the desk. He had to look up at his new DCI, the height difference much more apparent up close.

'This is not a sit-down meeting with coffee and biscuits, I'm afraid.'

'Oh.' Boyd had just been walking for fifty minutes. Sitting down, having a cuppa, would have actually been quite nice. Biscuits even better.

'My other DCI, Geoff Flack, is bogged down with an ongoing operation at the moment. So I'm afraid I'm going to have to dump this case straight on you.'

'What is it looking like?'

'It's looking very much like a murder,' said Sutherland.

Boyd felt a lurch in his gut. He knew he needed to be back and busy, for his own sanity, but heading up a murder inquiry as he – literally – walked through the door into his new posting was being gifted with too much too soon.

'You're aware I've been out of it for quite a while?' he said.

'Compassionate leave, yes.' Sutherland's perfectly round head wobbled up and down and threatened to roll off. 'I've read your HR file.' He paused to find something suitable to say. 'I really can't begin to imagine how horrendous it's been for you.'

Boyd nodded. How many times had he heard that bloody phrase or very similar? A year ago his therapist had told him over a Zoom session to write his own self-help essay on 'How to Deal with the Grieving' – to structure it like a list of do's and don'ts. She said he should print it out and pin it to his fridge, or even pin it to the top of his all-but-abandoned Facebook page. However, like every well-intentioned plan he'd put together, it had remained an unticked item on his to-do list.

'But,' continued Sutherland, 'this is probably the best way to get you stuck back into the job, don't you think?'

'A murder?' Boyd managed a look of incredulity mixed with sliver of sarcasm. 'I would have thought something less ambitious, maybe. To ease me in.'

'Nonsense.' Sutherland smiled and clapped him on the shoulder. 'I've read your record. You're a very capable detective, Boyd, and you've got a ton of experience. It'll all come back to you, I'm sure. It's like riding a bike.'

'Riding a bike?' Boyd sucked in a deep breath. 'Well, that's one way of looking at it, I suppose.'

Sutherland clapped his shoulder again. 'Come on, let's go and meet the kids.'

5

'All right – shut up, everyone. And sit down!'

Sutherland had a voice designed for the golden era of silent movies – it was pitched a touch higher than average with a burbly tone that sounded like a quick cough into a fist would clear it.

His voice filled the CID floor. 'Come on! Come on, people!'

The men and women of Hasting's CID pulled up chairs and perched on desk corners as Sutherland stepped to the side and gestured at Boyd, as though he was unveiling some new monument.

'This is our new DCI, William Boyd. Relocated down from London last week, if I'm not mistaken.'

Boyd nodded. 'I'm learning all about walking to work and the bloody steep hills of Hastings at the moment.'

'You'll be back in the car with cankles like the rest of us soon enough,' laughed the only female officer and BAME representative in the room. Boyd was used to more of a mix.

'Watch out for all the gull shit, boss,' said someone else. 'That stuff literally *rains* down from those bastards here.' There were murmurs of agreement. It seemed that Hastings had its own unique public order issues for the police to deal with.

'I'm sure you lot have heard the rumour that's linked to this yacht case.'

'Surely it's a Border Force case,' said one of the detectives. The floor filled with a collective moan and one or two pantomime boos.

'Yes, well, Chief Super has made the call that it's staying with us,' Sutherland said firmly, 'so some of you lucky boys and girls are going to be pulled onto this one.'

The room filled with another moan, and Sutherland flapped his hands like a supply teacher to quieten them. 'That's enough. The Chief Super has pronounced on the matter, so it is what it is.'

He turned to Boyd. 'DCI Boyd, you're SIO and I've already picked out a small team for you since, well... you don't know this lot of idiots from Adam.'

'Thanks,' said Boyd, looking at the officers before him.

'Don't worry. They're all good 'uns.'

Boyd nodded. 'Sure they are, sir.'

'Right. DS Minter, DC Warren, DC O'Neal and DC Okeke are this week's lucky winners on *Strictly Come Grafting*.'

The CID room erupted with a mixture of cheers and jeers, whistles and groans, as four of the eighteen strangers in front of Boyd got up. One of them was the 'token' officer. While the other three puffed wearily with resigned indifference, she was beaming with delight.

BOYD WAS GIVEN a temporary fish-bowl office opposite the Incident Room, as the larger room was being tidied after a previous case. The one-on-one interviews with his small team were punctuated by the sounds of doors creaking open and slamming shut as boxes of files, office stationery and the usual office crap were carried out and past his window.

Face-to-face interviews – they were a chance to weed out the gremlins before they got into the machinery of an investigation. He'd rather have a smaller team any day than a larger one with a potentially disruptive or toxic idiot in the mix. Through the interviews, he could probe his team for blind spots, chips on shoulders, personal grievances with another member of the team, or even inappropriate relationships that might bugger around with effective team communication.

His attention returned to the DC in front of him.

'How do I say your name? DC Samantha Oky... Okay...'

'Okeke,' she replied. 'Pronounced "car key". Like "Oh... my car keys".'

'Ah, great, thanks.'

'It's Nigerian,' she said.

He nodded thoughtfully, stroking the bristles on his chin. He'd have shaved this mess off his face if he could have worked out which cardboard box his electric razor was hiding in. Instead, with a week's scruffy growth on his cheeks and jaw, he looked like an overgrown and misshapen version of Rafe Spall.

'I had a colleague on the Met called Okafor – that's a Nigerian name too, right?'

'Igbo,' she replied. 'Same as me. That's the southern, non-Hausa part of Nigeria.'

'Okay, so I see here you're a fast-track placement. A degree in forensic sciences. That's helpful.' He smiled. 'Very useful to have a bit of science savvy on the team.' He wondered why, degree in hand, she'd decided to spend time in uniform. 'It says here you did a uniform year in the Kent police force before transferring here, where you did another two before joining the CID?'

'Yes, sir.'

'Why the transfer? Wasn't there a CID opportunity in Kent?'

She looked out of the window, irritated. 'Personality clash, basically.'

Boyd waited to see if there was any more. There wasn't. 'You don't want to talk about it?'

'I had three months of "Go get the tea, love". That was enough for me.'

'And you've been here six months?'

'Yes, sir.'

'How many serious crime inquiry teams have you served on?'

'None. I don't think I've actually stepped into the Incident Room yet.'

'Seriously? You've got a relevant bloody degree!'

'Yay, me,' she replied. 'Like that makes a difference.'

Her frustration was apparent, but the huge grin on DC Okeke's face when her name had been called out had told Boyd much of what he wanted to know about her. She was keen. She was obviously eager to prove herself, and clearly she was more than smart enough. Add to that – gender stereotyping aside – a little feminine intuition amid an all-male team could be invaluable.

'Well, good to have you on the team, Okeke,' he said. 'Enough of the small talk – you good to get going?'

DC Samantha Okeke cocked her head. '*Going?*'

'I want to go and get a look at the crime scene. I need your forensic eyes, if you think you're up to the job.'

She grinned. 'Excellent!'

6

They took a patrol car from the pool; DC Okeke drove. It started to rain as she pulled out of the forecourt.

Hastings this morning, absent of the weekend visitors, had the morose look of a ghost town. The half-arsed and meagre Christmas decorations, scattered throughout the retail end, should have been taken down weeks ago. The forced cheer of the pathetic, rain-soaked loops of lights, blinking pointlessly in the drab grey daylight, made the soulless west end look even worse.

Boyd turned to Okeke. 'So why are you in the CID room instead of the CSI room?'

Okeke took a moment to consider her reply. 'I can still apply the science knowledge while I'm out knocking heads together.'

He grinned. Good answer.

'Plus, as a detective, you get to see more sunlight than the technicians do.'

'True. But, still, you've got an untapped degree. Those things don't come for free.'

She signalled left at the roundabout and turned onto

Pelham Place. 'And I owe twenty grand in student loans. Truth was, I started uni doing medicine.'

'That's one hell of a course correction,' said Boyd.

'I wanted to work in A&E.' She sucked air through her teeth. 'But I don't know... solving crimes and walloping bad guys seemed far more interesting. So I switched.'

'Makes sense to me,' he said. 'There's something deeply satisfying about putting away some of the arseholes you come across.'

They were now heading along the coastal promenade. To his right, he could see a long apron of concrete parking; it was virtually empty now. Beyond that was the downward-sloping shingle beach, and the flat grey sea merged with the even flatter grey sky.

To their left, a procession of top-heavy, white-washed seaside apartment blocks seemed to compress the grubby-looking convenience stores and charity premises, accordion-like, beneath them. Ahead on the right he could see an old Ferris wheel and a flaky helter-skelter looming over a drab, tired-looking arcade.

He'd glimpsed the arcade on his walk down this morning. He pointed it out to Okeke. 'That area looks like a bit of fun.'

'Flamingo Arcade?' she said with a half-smile. 'You will never find a more a wretched nest of scum and villainy.'

'It's "hive".'

'What?'

'The Ben Kenobi quote,' said Boyd. '*You will never find a more a wretched hive of scum and villainy.*'

She looked at him blankly. 'Who's Ben Kenobi?'

'*Star Wars.*'

She shook her head. 'Sorry, sir. Never actually watched it.'

'Jesus...' His head dipped. 'I think a little piece of George Lucas just died.'

'George who?'

He rolled his eyes. 'Never mind.'

They passed a long row of scruffy souvenir shops selling a mixture of plastic beach tat, cheap printed T-shirts, ice creams and bargain no-brand booze.

'Have you explored the town much yet, guv?' she asked.

'Not really,' he replied. 'We only moved down last Wednesday and we've been unpacking ever since. It's never-bloody-ending.'

'How's your wife finding it?'

'It's just me and my daughter, Emma,' he said, a little awkwardly.

Okeke lifted her jaw. 'Ah, okay.' She was silent for a moment and then pointed ahead. 'So, that's the old town; one street back it's lovely. Very old and Harry Potter-like. It's all antique shops and cake shops and some very nice pubs.'

'Oh, good.' He nodded, appreciating the change of subject.

This was the end of Hastings he'd been admiring from the East Hill, the traditional fishing village bit – all quirky-shaped buildings with steeply pointed roofs jostling with each other for leg room along narrow streets.

As the road veered away from the beach and headed inland, Okeke turned right onto a single lane road flanked by tall fishing huts.

'Up ahead is Rock-a-Nore.'

'Rock-a-what?'

'Rock-a-Nore, sir. The little cove at the east end. That's where the yacht's secured.'

They passed a stone building that had once been a fisherman's chapel. It was now a fishermen's museum. That was followed by a small aquarium and yet another fish-and-chip shop. Hastings Old Town seemed to have a local economy that relied heavily on the sale of 'everything battered'.

The road ended with a height-restriction barrier that led to a small car park.

'That's the most expensive seaside parking place, guv,' said Okeke. 'If you drive into town, you should use the Pelham Parade car park.'

'I don't think I'll be driving into Hastings,' he replied. 'My house is just up that hill.'

She nodded and smiled. 'Oh, very nice.'

She drove the car into the car park and swung it round to the right. There was another patrol car directly ahead of them and a couple of very bored and very cold-looking PCs standing by an area cordoned off with perimeter tape. They were peering resentfully up at the spitting grey sky.

Beyond the coppers, Boyd could see the yacht secured to the side of the breakwater and beside it a small blue forensics tent.

Okeke parked next to the patrol car and they both climbed out.

Boyd flashed his warrant card at the policemen and they lifted the tape. Okeke and Boyd ducked underneath and headed down towards the yacht.

'DCI BOYD,' Boyd announced to the man waiting for them in the white paper forensics suit.

'Ah, you're our new DCI from the Met, aren't you?' He offered a gloved hand. 'Kevin Sully, today's lucky SOCO.'

Sully didn't look old enough to use the term. These days the fresh intake of eager forensic technicians tended to refer to themselves as CSI – quite probably the Sky Crime effect.

'Permission to board?' said Boyd with a hint of Long John Silver in his voice. With a Herculean effort, he managed to stifle the mandatory 'ah-harrrrrrr' that was on the tip of his tongue.

Sully shook his head. 'No Jim-me-bob-shiver-me-timbers-and-blistering-barnacles... etcetera, etcetera?'

Boyd grinned. 'Almost... but I thought that might be over-doing it.'

'Oh. Very disappointing.'

Boyd liked Sully already. CSI types, in his experience, tended to be a dour lot. Not that much fun at Christmas dos, or Friday drinks. Not that great at having fun at all actually, unless you could call pushing negatives or sample bags around on a light table having fun.

'Gloves and slippers please, folks,' instructed Sully, as he gestured to the tent. 'If you're well behaved, have some sea legs and not too clumsy, I'll let you forego the romper suit.'

Boyd turned to look at the yacht. A tarpaulin had been stretched over the boat's boom and tied down to the railings around the cockpit, creating what looked like a traditional boy scout's tent over it.

'The sodding boom's in the way,' said Sully, following his gaze. 'We couldn't get our forensic sheet up over the cockpit.' He nodded at his improvised solution. 'That works just as well, though.'

Boyd and Okeke donned rubber gloves and shoe mitts. Sully handed them a paper face mask each. 'You want some menthol rub on the outside?'

'Is it that bad?' asked Boyd.

'It's pretty ripe in there, to be fair.'

Boyd and Okeke nodded. Sully took back the masks, dipped his thumb into a tub of Vicks VapoRub and smeared a dab on the outside of each mask. 'Here. Get your glad rags on and I'll give you the fifty-pence tour.'

Sully stepped aboard first, offering a hand to Okeke. She raised a brow at him and hopped aboard effortlessly.

Sully shuffled along the side deck until he reached the draped tarpaulin. 'It's an interesting crime scene, this one,' he said, voice muffled slightly by the mask. 'We have a total of zero bodies but, on the positive side, oodles of blood and artful blood splatter patterns to analyse, and even one or two small chunks of meat bobbing around.'

He lifted the canvas flap, and blinding light flooded out from within. Boyd recoiled slightly and the boat rocked. He frantically grabbed for a halyard to stop himself toppling over the side.

'Oops, sorry,' said Sully. 'Should've warned you about that. We've got some serious stage lighting in here.'

He ducked down into the makeshift tent and gestured for them to follow.

Beneath the thick tarp, the light was dazzling. It was coming from a solitary 500-watt halogen bulb mounted in a protective cage on a low, robust tripod stand. The light reflected brightly off the white fibreglass of the cockpit. Boyd felt as though he'd emerged from a subterranean nightclub into a brilliantly sunny day.

The blood at the bottom of the cockpit, by contrast, glistened darkly as it rippled around like maple syrup.

Sully turned to Okeke. 'You walked through a murder scene before?'

She caught Boyd's eye and somehow managed not to eyeroll.

'Yes, actually, I have,' she replied politely.

He looked disappointed. 'Okay, then I can dispense with the caveats.'

Sully hunched over and shuffled, crab-like, along the bench seat to the rear of the cockpit, then round to the far side to give them a clear view of the floor. Boyd was too big and nowhere near as agile enough to follow suit, so he shuffled unceremoniously along on his bum, and Okeke crouched in beside him.

The three of them faced each other across the gently rippling pool of sepia liquid.

'We've had the helm and the collapsible wooden table removed for lab swabbing,' said Sully, pointing to a couple of bare fibreglass stands in the middle. 'That also means we can move around in here more easily.'

Boyd looked down at the blood. It was only a few inches deep and, as the boat gently rocked, the liquid sloshed its own tidal wave around, leaving shallows at the edges, where ragged shreds of flesh lay temporarily grounded.

'Is that human tissue?' asked Boyd.

'Yup.' Sully reached down with a gloved finger and scooped up a shred of flesh the size of a bottom lip. 'There was a lot of pretty amateurish hacking going on in here. Not somebody who was particularly good at the job, or had the right tools to hand.'

Boyd looked at the slither of wet tissue. It looked like a piece of muscle or tendon. 'I'm guessing this was a dismembering, to get rid of a body?'

'That or someone was prepping kebabs,' remarked Sully.

Okeke made a noise behind her mask. It took Boyd a moment to realise that she was chuckling. 'Well, there's another meal suggestion ruined for life.'

Sully let the piece of meat slide off his finger and splash back into the charnel pool.

'If I can draw your attention to these –' Sully pointed to the vertical sides of the cockpit – 'patterns of dried blood. We can see that the water in here was only about six inches deep.' He looked at them both. 'Rainwater, not seawater.'

'Does that tell us anything useful?' asked Boyd.

'Um...' Sully tapped his gloved fingertips together thoughtfully. 'It tells us it rained?'

'Hilarious. You should be on the stage,' said Boyd dryly. No doubt about it, he was going to like working with this SOCO.

'The spatter ovals have long tails,' he continued, 'which suggests high-impact velocity.'

'A fight?' offered Okeke.

Sully nodded. 'Swing-back momentum is a possibility,' he

said, miming an over-the-head striking action as best he could. 'You'd get that shape thrown from a knife blade if it's yanked out, raised quickly and then thrust down again repeatedly.'

'So maybe a fight out here, then,' said Boyd.

'Or it could be windborne?' suggested Okeke.

'Right.' Sully nodded again. 'We're outside, and we're at sea. If it had been gusty when whatever happened here took place, the wind could have been throwing the droplets around.'

Boyd could see thick circles drawn round most of the dried droplets, ID numbers written beside them. 'And this has all been photographed and logged now?'

'All done,' said Sully. 'Obviously, try not to rub against the sides if you can, but if anything gets smeared or scraped off, it's not the end of the world.'

Boyd took another look around the cockpit. 'What're the helm and table like?'

Sully's expression seemed to change beneath the mask. It could have been a grin or a grimace. 'A Jackson Pollock original.'

Okeke chuckled again. 'Nice.'

Sully gestured towards the hatch down into the yacht. 'You folks ready for down below?'

'There's more?' asked Boyd.

Sully smiled. 'Oh, yes.' He then shuffled along the bench and carefully stepped across to the lip of the hatchway. 'Mind you don't slip. One of my lot managed to do that. Took a bit of a dunking in the soup.'

Boyd followed him down the steps. At the bottom, he was pleasantly surprised to see he could stand up straight without bashing his head on the ceiling. The main cabin was also brilliantly illuminated by another 500-watt lamp squatting on the galley table.

'It really is a lovely sailing boat, this,' said Sully. 'I used to have an Esquire 32-footer. This puts it thoroughly to shame, though.'

The interior was what Boyd had been expecting from the sleek and modern design of the outside. Expensive. Beautifully finessed. To his right was a navigator's station with high-tech touch-screen panels: a marine radio, a depth sounder, weather radar, the works – all arranged above a mahogany map table like SpaceX Mission Control.

To the left, a galley with all the usual fittings. The cooking hob on a two-axis stabilising gimbal, a sink, an oven, a microwave, a preparation area with slide out add-ons – whoever had designed this had made ingenious use of the space.

The main cabin itself was dominated by a large C-shaped cream leather sofa, which surrounded a mahogany dining table, folded down on both sides to allow the CSI team space to move around.

'Nice, huh?' said Sully.

Okeke appeared beside Boyd. 'Whoa,' she said. 'So this is how rich people mess around on the water?'

The luxurious interior was somewhat let down by the lazy wave of seawater that was rolling from side to side across the lower deck. A scum line, a foot up from the boards, indicated that there'd been a lot more water down here earlier. Boyd looked questioningly at Sully.

'Yeah, we pumped most of it out. The water was almost up to the table level, and of course, because this thing has been bobbing around out there for some time, it's experienced some choppy periods where the water's been tossed around all over the shop.' He pointed at the navigation equipment. 'All that's water-damaged.'

'How long do you think it's been floating around out there?' asked Boyd.

Sully pulled a face. 'I dunno. Weeks. Maybe a month or two? It's hard to say.'

'Was the boat sinking?' asked Okeke.

'Very slowly. I think it would have gone under eventually. We caught it in time. There's a hole in the hull; you'll see that in the forward cabin. The seawater's been coming in slowly that way, plus whatever rainwater got in through the open hatch.'

'So what's the preservation like down here?' asked Okeke.

'Crap,' Sully replied. 'If you took a crime scene and put it in a washing machine and added several big buckets of pond water, you'd end up with what we've got. The cockpit, where the blood had a chance to dry out and leave permanent marks, has given us the most to play with. On the deck above too – we've got some trainer prints, thumb prints, hand prints in dried blood on the mast and sail. But down here –' he hunched over and scooped up a handful of scummy water mixed with tendrils of algae and other undefinable contaminants – 'all we've got is *goulash*.'

'And there goes another meal suggestion,' grunted Boyd.

Okeke snorted beneath her mask.

'Funny old thing,' said Sully. 'You never see CSIs invited to appear on *Come Dine with Me* or *Master Chef*. I suspect it's got something to do with the work.' He flung the muck off his fingers and back into the water. 'Pity really. I'm actually quite a good cook.'

'Looks like there's less blood in this water?' Boyd said, bringing Sully's attention back to the task at hand.

'Yup. It's been diluted by the sea. In terms of DNA, it's useless. There's some dead marine life, fecal matter from the toilet. A bit of everything really.'

Boyd nodded towards the end of the main cabin. 'How about in there?'

'The forecabin? Yeah, there's some decent forensics in there actually. Let me show you.'

'Does the water get any deeper?' Boyd asked, looking down at the waterproof slippers he was wearing over his shoes. He didn't fancy spending the rest of the day wearing socks and shoes that were soaked with this crap.

'You'll be fine. Come along, folks,' said Sully. 'Let me show you the en suite.'

He stepped past the folded table and the mast, which ran down through the floor into the keel below.

'Note the door and the hole in it,' said Sully, pointing at the door leading to the cabin. It had been battered with something that had left round indentations in the wood veneer. The area around the handle was splintered and shattered.

'Battering ram,' said Sully. 'I measured the diameter. It matches a standard marine fire extinguisher. We couldn't find one, so I presume that was flung over the side.'

'A murder weapon?' suggested Okeke.

'Quite possibly.' Sully opened the door, stepped inside and closed it again. He ducked down so that his face appeared through the ragged hole. 'Heeeere's Jonnieeeeee,' he sing-songed through the hole.

Boyd sighed. It certainly wasn't the first time a colleague had done that at a crime scene.

'So someone bashed the door in,' Sully continued, 'suggesting, obviously, that there was someone cowering in here, and well –' he opened the door – 'here is clearly where they died.'

He stepped to one side to reveal the A-shaped bed in the forecabin. The mattress and bedding were soaked and stained pink by the diluted blood. But, unmissable, was a large, oval, much darker stain that suggested a significant deposit of undiluted blood had had a chance to soak in, congeal and dry; it was now indelibly marked in the material.

Boyd followed him in. For the first time he had to duck slightly as the ceiling stepped down six inches.

'The boat was significantly lower in the water at the front

than at the back, which – and I'm no marine expert here – I suspect is because of that.' Sully pointed down and to the left. Where the floor planks met the moulded fibreglass of the hull slanting upwards, a ragged hole had been punched through.

'The yacht has an inner and outer hull. It's clear that someone used something like a claw hammer to smash a hole through them both. You can see the indentations where a round headed hammer was used. Then see those larger circles? They used the fire extinguisher again to try to widen the hole some more.'

'Somebody trying to scupper the boat,' said Boyd.

'To hide the crime scene,' added Okeke.

'Exactly,' said Sully.

The gentle rocking was beginning to get to Boyd; he felt queasy. The overpowering menthol taste of the Vicks rub wasn't helping much either. He tugged the mask down from his nose to get away from it.

'Uh, you probably don't want to –' started Sully.

Boyd inhaled.

Which turned out to be a bloody huge mistake.

7

As they drove back to the station, Boyd did his best to keep the conversation firmly on the subject – 'initial impressions of the crime scene' – rather than his stumbling, hurried exit from the boat and subsequent retching over the side. It hadn't been the most impressive first day for a veteran detective.

'I was thinking,' he said, 'it looks as though it started with an act of violence in the cockpit. The spatter patterns suggest a lot of motion at the time. Swinging arms, legs, so most likely some sort of struggle. But then, as you said, this is outdoors and at sea, so the wind could have been responsible for carrying the blood droplets some distance.'

Okeke nodded.

'And then,' continued Boyd, 'there's the smashed-in door below deck, the blood on the mattress in the forecabin.'

'Agreed. There's a lot of blood on that mattress, so the body was probably left there for some time,' Okeke added.

'Right. So what does all this suggest?'

'Could it be just two people involved?' she asked.

'A couple? Yes. I suppose. He finds out something from her

and in a rage attacks her in the cockpit. She escapes down below and he kills her in the cabin?'

'Lot of gender assumptions there, guv,' huffed Okeke.

'Well... yes,' he conceded. 'Sorry. It *is* possible it happened the other way round. It's just less likely.'

'What about the prints on the foredeck?' she asked. There'd been some trainer prints, barefoot prints, a whole palm print and a number of smears that didn't look as though they were going to yield anything usable.

'You thinking maybe there were other people on board?' he said, nodding. 'Possibly.'

'Or maybe that was the killer – pacing around afterwards?' she suggested. 'Wondering what the fuck he's going to do now?'

Okeke turned right off the promenade road, round the White Rock theatre and uphill towards Bohemia Road. Boyd was beginning to get his bearings now. This was the West Hill they were ascending. Hastings was, he thought, basically a town that nestled between two hills like a peanut lost down a cleavage.

'How are you feeling now, guv?'

'Like an idiot,' he replied. He turned to look at her. 'It was the rocking. Not the blood. I get seasick.'

She smiled and clacked her tongue.

'Really badly,' he added.

'If you say so, sir.'

'I do,' he huffed, hunching his shoulders and looking out of the passenger-side window again. 'I do say so.'

He could hear her chuckling beside him.

'Oh, yes... Ha ha, very bloody funny,' he muttered.

'Sorry, guv,' Okeke said, sounding more amused than apologetic.

~

BACK AT THE station Boyd swept into their recently acquired Incident Room to see how things were going with the other three members of the team.

DS Minter and two younger lads – DCs Warren and O'Neal – had set up the Big White Board and brought in some office chairs and some tables on which to set up their computers.

'Aaaand we're back!' said Boyd, throwing his coat onto the back of a chair.

He pushed the chair across the room to a table that had been placed beneath a window. He brushed the blind aside and savoured the spectacular view of the rear of the local Travelodge. On the windowsill was a skeletal spider plant in a pot of dried soil, and someone's dirty coffee mug, the contents of which seemed to be growing a furry blue skin that would have thrilled forensics. He grabbed the mug and the dead plant and dropped them into a bin.

'This'll be my desk, ladies and gents. The rest of you feel free to fight among yourselves.'

Somebody from IT had kindly placed a laptop on his table, even plugging it in. Boyd scanned the room; the furniture and basics were all there – they were about good to go.

'I want the meeting table in the middle,' said Boyd. 'Then individual tables as you want them.'

He checked his watch and saw that it was coming up to one o'clock.

'Right. Off you lot go and do what you do for lunch. Back here at two o'clock sharp for a team meeting and you can let me know what you found out this morning.'

He watched them gather jackets and coats and head for the door. Okeke lingered at the rear, holding the door open. 'Want me to pick you up something, sir?'

'What is there to have?'

'There's a half-decent canteen on the top floor, sir. But an even better option is the chippy down the hill at the pier. That's where we all normally go.'

Boyd patted his generous waist with both hands. 'I'll give the chips a miss for now. Might take a look at the canteen, though.'

She nodded and headed off after the others. He listened to their receding footsteps and the fading exchange of banter as the door swung shut, leaving him alone in the quiet of the Incident Room.

This is what you've needed, Bill. Only Julia called him that. *You spent nearly two years moping around at home. That's more than enough, love.*

She was right. He'd probably been ready to get back to this six months ago, maybe even a year ago. He just hadn't realised it.

'Quite right, love,' he said, picking up a pile of empty box folders and stacking them along the windowsill.

8

'Okay, everyone. Settle down, settle down. There's a bit of housekeeping to go through first, then we'll fill you in on our investigation this morning.'

Boyd gestured to the dark-haired officer who was taking a seat to his right at the central meeting table. 'DS Steven Minter will be my office manager and inquiry team leader.'

'Righto,' Minter replied, his Welsh accent slight but still unmistakable. Apparently he'd turned down playing rugby for Swansea and joined the police. By the look of him, Boyd reckoned he could still hold his own on the pitch with that solid physique.

Boyd smiled and turned his gaze to DC Eddie Warren. He looked, to Boyd, as though he'd just finished his GCSEs and was enjoying his first work experience with the grown-ups. He was in his late twenties and obviously competent enough to have become a detective, but he looked so incredibly young. Put him in a school blazer and a tie and he could easily go undercover in a sixth form common room. He was spindle-thin, had a mop of floppy wavy auburn hair and had begun an embarrassing experiment with what looked like a pitiful attempt to grow a handlebar moustache.

'Warren, you're my exhibits officer,' he said.

'Yes, sir.' Warren nodded enthusiastically.

Next, Boyd turned to DC Darren O'Neal, another young-looking officer. Boyd mentally shook his head as he glanced around at them; they looked young enough to be friends of Emma's. O'Neal was stocky and short and reminded him of the chirpy chappy who delivered the weather for Charlie and Naga on the morning news.

'O'Neal – you'll be disclosure liaison… if we get a suspect to charge. And, Okeke, as you may have guessed you're CSI and crime scene manager liaison. The usual rules apply: no gossiping with non-team members, no comments to press, all inquiry tasks go via Minter's action log but that doesn't mean to say don't use your initiative if you see something I've missed. What else…?'

Boyd hadn't made this speech in some time. It was funny how quickly a routine could fade from memory.

'Umm…' He was dimly aware his small audience were exchanging glances as he tried to remember what was missing.

Okeke stepped in to save his bacon. 'Guv, what about press liaison? Are you handling that? Or is that Sutherland?'

'Ah yes. Thanks, Okeke. To be advised…. I suppose it'll depend where this inquiry heads. If it's a straightforward murder, then it may just pick up some local press. If it's contro-versial in any way… then…' He shrugged. 'Sutherland or even Hatcher may end up with their faces on the evening news.'

'Sir, is it likely to be?' asked Minter.

'TV worthy?' Boyd shrugged again. 'Who knows? I suppose it's down to how slow the news is and whether they have anything more interesting to cover.'

'If it's a migrant attack, though, boss?' said O'Neal. 'That'll be –'

The phrase sounded ridiculous to Boyd. 'Migrant attack? What the hell's that?'

'When they swarm a rescue boat, sir, and take it over.'

'Has that ever happened?' Boyd looked at him. 'I'm sorry, is that a *thing* down here?'

O'Neal shrugged. 'It happens. You get gangs of migrants giving the locals trouble.'

Okeke shook her head and rolled her eyes. Boyd suspected the same divisions existed down here in East Sussex as they did in London – those who saw racism and those who didn't.

'The Channel's crawling with migrant boats,' added Warren. 'The yacht could easily have encountered one of them.'

'And what? Been attacked? Like Blackbeard's gang of hearty pirates?'

'Just saying – it happens, sir.'

Boyd managed to contain his dismay at that statement to an eye roll. 'What about the time of year. I thought migrant boats were a summertime thing?'

'It's all year now, sir.'

'If you read the *Sun*, it is,' muttered Okeke.

'Well, we're not going to jump to any assumptions yet, Warren,' said Boyd. 'We're at the gathering info stage. Speaking of which... Okeke, where are we with Sully and his merry men?'

'The forensics report is being put together. As he said, there's a lot of messy cross-contamination with the blood samples due to weather, the seawater, that kind of thing. So they're still at the boat, taking swabs at a number of different locations.'

'Did he give you an ETA?'

'Tomorrow,' she replied. 'Or the day after.'

'Anyone got anything on the boat?'

Minter cleared his throat. 'Yes, boss. The yacht has a berth in Sovereign Harbour Marina, Eastbourne.'

'And have we got an owner?'

'Not a *name*, sir, no. But we have a company.' Minter checked his notes. 'McGuire Mackintosh – they pay for the marina costs but I don't know yet whether the company actually owns the boat.'

'Okay, good. Someone check Companies House and let's get a name. The boat... what's it called again?'

'*Magpie*,' said Okeke.

'The *Magpie* may be just some corporate entertainment toy, or she could be some tax-dodger's asset-hiding wheeze.' Boyd checked his watch. It was three thirty. 'Who fancies a drive over to Eastbourne?'

The room was perfectly still.

'No one?'

'It's the traffic, boss,' replied Minter. 'At this time of day, the A27, you'll be smacking right into rush-hour traffic coming back from Brighton. It's a crappy single-lane road.'

Okeke raised her hand. 'I'll go.'

Boyd smiled. 'Thanks. Take someone with you. Take O'Neal. Okeke, you lead; O'Neal, you're along for support. See if you can get hold of a marina manager on the way there and tell them to make sure they stick around for you.'

Okeke nodded, as did O'Neal.

'Warren? Make a start on compiling recent misper cases for the area. Minter, if you could open up an action log, get a crime scene timeline from the CSM. Who's the crime scene manager here?'

'Leslie Poole, boss,' replied Minter.

'Right.' Boyd clapped his hands together. 'That's the first meeting done with. Back to your desks, people.'

They all started to rise, pushing their chairs back noisily, as Boyd had one last thought.

'Can someone get a coffee machine in here?'

They looked at each other.

'Well, I saw Flack's team had one of those Nespresso ones...' Boyd added.

'That's Flack's from home,' said Warren.

'Ah, right. A kettle and instant it is, then.' Boyd could just imagine Emma's face if he suggested relocating their machine to the station.

He stood up and grabbed his notepad, glancing at his hastily scribbled to-do list. Item number one was to check the Inquiry Team budget with DSI Sutherland. Each police force had its own in place, and even that varied from station to station when it came to financial considerations like overtime hours and material costs. He'd have to talk to Sutherland at some point about what sort of discretionary budget he'd get to play around with. Although that particular conversation was almost certainly going to be pushed uphill to the Chief Super or 'Her Madge' as they discreetly referred to her.

He'd asked Minter earlier: 'Why "Her Madge"?'

DS Minter explained. 'Her full name's Margaret Hatcher. She knows we use it behind her back. I think she actually likes that. But... it's best not to say it within earshot, boss. She'll rip your balls off.'

Boyd had smiled. The iron lady and wannabe queen. *Her Madge.* Obvious, really.

He had a couple of hours of paperwork – the usual investigation set-up box-ticking – left to do before he could call it a day.

But, administrative tedium aside, he had to admit that after two years of compassionate leave and a lot of long dark days it felt good to be busy again, to get his mind off Julia and Noah for a while.

9

Oh God, no. Oh God, no.

Boyd was staring at too much blood. Fatal amounts of it. Not just blood. Solid matter. She was right beside him unable to look back, unable to move, only able to stare up at his face and whisper over and over.

'Noah? Noah? Noah?'

'He's fine, love. He's fine. Just keep still.'

'Bill?'

'You're fine.'

Only she wasn't. She was far from fine. She was almost completely in half. Nothing at all salvageable here, just end-management pain control if the shock-trauma endorphins didn't last long enough to carry her off.

BOYD'S MIND was mercifully jerked away from that fucking awful memory by the persistent buzzing coming from his jacket pocket. He pulled out his phone and saw Emma's gap-toothed smile on the screen. A picture taken when she was still at primary school. It always made him smile.

'Hey, Ems.'

'Supper's nearly ready, Dad. Fifteen minutes or so. I can keep it warm if –'

'I'm on my way back,' he replied.

'Do you want me to come down and give you a lift?'

'No. The walk's good for me. Clears my head while I burn those calories.'

'Okay. How long do you reckon?'

It had taken him forty-five minutes this morning to walk to work. But then most of that journey had been downhill.

'Maybe an hour?'

'An hour! You sure you don't want a lift?'

He was emerging onto the promenade now – the pier directly ahead of him. He turned to look left and saw a long straight walk ahead, with the faint line of the East Hill on the horizon and the grey sea churning restlessly.

Stirring stuff.

Inspiring stuff.

It started to rain.

'Oh, sod it – yes please,' he said.

Five minutes later she pulled up beside him. He opened the door of the Captur and hopped in. 'Thanks, love.'

Emma waited for a gap in the evening traffic, then pulled back into the road. 'So? How was your first day back?'

'Busy. Very busy. There was a yacht brought in below East Hill. CSI team crawling all over it.'

'A murder?'

'Uh-huh. *Murder*.' He said 'murder' like 'moi-duh'. An old joke between them. They used to watch *NYPD Blue* repeats when she was younger.

Her eyes widened behind her glasses. 'Really? Day one?'

'Yup. And it's dropped straight into my in-tray.'

'What? I thought you said they'd give you a week or so to bed in?'

'Nope. Straight in.'

She fiddled with the wiper speed. The rain had suddenly got heavier, turning the windscreen into the rippled surface of a pond.

'I suppose they're like every other force, Ems, short-handed and under-budgeted. Just shitty timing, I suppose.'

She glanced his way. 'Or good timing?'

'No, definitely *bad* timing. I could have done with an easy first week.'

Emma pushed her glasses up her nose. 'So is there, like, a body on the boat?'

'No.'

'So how do you know it's a *moi-duh*?'

'Because I'm a DCI and – I dunno – *detecting* is what I do for a job.'

She flashed him a sarcastic smile. 'Oh, of course.'

'And the blood. That was a big clue. Lots of blood.'

She drove them along the front, past the seafront parking, a mini crazy golf course and an amusement arcade, then turned inland and up the side of East Hill. She turned right onto Ashburnham Road and parked outside their new – way too large for the pair of them – home.

The rain was pouring down and they huddled beneath the porch roof as he jiggled through his keys to find the one for the front door. He finally found it and let them both in.

The house was cold. The house was old and cold. And enormous. The estate agent had told them it had been used as a guest house 'back in the day', whenever that was. It was all very Victorian; the ceilings were ridiculously high with cobwebs and dead spiders above the coving. In the lounge they had a large, cracked, oval ceiling rose that either needed to come down or be patched up at some point. It had been very grand, once upon a time.

He rubbed his hands together. 'Dinner smells good. What is it?'

'Bolognaise.'

'Nice. Do you want a glass of red, Ems? ... Where you going?'

'Getting a jumper... and yes please,' she said as she disappeared from view up the stairs.

Boyd headed down the hallway towards the kitchen and dining room at the back of the house. Every room in this place echoed. It was all old-varnished floorboards, no carpets anywhere. They'd unboxed some of their belongings but, the fact was, this house was three or four times the size of the one they'd just moved from and it was going to be a while before they'd accumulate enough stuff to fill their new home and soften the acoustics. For now, every room sounded like an empty village hall as you entered it.

He made his way across the dimly lit dining room. The walls were dark aubergine, and the white picture rail and ceiling had been so discoloured over the years by pipe smoke they were now a horrible mustard colour.

There was a chandelier that sported six light sockets and only three dusty bulbs – another thing on a very long DIY to-do list he had in his head. Julia would have been on that the first day they'd moved in. She'd have loved this insanely large house with its high ceilings, grand chandeliers, tall windows, genuine wooden floors. It would have been the kind of project she'd have lapped up...

From the dining room, Boyd entered the tiniest room in the house: the windowless kitchen. It was about twelve feet by six. There was an ancient built-in gas cooker, a sink and drainer, and about enough counter space to play a game of Scrabble. There'd been room in the corner – thank God – for their fridge freezer, which stood like some large white sentry tower glowering at its inadequate new home.

He squatted down in front of the oven and peered through its grimy window. There was a crockpot sitting in there. He was about to open the oven door when Emma came in, shrugging on a thick cardigan. 'Dad! No fiddling!'

He raised his hands and stood up. 'Sorry, guv.'

'Go set the table and open some wine,' she said, shooing him away.

He did as he was told, leaving Emma to serve up while he pulled a bottle of red from the pantry cupboard in the corner of the dining room. Their Ikea dining table looked tiny in the large dim room; it had been far better suited to the terraced house it had spent the last ten years in, presiding over Emma's homework, Noah's Play-Doh creations and Julia's copy-editing – it had been the hub of their family life.

Baked into that oak-veneered MDF were a decade of memories. Happy ones. Although the table looked lost at sea in this room, he was damned if it was going to be demoted or, worse, skipped.

He poured them a glass of wine each and sat down as Emma came in, carrying two steaming plates.

'Hot,' she cautioned as she set it down in front of him. She placed hers on the table and sat down. 'God, it's dark in here.'

'I know.'

'Hold on.' She disappeared back into the tiny kitchen. He heard some rummaging around then: 'Aha!'

She returned with candles and a lighter. A few moments later, the dining room felt less like a mausoleum.

'Want to know about my day?' she asked.

Boyd smiled. 'Of course.' Poor Emma... She should be out with kids her own age, he thought, not for the first time. At university getting drunk and skipping early morning lectures –

not stuck here in this creaking old house babysitting her father.
'Did you go exploring?' he asked.

'Indeed, I did. There's a decent Indian takeaway down the
hill that might be worth trying. I walked along this totally cool
old street called George Street. It's like something out of
Charles Dickens; old, tilting-forward buildings, lovely-looking
pubs, antique shops. Did you walk down it to get to work?'

'I walked along the front,' he said. George Street must have
been the one that DC Okeke mentioned to him on their way to
look at the yacht.

'Oh, and I met the neighbours.'

'Yeah? What are they like?'

Their house was half of a much grander-looking property.
While their side had once been a B&B, sometime before that
someone must have owned the entire building – and 'mansion'
really would not have been too much of an overreach to
describe it. Looking at the grand houses on this side of
Ashburnham Road, he was hoping for a nice, quiet retired
couple. No teenagers slamming doors or pumping irritating
bass lines through the partitioning wall – just a pair of sweet,
quiet old dears.

'They're a lady and a parrot.'

'What?'

Emma chuckled. 'I crap you not. An old lady with a parrot,
or a parakeet, on her shoulder.'

'A real one?'

Emma raised a brow. 'Well, if it was a plastic one, I'd probably have called social services to come and have a look at her,
Dad. *Of course* it was real.' She shook her head and chuckled
some more. 'She's a character.'

'In what way?'

'You mean apart from having an exotic bird on her shoulder? Umm... just totally. I don't know – all ditsy gypsy-ish,
scarves, bangles, beads and... who was the Harry Potter teacher

with the googly-eyed glasses? The one played by Emma Thompson?'

He didn't remember the name, but now he had a good mental image. 'You're kidding me?'

'She's barking mad, Dad!' said Emma, smiling. 'In a good mad way.'

'How does *that* work?'

'She's eccentric. She said she does seances, tarot reading, crystal therapy...'

'Oh, for God's sake.'

Emma was grinning. He could see his daughter loved the woman already. 'You totally have to meet her. She's absolutely bat-shit crazy.'

'Great. Well, doesn't that sound something to look forward to,' he said.

'And Ozzie. Don't forget Ozzie's arriving tomorrow.'

He had a blank moment. The name was pinging something in his head... 'The rescue dog? Ah, yes.'

'You'd forgotten!' she said.

'No, it's just... there's lot of stuff being shoved into my poor brain at the moment.'

'The Spaniel Aid people are dropping him off about lunchtime. Do you want to come back in your lunch break to meet him?'

'I don't know. It might be busy tomorrow. I'll try,' he promised.

Getting a rescue dog had been entirely Emma's idea. She had researched it online and found a good charity that took the adoptive vetting seriously. She'd done all the paperwork, answered the questions, done the phone interview and the home visit. But, although she'd always wanted a dog, he suspected she'd done this with him in mind.

This was her – less than subtle – way of trying to rescue her dad from spiralling into a black hole of loneliness. A dog would depend on him, would need him to keep his head together. A dog would force him to spend time outdoors, getting at least some exercise every day. Perhaps he'd meet other dog walkers? Perhaps he'd meet someone else? In his daughter's mind he imagined it was the perfect solution. *Carpe Diem* therapy for Dad, and a cosy home for a lovely old boy called Ozzie.

Sorted.

10

'So how did it go in Eastbourne yesterday?'

DC Okeke's eyes were on her computer monitor. She was a million miles away, unaware that Boyd was standing beside her.

He waved his paper coffee cup in front of her screen. Her eyes flashed with irritation as she dragged them away from whatever she was looking at.

'*What?*' Then: 'Oh, sorry – didn't know it was you, guv.'

'That's all right,' he said, smiling. 'Glad to see you're getting stuck in. How'd it go in Eastbourne?'

'Fine,' she replied. 'And the traffic wasn't too bad after all.'

She tapped her mouse and saved whatever she was doing. 'I spoke to the day manager at the marina.'

'And?'

'*Magpie* checked out of the marina about three months ago.'

'Three months? Fits in with Sully's timeline...' he muttered to himself.

She nodded. 'The owner registered an intention to take a long weekend break across the Channel and completed a –' she flicked through a tray on her desk – 'a BF1331d form.'

'What the hell's one of those?'

'You have to get one rubber-stamped if you're intending to sail outside UK waters into European waters. It's a new Border Force thing.'

'So, what then?'

'The marina holds a copy on file. The boat owner takes the original with them, which they're meant to show to EU officials when they arrive wherever they're going. More lovely bureaucracy.'

She handed him a photocopy. 'All part of our brilliant New Normal,' she said, her voice heavy with sarcasm.

Boyd bit his tongue. In his experience, politics – particularly of the Brexit variety – was best kept away from work, having the tendency to escalate into a full-blown argument in the blink of an eye.

He frowned as he tried to decipher the spidery handwriting on the form. 'So who's M. E. Heff? Huff? Hoff?' The handwriting was scrawled so badly it was barely legible. 'Is he the boat's registered owner?'

'Not necessarily,' she replied. 'The monthly fee to berth at the marina is paid by a company called Maguire Mackintosh. It could be a company director's yacht.'

'How long's the boat been kept there?'

'Seven months, I think.' She checked her notepad. 'Yeah. Seven months.'

'And who's this Huff-Heff...? Any ideas?' He looked around. 'Anyone?' He turned to Minter. 'Who's checking Companies House?'

'O'Neal?' Minter shouted across the room.

'Huh?' O'Neal looked up from his computer screen and pulled his earphones out.

Minter sighed. 'No fucking headphones! Companies House. You on that? You got details yet?'

'Oh, crap,' was O'Neal's answer, his face pinking. 'Sorry.'

'You *forgot?*'

'No, no... I didn't. I tried yesterday, but their server was down all afternoon. So –'

'Try it again, then.' Minter looked back at Boyd. 'Sorry, boss.'

Boyd turned to Okeke. 'Did the duty manager know this M. E. Heff?'

She shook her head. 'No. She said she didn't recall dealing with that specific owner.'

'Well, did you ask if it's an odd thing now? You know, people taking their boats out for short hops to Europe?'

'Of course. She said it still goes on, maybe less so because of the additional paperwork hassle, but she didn't *specifically* recall the *Magpie* checking out.'

'Can boats *sneak* out?'

'I also asked that, guv.'

'Good. And?'

'No. They have a camera and sensor at the marina exit. Boats going out or coming in – trigger the sensor and the duty manager has to log the boat's name.'

'What about at night?'

'Same thing. Night duty manager logs it.'

'Okay. So, in theory, any boat leaving, whether for five minutes or five months is in their records?'

'Yes.'

He stared back at the photocopied form. 'Have the names on this form been checked?'

Okeke shook her head. 'The manager said that many of the boats are hired or lent to mates. So – although they should verify the name of every passenger – often they don't.'

'World-beating high-tech border security, eh?' Boyd muttered to himself.

She pulled a face. 'Quite.'

He studied the scribbled names. M. E. Heff or Huff-something, Z. Kov-something, G. E. Kov-something. The hand-writing was shite to read, but at least they had a number of passengers now.

'It looks as though there were three people on board,' said Boyd. Then he stared at the scrawled dates. 'So three folks... going for a trip for up to seven days, left on November the twenty-seventh...'

'And never checked back in,' Okeke added.

'The manager was certain of that? They didn't come in and leave again?'

'No, guv. She said it was *unlikely but possible*. I mean... if she'd been on the loo, or dealing with something else, a boat could have wandered in and out. She said there had been the odd occasion when the sensor hasn't triggered, but it's very unusual.'

'Great.' He sighed. 'And when the boat didn't come back seven days later, the marina manager didn't think to flag that up with anyone?'

Okeke shook her head. 'They have the form on file. When the boat returns, they dig the same form out of the filing cabinet and sign it back in.'

Boyd sighed again. British bureaucracy at its best: the forms were simply face-saving bureaucracy. A paper mountain created simply to spare some politician's blushes.

He looked again at the scribbled names. Were they even real? At least there were some parts of the form that were legible. He pointed to one of the boxes. 'Scheduled departure – eleven thirty... Is this form a thing you fill in *just before* departure?' he asked, not really expecting an answer.

'I don't know, guv,' Okeke replied. 'I would think it's something you'd have to do the same day.'

'You said there's a camera at the marina exit. They should have CCTV cameras all around too then. You'd think so, wouldn't you? Can you check for me?'

'On it, guv,' she said, turning back to her computer.

LATER THAT MORNING Boyd had the press briefing to deal with. He'd done about half a dozen in his career so far, and each time he'd got a little better. The objective, really, was to say as little as possible, in the dullest manner possible and then, when the questions came at the end, to answer as few of them, with as little information as you could sensibly get away with. He wondered why journalists even bothered turning up for these things.

This one had pulled in a modest audience of a dozen or so local journalists. So the story had attracted a fair bit of interest, he noted.

He surveyed the room, looked down at his notes and began.

'On Sunday the sixth of February, at two in the afternoon, a Danish merchant ship sighted the yacht *Magpie* drifting in the English Channel. It was formally reported some four hours later and the local RNLI launch team was alerted. They located and boarded the yacht to find no sign of any passengers and significant impact damage to the hull, which was causing the boat to slowly sink.

'There were forensic indicators on the boat suggesting foul play, which is why the CID has been involved and an inquiry team has been put together. At this stage we do not have any confirmed names of those who might have been aboard. But we do know the boat was berthed at a marina in Eastbourne.

'We are asking the general public – particularly those living along the south coast of England – if they have concerns about missing family members, if they own a yacht, or know someone who owns one by that name, to call the inquiry line number.' He looked up from his notes. 'I'll take one or two questions now.'

The conference room seated fifty, the chairs arranged in rows of eight to ten. Only the first two rows were occupied, and a solitary BBC cameraman stood at the back. With the spotlights from the spar above shining down on him, it reminded Boyd of a really shitty open-mic night.

A few hands went up. Boyd picked one on the front row.

'There are rumours that this boat encountered a distressed migrant dinghy and was swarmed by them. Can you comment on that?'

Boyd sighed. Not this again.

'Rumours? Really? From where?' he shot back. Rumours were the bane of his bloody life. The journalist might as well have said: 'In my opinion...' or 'I read on Facebook that...'

The young journalist's face blotched a rosy pink. He'd obviously not been expecting to have to back it up. 'Various sources,' he muttered.

Boyd shook his head and tutted. 'No. There's no evidence at all that something like that occurred.' He looked around for another raised hand.

'Yes?'

'There's –'

Don't say 'rumours'.

'– *word* that the boat may have been drifting for quite some time? Can you say how long?'

'Well, we're not talking the *Mary Celeste* here,' Boyd deadpanned to the silent room, 'but... we have an indication that it departed from Eastbourne last November. Whether it has been drifting or berthed somewhere for that time, we don't yet know.'

He took another question.

'You suggested foul play. Do you mean murder?'

'We don't have enough information to comment on that at this time.'

Pinky Face in the front row had raised his hand again. Boyd

decided to be magnanimous and give him the opportunity to look less like a prat.

'Do you believe the boat may have been used in trafficking? Migrants? Drugs?'

'It's not something we've ruled out, but at this stage it's certainly not our leading theory.'

'What is then?' he asked, before Boyd could move on. 'What *is* your leading theory?'

Boyd mentally eye-rolled. He couldn't believe he'd used that word. *Theories* tended to have a habit of circling around and biting you in the arse. He gave Pinky Face a forced smile. 'When we have more information, we'll update you.'

Moving on, he pointed at a raised hand at the back. 'Yup?'

'There are reports of lots of blood on the boat. Can you confirm that?'

For fuck's sake. With great effort, Boyd kept his poker face on. 'At this stage I'm not going to comment on any forensics until we have the scene-of-crime report. Thank you.'

'The term *bloodbath* was used,' called a voice from the back.

This shitshow was really beginning to piss him off now.

Some arse on the team had obviously been talking to someone. Minter and Okeke seemed smart enough not to gossip. But the two younger lads? He would definitely be keeping an eye on them.

'*Bloodbath?*' Pinky Face was quick to latch on to that. 'Is that phrase in the forensics report?'

'No!' snapped Boyd, grabbing his statement and turning to go, 'but it's the kind of language I'd expect from a tabloid hack or some twat on Twitter.'

The room fell completely silent.

DSI Sutherland, with his cheery Penfold face smiling full-beam, stepped hastily forward to wrap up the press briefing with the standard 'That's all, folks. Nothing to see here!'

Five minutes later they were back in Sutherland's glass-walled office.

'Interesting choice of word there, Boyd.'

Boyd grimaced apologetically. 'I meant *twit*. I actually meant to say *twit*. It got tangled with *Twitter* and... honestly... anyway, I'm sorry, sir.'

Sutherland nodded. 'That's okay. Just be mindful that the journos can be utter arseholes and write whatever rubbish they want... but let's not give them something like that that they can actually quote, eh?'

'Yup. It's been a while since I've done one of those.'

'Sworn at a press briefing?' Sutherland grinned. 'I'm pretty sure the Beeb will bleep it.' The DSI steepled his fingers together on the ink blotter in front of him. 'But best to remember to mind the language in front of the children in future, eh?'

11

Boyd was greeted with a ripple of applause from his team when he stepped back into the Incident Room.

'All right, all right,' he said, raising a hand to shut them up. 'Twit, twat. It's just one bloody letter. Could have happened to anyone.'

They eventually quietened down and got back to work. Boyd realised he'd just banked a few brownie points with his little team. He doubted there was a cop in the country who wouldn't *love* to hurl a deliciously vulgar expletive at a room of gutter-press hacks.

Minter came over to Boyd with a folder tucked tightly between his pecs and a bulging bicep. 'Hey, guv – we've got an update on the corporate owner of the yacht.'

He put the folder on Boyd's desk. 'The company is, as we know, Maguire Mackintosh. They own the yacht and pay its marina bills. Their address is registered in Guernsey as –'

'Oh, well, there you go – a letterbox company.'

'Sir?'

'Letterbox as in "PO Box". No actual company premises –

just a shared address with their PO box number on a cubby-hole. It's a shell company.'

'Oh, right, yeah.'

'Do we have a director name?'

'Only one.' Minter opened the folder and screwed up his face as he tried to pronounce the name.

'Let's have a look.' Boyd spun the folder round.

Director : Xin Gi

He didn't attempt to try and say it out loud either. 'Chinese, it looks like.'

'You reckon it's dodgy money?' asked Minter.

'Who knows? The UK's a magnet for it these days.' It was no big secret that England was the easiest place in the world to register a business under a false name. 'Let's put that name into LEDs and see if anything pings up. We might get lucky with a misper.'

'Righto, sir.' Minter picked the folder up and turned away. 'O'Neal? Got some more arse-ferreting for you.'

Arse-ferreting? Boyd shook his head and snorted. He wondered where the hell that term came from. Another Welsh thing? Or was it a local one?

BOHEMIA ROAD LED DOWN to White Rock Road and a seaside theatre that overlooked the shingle beach and Hastings Pier. Boyd took advantage of a brief window in the miserable February weather to walk down to the pier to see if he could clear his head and grab some chips for lunch.

He was disappointed with how little there was on the pier itself. He'd expected wonky rides that flaunted safety regulations, candyfloss, hotdog stands, penny arcades and rows of deckchairs with leathery-looking pensioners on them. There was sod all of that – just a wide minimalist platform that ran out several hundred yards and a few desultory huts perched along the side, with something that looked like a large grey Lego brick two thirds of the way along.

As he got closer, thunking his heavy-footed way along the decking, he could see the Lego brick was actually a pub. The roof had tables and chairs on it – a rooftop beer garden surrounded by a tall glass windbreak.

It was all very modern-looking.

The pub was called the Bier Garden. Bier – as in Pier. Very clever. He walked around it, mildly tempted to wander in and give it a try. But the smell of frying chips and fish in batter that was wafting from the café near the pier's entrance proved too much of an enticement. He doubled back, picking up his pace, and entered the café.

It was busy. A queue snaked along the counter, almost to the door. Boyd spotted several uniforms in the line and recognised a few faces from the CID pool.

It took him the entire length of the queue to decide what he was going to have and at the very last moment he settled for play-it-safe cod 'n' chips.

He emerged from the café with a warm polystyrene box and a paper coffee cup, both burning his hands as he headed over to one of the wooden picnic tables on the pier.

'All right, guv?' It was DC Okeke. She was sitting on her own with an identical meal. 'You want a seat?'

'Oh, hello.' He smiled. He'd have preferred his own table and some thinking space but couldn't think of a polite way to avoid the inevitable. She was already clearing away the paper wrapping and ketchup sachets to make space for him at the table. It would, he supposed, be a good opportunity to learn some more about his team.

'Sure. Okay. Thanks.' He sat down and relieved his burning hands. 'Chips good here?'

'Chips are chips. It's the fish you got to judge it on,' she informed him.

He nodded towards the east end of Hastings where the fisherman's huts and boats were all crammed together. 'Which I imagine is fresh?'

'Very likely caught this morning.'

He tried ripping the corner of his ketchup sachet, but it required a little help with his teeth. He managed to get the corner off and pipe the ketchup out across his chips in zigzag lines.

'Oh, I see you're a *spreader*, not a *dipper*.'

Boyd looked at Okeke's meal; the sauce was pooled tidily in one corner.

'It's a habit from my patrol car days,' he replied. 'It's hard to pursue and dip chips at the same time.'

She laughed at that, though she wasn't entirely sure whether he was joking. Then her serious work face returned. 'Oh, guv... the marina manager called me and said their CCTV archive goes back six months. She's going to look up the footage from the twenty-seventh of November and drop it on our Lockbox server.'

'Excellent. Hopefully we'll get something usable from that.'

He dug his plastic fork into the bloody crime scene of ketchup-spattered chips.

'So how are you finding it, guv? Out here in the primitive wilderness of Sussex?' asked Okeke.

'Boyd,' he replied. 'Off the clock you can ditch "guv" and call me Boyd.'

'Right. In that case, off the clock... it's Sam.'

He nodded. 'Hastings? I like it,' he said. 'Loads of character.' He gestured at East Hill and the fishing huts. 'That end anyway.'

She nodded. 'It's a town of two halves.' She speared a chip and dunked it. 'Not too parochial for you?'

He laughed softly. 'Nope. It's nice – the boats, the huts, the seagulls, the sea. I spent a few summers here actually, when I was a little boy.' He looked around. 'I thought I remembered it pretty well, but I suppose I have a kid's memory of it all. Including the pier apparently. I seem to remember it looking like something out of Willy Wonka.'

'It burned down – that's why it looks different,' she replied. 'Big fire back in the noughties. They completely rebuilt it.'

'Ahhh. Okay. That explains it. He paused. 'I gave Brighton some thought when relocating, but the property prices are almost London-like. Here, though...' He shook his head. 'I can't believe how much you can get for your money.'

'That'll change,' she said. 'The DFLs will drive the local prices up, I bet.'

'DFL?'

'Down From London.'

He smiled apologetically. 'Sorry about that. Do you own, or do you rent?'

'I rent,' she replied.

'Ah, I'm *really* sorry, then.'

She smiled. 'Not your fault – just market forces, isn't it? You'd be dumb not to cash out before London prices start to tank.'

He stabbed a large chip and blew on it to cool it down. 'It wasn't all about the money, to be honest.'

'Fed up with city life?' she asked.

'I needed a new start,' he said. 'A reset button.'

She frowned, curious. 'Oh?'

'Didn't Sutherland mention it?'

She shook her head. 'No. What?'

'I've been on compassionate leave for a while. I lost my wife and my son not so long ago. Actually –' he paused – 'it's been over two years... Christ, time flies.'

'Oh, I'm sorry. That's...' Okeke suddenly looked awkward.

'So you moved out to Hastings.'

'With Emma, my daughter. That was basically a part of our recovery. A big part, truth be told. I think the distraction of moving and starting again has been good for us.'

She nodded. 'Your new start.'

'Precisely.'

'How old is your daughter?'

'Twenty-one,' he replied. 'Nope. Correction, twenty-two. She's been stalling university for the last two years to look after her old man.'

'You don't *look* like an old man.'

'Six days of growth and a full head of hair hide a multitude of sins,' he said, smiling. 'I'm staring down the barrel of fifty. Well, I will be in a few years.'

'Oh... okay,' she chuckled.

'What's so funny?' he asked.

'I thought you were older than that.' She chuckled again. 'One of those blokes who's managed to age well.'

Boyd wasn't entirely sure how to take that. 'Now what am I meant to say? *Thanks* or *screw you*?'

She laughed. 'Put my foot in it, I think.'

'Right.' He popped the now-cool chip into his mouth. 'None bloody taken, by the way.' He speared another. 'Julia – that's my wife – always said she was in for the long game. That although I was an ugly sprog of a young man, she was banking on me ageing well.'

Okeke smiled. 'Like cheese.'

'I was going to say wine actually –'

'Shit! Guv! Watch out!' Okeke ducked down.

For Boyd it was a white blur. One second of terrifying chaos.

A hit-and-run and his battered fish was gone. The whole bloody thing.

'Fuck's sake!' He watched the seagull swoop up into the sky with his lunch. 'Thieving bastard!' he called out after it.

'They do that here,' said Okeke, trying not to laugh. 'Little thugs. Sorry, I should have warned you about that.'

12

On their return, Okeke had a call from the Sovereign Harbour Marina – the video files from two different CCTV cameras for 27 November were now uploaded onto their secure public server and ready to view.

All forty-eight hours of it.

'I guess that's you sorted for the next few shifts,' said Boyd.

DC Okeke rolled her eyes at him and turned towards her desk. 'Lucky me.'

'Don't forget to log what you're doing with Minter,' he said.

She pivoted and changed course.

Boyd had learned from bitter experience to keep the action log up to date. Policing, particularly in the Met, had become very political in recent years. The further up the ranks you got, the more of your time was invested in arse-covering. It paid to have a constantly up-to-date record of actions, just in case a senior officer came looking for a scapegoat or something went wrong. If a suspect escaped arrest, or a piece of evidence became compromised, and the general public or the IPCC came looking for a scalp – as SIO you most definitely needed that logbook explaining the whys and wherefores behind the decisions you'd made.

Boyd had just sat down with his coffee – frothy, milky and sugary as he preferred it in the afternoon – when a broad shadow spilled across his desk.

He looked up to see Minter looming over him like a budget Ant Middleton. His dark hair was soaking wet and there were wet patches across his shirt.

'You all right, Minter?' he asked.

'Huh?'

'You're all wet. Is it raining again?'

Minter shook his head. 'Just got back from the gym and shower, boss.'

Boyd nodded. 'Right. Makes sense. Nothing like punishing your body during lunch break to unwind, eh?'

Minter raised a brow at Boyd's first trimester food baby. 'Wouldn't do you any harm, sir.'

'Cheeky bastard.' He pulled his chair forward slightly to hide the pouch. 'So what're you loitering over me for. Got some news?'

'I've got a list of the misper cases from the last three months.'

'Regional or national?'

'National. Just over twenty thousand of them.'

Boyd took a slug of his cappuccino. 'You can farm that out to...'

'Okeke?'

'She's already busy,' he replied. 'Try O'Neal.'

'He's already busy too, boss.'

'Then Warren.'

'I sent him boat-knocking around the marina, boss.'

'Ah, good call. Well, when O'Neal's free again and Warren gets back, put the two lads on it. Get them to go through the whole list. Given it's a corporate boat, I'm going to presume these aren't young adults or kids. Get them to screen out anyone younger than twenty-five and older than –' he pulled in a sharp breath – 'let's say seventy. That should trim it down a bit.'

'Righto. Will do,' Minter replied, and headed back to his desk.

Boyd checked his watch. It was five past two. There were three hours of his working day left. He decided to chase up Sully and his forensics team for that crime scene report. It should have been on his desk by now.

'Ah! DCI Boyd... I was just about to email you my SOC report.'

'Sully?' Boyd did a double take as he addressed the man in front of him.

'Yes, of course.'

'Sorry, I didn't recognise you out of the forensics suit and mask.'

Sully was skinny to the point of looking unhealthy to Boyd. He had an Adam's apple that bobbed like a fishing-line float, and frizzy almost albino-blonde hair on his head, so fine it was almost a mist.

'Have you got a hard copy for me?' asked Boyd.

'We try and be as paper-free as we can here, sir. It's all about the environment. I'll email it to you. Think of the children.'

Boyd couldn't tell if Sully was being sarcastic or not. His Jack Dee-style dry delivery so far had been difficult to decipher. 'I'd like a hard copy if that's okay. I'm a big fan of making margin notes.'

Sully huffed. 'On my stationery budget, I suppose?'

'Exactly.'

Sully sighed. 'Right.'

'You got any exciting bulletin points to flag up for me in the meantime?' asked Boyd.

'There were three distinct DNAs in the dried blood,' Sully said, 'and a mish-mash of contaminated DNA. I gave up trying on the wet samples; the seawater had turned them into stew.'

'Nice. Well, that ties up with our investigation so far.'

'The splatter markings in the cockpit are more likely wind-borne than arterial,' Sully confirmed.

'Why do you think that?' Boyd asked.

'They have a uniform spread direction,' Sully replied.

'So the blood...'

'Was most likely post-mortem.'

Boyd nodded. They both knew what that meant. It hadn't been a fight then, but –

'Dismemberment,' said Sully matter-of-factly. 'That's what was going on in the cockpit, Boyd. The cutting up of bodies.'

'Right. Thanks for that. Anything else that I should jump straight to in the report?'

'There were finger, palm, feet and shoe prints on the fore-deck. Quite a lot of those,' Sully said.

'Indicating *more* than three people?'

'Hard to say, *at least* three distinct individuals. There could have been more. But certainly no less.'

'So what's the story you're getting from this?' Boyd asked.

'That's your job, Boyd, not mine,' Sully replied, waggling his finger.

'Off the record...' Boyd smiled. 'For fun. I'm not going to hold you to it.'

Sully tapped his lips. 'There were at least three people on board. A murder down below. Maybe two. Followed by lots of cutting up in the cockpit area. On the foredeck there are a lot of bloody trainer prints from what looks like the same person. But there are also other shoe prints, which... were probably made later. There are scuff marks on the side of the boat, the hull, the gunwhales – could've been caused by another boat bumping against it.'

'A lifeboat?'

'Possibly. A collapsible or inflatable one.'

'And the hole in the hull – you're certain that was definitely done with intent?'

'Ah... yes. There are claw hammer dents in the fibreglass on the inside. It was definitely created from within. The fibres splay outwards not inwards.'

'So somebody had a good go at trying to sink it then,' muttered Boyd.

Sully nodded. 'Makes sense. Way easier than trying to clean up the crime scene. Just sink the whole bloody thing out at sea. Only, of course, the thing *didn't* go down.'

'Murphy's law. Bloody boats – you *want* them to sink and they *don't*. You *don't* want them to sink and they do a *Titanic* on you.'

'Right. I'm not really a big fan of sailing,' said Sully. 'All that drowning.'

'It's safer than flying, I believe,' Boyd pointed out.

'My parents kept nagging me to go on a cruise with them before the Covid outbreak,' said Sully.

'Floating plague ships not your thing?' Boyd could think of a hundred ways he'd rather spend his holidays. With or without parents.

'I saw *The Poseidon Adventure* when I was young. The thought of being stuck in a windowless cabin at the very bottom of a sinking ship...' Sully actually shivered. 'Anyway, cruise ships... You're right, Boyd – they're giant germ factories.'

'So, what with all the lockdowns, they must have given up nagging you to go along with them, eh?'

'Well, yes.' Sully's face suddenly went blank. 'They're dead.'

Boyd let his mouth drop open slightly, hoping it would come up with the right thing to say. He'd been on the receiving end of awkward platitudes for the last two and half years – everyone trying to avoid the obvious clichés but creating new ones instead. 'Sorry to hear that...'

Sully's long and silent expression gave way to a smirk. He winked. 'Just messing with you, Boyd.'

Boyd frowned and shook his head. 'Right. Hilarious. You're very funny, Sully.'

Sully grinned. 'I know. I'm totally wasted here.'

13

An hour later, Boyd was busy making notes and underlining pertinent sections of the SOC report when DC Okeke called out to him from her desk.

'What is it?' Frankly he was relieved to set the bloody thing down for a moment and rest his eyes. Sully's writing style was so dry he felt like he needed to bathe his eyes in Optrex. 'What have you got?'

She waved him over. 'CCTV from inside the marina shop, guv. From the same time that departure form was rubber-stamped.'

Boyd went to her desk and squatted down beside her. Okeke reached into a box of mini doughnuts on the desk, grabbed one and took a bite. 'Let me just dial this back a few minutes.'

The image on the screen flickered as it rewound, then she let it play again.

'Oh, sorry, sir, want one?'

'Please don't force me,' he said. 'I'm trying to be good but my willpower's not great.'

'Well, I'm not going to put a gun to your head.' She laughed and gestured towards the box. 'Help yourself if you want.'

He sighed, reached in and grabbed one topped with chocolate sprinkles.

Unsurprisingly, the image quality of the CCTV footage was shockingly poor. They had three picture-in-picture angles to look at: a view from behind the shop's counter that covered most of the store, its window and entrance; one view of the alcohol section; and one of the frozen-food aisle.

'So here we are,' she said. She pointed at the entrance. The motion was the usual stop-start, one-frame-every-half-a-second kind. A pair of feet appeared in the frame. The glass door opened, and a woman in jeans, an anorak and a baseball cap came into view.

'A woman,' he said softly.

'Well done, guv,' said Okeke, grinning.

The woman made her way straight towards the counter and appeared to be talking to the marina manager for a short while. She pulled out a folded sheet of paper from her anorak and pushed it across the counter. The manager looked it over, then disappeared from view with it.

'That, I presume, is this Border Force departure form?' said Boyd. 'I guess she's making a copy of it.'

The woman leant forward, elbows on the glass counter. Not looking up. Not looking around. Keeping the peak of her baseball cap low.

'You notice that?' he said.

'Keeping her face down?'

'Uh-huh. I think that comes under "suspicious behaviour".'

The woman glanced quickly over her shoulder towards the entrance.

'She looks nervous to me,' said Okeke.

Definitely. He found himself agreeing. *But why?*

The manager returned with the piece of paper and handed

it back. The woman took it and tucked it away but lingered at the counter.

'Are they talking?' asked Okeke.

Boyd narrowed his eyes, as if that might help him to see better. The resolution and frame rate were too poor to pick out lip movements. But the woman seemed to be gesturing or pointing at something.

'They're definitely saying something.' Boyd looked at Okeke. 'Is the woman behind the counter the one you interviewed?'

'Looks like her, yeah, guv.'

'And she didn't recall talking to this woman?'

'No.'

'Nothing? No sense that she looked uncomfortable? Nothing out of the normal?'

'No. Nothing at all.'

The exchange was short. The woman with the baseball cap and the anorak turned round and headed for the store's glass front door. As she pulled the door open, Boyd caught a blur of movement near the top of the image.

'Pause it.'

Okeke hit the space bar and the CCTV image froze. Boyd straightened up, wincing at the pain in his thighs – no doubt courtesy of all the Hastings inclines. He grimaced and resolved to take the sodding car tomorrow. He leant over Okeke's shoulder and pointed at a smudge of grey.

'Feet. In shot. See up there?'

She nodded. 'Let's see if they're heading in or waiting.'

She hit the space bar again and the jerky motion of the CCTV footage resumed. The woman emerged from the store and let the door swing shut behind her.

She walked out of shot and was followed by two pairs of feet. The image revealed the lower half of both sets of legs as their path descended further into the camera's field of view. But hip height was as good as it got before they disappeared completely. Boyd and Okeke watched the footage for another minute to make sure that there was nothing else, then Okeke pressed stop.

'One woman. And two men waiting for her outside,' she said. 'They look like they were *with* her. Do you agree?'

Boyd nodded. 'Looks like it'. As best he could make out, those legs did seem to belong to two men. But they couldn't be sure.

'Is there another CCTV camera on the boats in the marina?'

She nodded. 'There's one covering the main jetty. The one the *Magpie* was tied up on. The owners were looking into it for me. I'll chase it up and see if they found anything worth sending over.'

'Good job. Oh... Okeke?'

'Yes?' She followed his line of sight and suppressed a grin.

'Could I have another one of those...?' Boyd nodded sheepishly at the box of doughnuts.

IT WAS GETTING LATE. Boyd had his coat over one arm and was making 'getting ready to go' noises when Minter appeared in front of his desk. Boyd wished he could just wave him away. His stomach rumbled loudly in agreement.

'Boss, just a quick update on the mispers list.'

Boyd sighed and sat back down. Minter's 'quick' updates, he was beginning to realise, could take some time. 'Are we down to less-than-stupid numbers?'

'Under three thousand now.' Minter pulled out a chair and sat down too. 'I've got O'Neal crunching his way through them. Warren's on his way back from Eastbourne.'

'I'm sure common sense will prevail but, just in case it doesn't, we're looking for people with a *possible* Chinese connection, with an interest in yachting, who own a boat, and are ideally assumed missing from about three months ago, but not necessarily reported missing three months ago. It could be a misper report raised yesterday... if you get what I'm saying.'

'Yeah, O'Neal knows all that, sir.'

'I'm sure he does. But always worth double-checking, right?'

'Absolutely, boss,' replied Minter.

Boyd eased his chair back, picked up his bag and stood up. He was six foot two, several inches taller than Minter. Minter, despite being infinitely fitter, stronger and undoubtedly more rugged than Boyd, seemed to shrink ever so slightly into his chair.

'Excellent,' said Boyd, striding towards the door. 'Good work. See you tomorrow morning.'

14

Boyd had completely forgotten about the rescue dog. It all came flooding back to him as he opened the front door. He was supposed to have rung Emma to let her know whether he was coming home at lunch time to meet him.

'Bollocks,' he muttered as he closed the front door behind him.

'We're in here,' she called out.

He hung his coat up, flung the car keys onto the hallway shelf and steered himself into the lounge. Emma was sitting on the wooden floor at one end, a white-and-ginger-patched spaniel was sitting at the other. One of the patches surrounded his right eye – he could have been in a Kiss tribute band.

'You two fallen out already?' he asked.

'He's very nervous,' she replied.

'Oh, he just needs to be broken in with a good ear ruffling, Ems.' Boyd strode towards the dog. As Boyd approached and loomed over him, Ozzie began to issue a low warning grumble.

'Dad, careful. You're scaring him.'

'He's just –'

The grumble became a full-on growl, stopping Boyd in his tracks. 'Okay, maybe I am a bit,' he conceded.

He backed up and sat down on the floor beside her. 'How long have you two been like this, staring at each other from across the room?'

'A couple of hours. The Spaniel Aid lady said you've got to give them time and space to settle in.'

'Did she mention anything about bribing him with food?' He reached into his jacket pocket and pulled out a half-eaten doughnut wrapped in tissue. He'd planned to finish it on the walk home.

'Um, Dad... he's meant to be on dried kibble. *Very* plain food.'

'Aw, come on. Just this once. Call it a welcome home cake.'

Boyd peeled the tissue away and placed the caramel-topped doughnut on the floor in front of him. 'Here you are, Ozzie,' he said softly. 'Come and get it.'

Ozzie, sitting very stiffly in front of the fireplace, remained wary and uninterested.

'There, your cheap attempt to buy his love has failed miserably,' said Emma.

'Give it a second. The smell's got to reach him first.'

'Errr... Dad? You know he can see it, right?'

'Yes, but he won't know it's food until he can smell it, will he?' replied Boyd. 'I could have put down a balled-up sock as far as he's concerned.'

Ozzie's wet nose began to twitch, his muzzle lifted as he probed the air in front of him and he leaned forward slightly.

'Aha!' he said smugly. 'See? Everyone has a price.'

'Come on, Ozzie,' coaxed Emma.

Boyd eased the doughnut further forward. 'Come on, Oz. How much do you want this delicious, yummy thing, hmmm? Not just any doughnut, old boy – it's a deep-fried, caramel-topped and lovingly sprinkled Krispy doughnut.'

The sales pitch seemed to be working. Ozzie got up, took a step forward, then another.

'That's it, you bribable old bastard – come and get it,' he cooed gently.

'Oh, don't,' Emma scolded. 'Poor thing's been through a rubbish few days.'

Ozzie took another few wary steps, then halted a foot short of the offering.

'What's he doing?' muttered Boyd. 'Just take the bloody thing, mate, and let's be friends.'

'He's been abused in the past, Dad, remember? He's been beaten, thrown out, left to rummage in dustbins. You can't blame him for being wary.'

Ozzie stretched his head forward. Finally a pink tongue shot out and took a testing swipe at the caramel topping. The decision process was pretty rapid. He lurched forward and downed the half doughnut in one gulp. Then, quick as a flash, he was back in his spot in front of the fireplace.

15

Boyd was trying to decide whether or not he should invest in a bicycle for his morning commute. It had occurred to him that if he didn't have to stop for any red lights or old ladies, he could probably get all – if not most – of the way to the police station from his house on the hill without a single pedal.

Of course, the corollary of that was that he'd be pedaling uphill like a bastard all the way back home.

Sod it, he thought. The walk would give him a bit more thinking time, and he supposed his thighs would get used to it at some point.

As he headed in, to what would be his third day at work, he realised that it already felt as though he'd been there for weeks. He'd expected to get to know the CID department *gradually* as he fumbled his way around the new job, new town, new home... his new *life*. But instead he was getting a frantically crammed crash course.

Oddly, though... it all felt invigorating rather than draining.

He emerged from the end of the fabulously Dickensian-looking George Street to see the apron of seafront parking and the sea beyond. It was lively this morning, and high tide too; waves were surging their way up the beach and throwing up rooster tails of froth onto the long shingle berm at the top.

Four weeks ago, the prospect of packing, moving and meeting new colleagues, let alone heading up an investigation, had been a mountain he'd thought he couldn't climb. Four weeks ago, just getting out of bed, putting on a dressing gown and making a cup of tea had been a project that needed careful evaluation.

What most people don't seem to get, Boyd thought, is how bloody exhausting grief is.

He arrived at the station at five to nine, flashed his warrant card at reception and buzzed through the side door, with just enough time to take a piss and grab a coffee from the canteen upstairs.

He was mid-flow, his mind a million miles away in what now felt like another lifetime, when he was jerked unceremoniously back to the present.

'Boss.'

He turned to see Minter at the urinal next to him, promptly unzipping and letting rip. 'I think we've got a hit on one of the mispers. It –'

'Errr... Minter, I'm busy...'

Minter either didn't hear or didn't care. 'It only came in a fortnight ago and you won't believe how it flagged up –'

'Mate, I'm actually having a piss right now. Time and place?'

'It was bloody typo error that –'

'Can I just have five. Bloody. Minutes. Please, Detective Sergeant?!'

Minter stopped. His mouth snapped shut. He looked uncannily like a scolded puppy.

Boyd suddenly felt guilty. 'You want a coffee?' he asked. 'I'm going up to grab one. I'll meet you back in the office in a min.'

Ten minutes later, illicit bacon roll in hand, Boyd was back behind his desk and sipping scalding black coffee, listening to the rest of Minter's explanation.

'O'Neal with his thick bloody sausage fingers typed the name in arse-backwards so that he accidentally did a database search on NIX instead of XIN. And guess what. We only got a hit back! One Gerald Ian Nix. A misper that was only logged a couple of weeks ago.'

Minter dropped a printout on Boyd's desk.

'Here's the report. It was made by his ex-wife, Jo Bambridge.'

Nix was a surname Boyd was sure he had stumbled across before. Not in a work context, though. Where was it? Wasn't there a writer with that surname? He vaguely recalled books on Emma's shelf about the time she was at secondary school. He dragged his attention back to the present. 'So we got a lucky lead because one of my team's dyslexic?'

Minter nodded, grinning like a Cheshire cat.

'Sherlock Holmes would be so proud of us.' Boyd picked up the printout. Jo Bambridge lived in Bexhill-on-Sea, just a few minutes away. A conveniently close, lucky lead.

'So what do we reckon? This missing G. I. Nix decided to register a business at Companies House with his name written backwards as Xin Gi? And, remind me, the company is...'

'Maguire Mackintosh,' said Minter. 'Which is the same company that pays for that yacht's marina costs.'

Boyd scratched at the thickening growth on his chin. He really needed to find his electric razor sometime soon. Even a shitty Bic would do. He was in great danger of growing a proper Uncle Albert beard in the very near future.

'Okay, this is good. Very good. We've got our first lead.' He looked up at Minter. 'I bestow on you, Detective Sergeant, the honour of pinning this misper report to the case board and, yes, you may do the twirly red cotton link-line too.'

'Aww, thanks, boss.' Minter picked up the report. 'I've

always wanted to do my very own twirly red cotton thingy.'

THE EX-MRS NIX lived in Bexhill-on-Sea. Another small town, Boyd learned from Okeke, on the seafront that had merged seamlessly with St Leonards and Hastings. If there was a notable variation between these three elderly seaside sisters, it was probably in their character. Whereas Hastings was charming and quaint, St Leonards was the older sister who was having some cosmetic work done. Which made Bexhill-On-Sea the batty oldest one with ten cats and a gin habit.

Boyd had a fleeting childhood memory of passing through Bexhill – his mum pointing out the grand Edwardian town-houses overlooking the promenade with their wrought-iron balconies, the French doors, the porches with their proud Doric columns. Everything was gleaming, freshly painted white and beautifully maintained like the 'Who Will Buy?' scene in *Oliver!*

In recent times those same palaces by the sea had become scruffy guesthouses put to work homing ex-cons, alongside vulnerable youngsters and bewildered asylum seekers.

Boyd had asked DC Okeke to accompany him firstly because she was smart and he liked her, but also because she was the only woman he had on his team. During the phone conversation he'd had with Jo Bambridge earlier, he'd got the distinct impression that she wasn't particularly keen on men. He thought Okeke might be able to get more out of her. She could offer a little feminine solidarity, perhaps.

'How's the CCTV stuff going?' asked Boyd as she signalled right and steered them away from the seafront.

'Not much that's useful on the jetty camera. It's just off where the *Magpie* was berthed. You can see the front of the boat but not the back, which would have been far more useful.'

'Aft,' said Boyd.

'Sorry?'

'Sailors call it the aft of the boat, not the *back*.'

'The arse?'

'Aft!'

She laughed. 'Sorry, guv. Duly noted.'

'Are there no other cameras?'

'Not belonging to the marina, but I'm waiting on the neigh-bouring businesses. There's a shared parking area that might be covered by one of them.'

'Good thinking.' Boyd moved onto their imminent appoint-ment. 'So this Jo Bambridge. I spoke to her on the phone. She's not the worried tearful wife by any stretch. She was actually quite combative.'

'Combative?'

'She was dumped by Nix some time ago for some – and I quote – "young tart". I got the distinct impression she'd be more than happy to bury an ice pick in both their heads. I'm going to lead the questioning but if this turns into a gender-war thing, if she looks like she'd prefer to talk to you...'

'Step in? Sure, no problem, guv.'

'Good. Thanks. He's obviously done a number on her and I'm not sure she's all that keen on any men at the moment.'

Okeke followed the directions on her phone, taking them away from the smart, white-washed seafront façade into a warren of narrow roads flanked on either side by nose-to-end parked cars and low terraced houses that sported seventies pebble-dash veneers and windowsills that were shedding paint like a bad skin condition.

'Here we are,' she said, looking for a gap to shoehorn the patrol car into.

This was another part of Bexhill Boyd vaguely remem-bered. And this part *hadn't* changed.

16

'This is DC Samantha Okeke and I'm DCI Boyd,' said Boyd, smiling at the stressed-looking woman, in front of them.

'You took your time,' Jo Bambridge said harshly.

He was momentarily taken aback by that. 'We only spoke twenty minutes ago.'

'No, I mean since I reported my ex-husband missing. That was over a fortnight ago!'

She led them into the front room and gestured to them to sit down.

Jo Bambridge was a woman in her early fifties with long blonde hair that was well on its way to becoming grey, pulled back tightly into a ponytail. She'd clearly been crying before they'd arrived; her make-up wasn't doing a great job at masking the red eyes. There were photos of her on the windowsill from when she was younger, slimmer and happier. Pictures of her on a horse. Pictures of her helming a sailing boat. Glamorous pictures of a woman enjoying a much better life than the one she was living now.

'Sorry about the time this has taken, Mrs Bambridge –' Boyd said.

'Just call me Jo, for God's sake. I'm not officially divorced from that bastard yet. But I'm using my maiden name.'

Boyd nodded. 'Jo it is, then.'

'So have you found the shitty little weasel?'

'Gerald Nix?' He shook his head. 'We found his yacht, though.'

'*Magpie*?'

Boyd nodded again.

Jo pointed at the picture of her sailing. 'That's the *Magpie* and me, about seven years ago.'

Boyd and Okeke turned and looked at the photo. Neither of them really knew what to say. It was a picture of her and a tiny bit of the boat's helm.

'The *Magpie* was found drifting in the Channel, deserted,' said Boyd. 'There was some damage to the hull and –'

'I saw the news,' said Jo. She almost smiled at him. 'And your amusing bleeped press conference. Something happened on board, didn't it? There were reports of blood. Was someone murdered? Was it Gerald?'

'Well, that's exactly what we're looking into, Jo,' said Okeke. 'We think there were three people aboard.'

'Gerald and his trophy bitch being two of them, I suppose?'

Okeke nodded. 'We think so. We've got CCTV footage of a woman, and possibly two other men.'

'Was the woman young and slim? Tits out and tarty looking?'

Boyd caught Okeke's eye, trying to keep a straight face.

Okeke bit down on her lip and shrugged. 'We didn't get a close look at the woman. She didn't look particularly glamorous, if I'm honest. She seemed to be wearing an old parka. She had a baseball cap on too. Looked quite scruffy actually.'

Boyd liked the way she handled that. On side with Jo at the first opportunity.

'Tell me about her,' Okeke pressed.

'All I know about *her* is that she's twenty years younger than me and she's basically stolen my husband, my home, my business and my money. Gerald – he hits his mid-life crisis and, instead of buying a motor bike, ditches me for someone young enough to be his bloody daughter!'

'He sounds like a real prize, Jo. Do you have any children?'

Jo shook her head. 'He didn't want any. To be frank, neither did I.'

'What do you know about her?'

Jo shrugged. 'Not much.'

'Do you know her name?'

'Zophie something.'

'Sophie?' asked Okeke.

'No, Zophie with a pretentious "Z" at the beginning. I suppose she thinks it makes her sound more exotic.' Jo tutted and rolled her eyes.

'How did she meet Gerald?' Okeke asked, as Boyd jotted the name down in his notebook.

'Online. The dirty old bastard chatted her up online. What a cliché. Obviously she saw he had money and that was that... She dug her claws in and it was out with the old, in with the new.'

'Have you met her?' asked Boyd. 'Could you identify her?'

'I could probably identify her breasts if you want. I saw those on his screen.'

Okeke gave Boyd a '*let me handle this*' look.

'When was the last time you spoke with Gerald?' she asked.

'Eighteen months ago. When I left him,' said Jo.

'So what happened? How did you find out what he was up to?'

'I discovered he'd been texting – sorry, *sexting* this girl.

They'd been sending pictures to each other.' The hard tone in Jo's voice began to waver slightly. 'It had been going on for weeks, months. When I confronted him, he didn't even try to deny it. He didn't even try to lie his way out of it...' She cleared her throat. 'I don't want to cry again. I've just put make-up on.'

'It's all right,' said Okeke, resting a hand on her arm.

Boyd found himself gazing awkwardly out of the window. This Nix guy sounded like a total arsehole.

Jo dabbed her eyes lightly with the heel of her hand. 'He doesn't fucking deserve my tears. Really...' She took a deep breath and continued. 'He just admitted it. Said it was over between us and that maybe I should move out.'

'Just like that?'

She nodded. 'It was like he'd been *hoping* I'd find out. Waiting for a chance to tell me to sod off. And there it was.'

'Did you leave?'

'I packed a couple of bags and left. Yes.' She dabbed at her face again. 'To be honest, I thought I'd be out for one night and back home the next day, listening to him begging me for a second chance. Well, that didn't bloody happen, did it?'

'Have you been back since?'

She shook her head, more tears spilling from her red and puffy eyes. 'I'm stuck here,' she mumbled pitifully. 'Renting.'

Boyd gazed around the front room and noticed for the first time how bare it looked. The furniture was generic Ikea stuff, just the basics: a sofa and chairs, a small dining table, a TV cabinet, a shelving unit and a couple of bland, framed prints on the wall. The only personal items in the room were the few photographs of Jo's younger self.

'So all your things are still in your house?' said Okeke.

Jo nodded. 'I haven't been back in. He changed the front door lock. And it *is* my house. I made it our home, not him.'

'You've not spoken to him?'

'I tried. I texted him a few times. He wouldn't answer. A

week after we split, he said that he was going to get the divorce arranged and I'd get a cash settlement when it was all done.' She shrugged in resignation. 'And that was it.'

'You reported him missing a fortnight ago.' said Okeke. 'Why then? What changed?'

'I got a solicitor three months ago and she's been trying to get him to respond. And, of course, there was nothing. No replies to her letters or calls. So I went to the house. Knocked on the door. Nothing. Looked in all the windows... ' She shook her head. 'There was no sign of him.'

'Where do you think he could have gone?' asked Boyd. 'Could he have gone to visit family?'

Jo shook her head again. 'No. Like I said, we don't have kids. He's not that close to his brother, and his parents are both dead. Besides,' she added, 'his car was there. I supposed he was off sailing somewhere with his tart in tow.'

Okeke tutted. 'He sounds like a right piece of work.'

Jo's eyes flashed. She nodded her head vigorously. 'Oh, God, but he *is*! A complete, selfish arsehole. We were together twenty-two years, building up the business together, then he just dumps me for a younger model.' Her voice quivered again and Okeke instinctively placed a supportive hand on her shoulder.

'What was the business, Jo?'

'Financial consulting,' she said. 'Investments, tax advice... that kind of thing.'

'You worked together?' asked Boyd.

'Yeah, on the High Street. I ran the office, admin, marketing, business accounts... the appointments, the client handling; pretty much all he did was the consulting. He owes me for that. He bloody well owes me for all the years I put into it all.' Tears spilled from her raw eyes.

She dabbed at her cheeks again. 'It's the betrayal that hurts, you know? You think you know someone. You think you're working together as a team for a beautiful, happy retirement, then...'

'I know...' said Okeke. 'I know what men can be like.'

Boyd sat back to give them a little more space.

'So you think he took *Magpie*? Took the yacht out?' Okeke asked.

Jo nodded. 'That's what I thought. Maybe he was showing off to his new girlfriend. Maybe just swanning around for a bit.'

'What about his office? Have you been to –'

'Gerald closed that down nearly a year ago. There's no office any more. It's a hairdresser's now.'

'Right. So you called the police to make a missing person's report because...?'

'Because I could see post piling up in the hallway. Because he wasn't answering my solicitor. Because there was no sign of him... and because *Magpie* was gone.'

'You went to the marina?'

She nodded again. 'I thought I might find him... *them*... there.' She looked up at the ceiling. 'I thought that if they were there, then maybe I'd have the chance to tell this girl about the life she'd just destroyed. Or maybe I'd have just slapped her.'

'And the yacht was gone,' said Okeke.

'Yes. The lady behind the counter said *Magpie*'s berth had been vacant for several weeks.'

'And that's not normal?'

'He barely used it. An afternoon here and there. He's not a very confident sailor.' She looked at Okeke. 'To be totally honest with you, I thought he might have emptied the bank accounts and gone off into the sunset with her and all our retirement money. *That's* what made me call. I don't have much money left,' she whispered. 'I've been living off what was left in the only account I have access to.'

She reached into the pocket of her trousers and pulled out a blue plastic name badge. 'This is how I'm paying the rent now. Tesco.'

Boyd glanced at his notebook. 'Jo?' She looked up at him. 'Can you think of anyone who might have a reason to harm your... to harm Gerald? Anyone he might have crossed swords with?'

She gave that a moment's thought. 'Not really. Maybe through his work. Wait. There was a client.'

'Who?'

'Well, I'm... I can't really say the name because of client confidentiality. But there was an investor who lost a lot of money through us. I mean it wasn't our fault. But he blamed us. Blamed Gerald specifically.'

'How much? A lot?'

She nodded. 'Enough that he tried to pick a fight with Gerald in our local a few years back.'

'Words or fists?' asked Okeke.

'Oh, fists,' she replied. 'I mean it was a proper fight. Drinks were spilt. Gerald got a bloody nose.' Jo smiled at the memory.

'Did Gerald call the police?'

She shook her head. 'He didn't want it to escalate. He hoped his bloody nose would be the end of it.'

Okeke lowered her voice. 'Give me a name. It'll save us having to go to the pub to ask there.'

'Well, yes. Okay, I suppose...' She clacked her tongue. 'It was a man called Aiden Rigby.'

'Do you know where he lives?'

'No, I don't. He used to live in Rye. I think.'

'Do you mind if at some point we pay a visit to your old house?' asked Boyd.

Jo shook her head. 'Please, do. Do whatever you need to.'

'Can we have the address?' asked Okeke. 'It's not far, is it?'

'It's also in Rye,' she replied. 'So, no, not very far.' She gave the address to Okeke who jotted it down.

Boyd decided they had probably put Jo through enough for one day. He thanked Jo for her time and asked Okeke to hand over one of her business cards.

'If there's anything else you can think of, you call Samantha, okay?'

Jo Bambridge nodded, relieved it was over for now.

17

Back in the car, Boyd called Minter. 'We've got a name. Can you check it for me please?'

'Fire away, boss.'

'Aiden Rigby. He may or may not be on LEDs. I need a current address.'

'Righto.'

'Me and Okeke are going to drive over to Rye to visit Nix's house.'

'What's your reason, boss? For the log.'

'Reason for visit – to look for evidence of forced entry or abduction.' Boyd could hear Minter repeating it word-for-word as he tapped away at his keyboard. 'As soon as you've got an address for Rigby, you call me, okay?'

'Roger that.'

He ended the call and turned to Okeke. 'So how far away is Rye?'

'It's about half an hour or so, guv,' she answered.

'What's it like? Big place? Small place?'

'It's an exclusive and expensive place,' she replied. 'It's

where the posh folk have out-of-London homes.' Okeke finished setting up the route on her phone. 'I think Johnny Depp is supposed to have a place near there.'

'Lucky old ladies of Rye.'

Okeke started up the patrol car and managed to wiggle it out from its tight parking space.

'So what did you make of the ex-Mrs Nix?' Boyd asked once they had pulled away.

'Understandably pissed off,' said Okeke. 'If I'd been married to someone for twenty years, built something up, bought a house – there's no way I'd just walk out with nothing. I'd make *him* leave.'

'Hmmm.' Boyd asked the obvious question. 'So... motive, then?'

'What? Her? To kill Nix?'

'Yeah.'

She gave that some thought. 'I could imagine her wishing him dead. I think I would too, but...'

'But?' Boyd had his doubts too.

'She seemed too openly angry with him. I mean, if she had anything to do with his disappearance, she would have been a bit more guarded with us, surely, guv? Less of the obvious vitriol?'

'She also referred to him in the present tense,' said Boyd. 'I know that sounds a bit Detective Columbo, but it tends to be an accurate tell.'

'Who's Columbo?'

He looked at her. 'Christ alive. What are you... a bloody millennial?'

She tutted. 'No. I just don't watch TV crime. I find the inaccuracies irritating. I presume that's what he is... *was*?'

'Correct. A US show.'

'Well, that's even worse, then.'

Boyd checked the journey time on her phone. Thirty-three minutes. Was it worth sending someone from the team instead? Probably not. They were already partway there and this would hopefully be nothing more than a 'knock on the door and peek through the window' situation.

'You've got to feel sorry for her, though, Jo Bambridge,' said Okeke. 'A few years ago she had a nice place in Rye, a yacht, her own business... and now she's in a two-up, two-down in a Bexhill backstreet and working in Tesco.' She glanced at him. 'I mean, that's all she's left with after twenty-plus years with Nix? Not even any kids to show for it?'

'Yeah, that's pretty shitty, to be fair.' He couldn't ever have imagined a similar scenario with Julia. They'd had just over twenty-five years together, and those years had shot past in the blink of an eye. Happy days. Yes, there'd been one or two bad ones, but overwhelmingly they'd been good. If either of them could *conceivably* have grown tired of their relationship, it wouldn't have been him. It wasn't that he was blinded with rose-tinted nostalgia, it had simply been a wonderful relationship. One of those lucky and sublime carpentry joins where two pieces fit together perfectly.

'So the woman in the CCTV, she's the "Z-someone" on that form and therefore this "Zophie",' Okeke continued.

Boyd nodded. 'Okay, let's say that she is. One of those sets of feet outside was presumably Gerald Nix. So, it's the other pair I'm interested in.'

'You think it could be this Rigby guy, guv?'

'Well, according to Jo, he has previous when it comes to Nix. And Nix has apparently double-crossed him, so there's a possible motive right there. At the moment that puts Rigby in pole position.'

His phone buzzed on the dashboard and fell into the footwell. Boyd heaved against the seatbelt and rummaged around, cursing until he finally retrieved it. It was Minter. He answered and activated the speakerphone.

'Hello again, boss. I've got an address for Aiden Rigby. And, yes, he is on the PNC. With some form.'

'Form for what?'

'Fraud. He was done a few years ago for running a telephone scam on old people. A right nasty piece of work by the look of it.'

'Any history of violence?'

'Nothing on the PNC. But just a general shit piece of work.'

'What's the address?'

'31a Denham Way, Camber.'

'That's just beyond Rye,' said Okeke.

'We can go to see Rigby, then see the Nix place on the way back?'

She nodded. 'Makes sense.'

'Okay, Minter... change of plan. Me and Okeke are going to knock on Rigby's door first, then drop by the Nix place on the way back.'

'What do you want me to put down for this Rigby visit?' Minter asked.

'He had a violent altercation with Nix a few years back. Put him down as a possible suspect. We're just going to ask him a few questions.'

'Okay, it's logged in, boss.'

Boyd hung up. 'You want me to tap that address into your phone?'

'No need, I know Camber. I know Denham Way.'

'Good. Well, that makes me happy – three visits, one journey, all very efficient.' He flung his hand forward. 'Proceed.'

Ten minutes later they pulled up outside a small council house at the end of a scruffy-looking cul-de-sac. It had all the usual garden decor: the abandoned sofa, the inevitable discarded shopping trolley, a gravel driveway packed with cars either partly dismantled or partly repaired – it was hard to tell which.

BOYD AND OKEKE got out and headed to number 31a. It had the look of a rotten tooth, about ready to fall out. A concrete path, overgrown with weeds, led the way to a paint-chipped front door, flanked by grubby, bare windows.

'He lives alone,' said Boyd.

'How do you know that?'

'Blokes don't bother with curtains.'

'That's a sweeping statement, isn't it?' She glanced sideways at him.

'Want a wager? Five pounds?'

'No, you're all right, guv. I can't go taking money from you...'

They walked up the path and Boyd knocked heavily on the door. He waited an indecently short amount of time and then knocked again, harder.

A neighbouring door opened and an old woman poked her head out. 'What's up, love?'

He raised his voice. 'Do you know if Mr Rigby's in?'

'Ade? Oh probably not, love. Not at this time of day.'

'Well, do you know where I might find him?' he called.

She glared. 'I'm old, not deaf, love! He's probably at his work. Got a unit somewhere over at Duke's Park.'

Boyd looked at Okeke. She nodded. 'I know it. It's a small industrial park.'

'Do you know what his business is called?' he asked hopefully.

She frowned in concentration. 'Something ... *Medicines*, I think.' She shook her head. 'I'm not sure.' Then she pulled her head back in and shut the door.

Boyd turned to Okeke. 'Well, I guess that's that, then. Is it far?'

'No. Two minutes. It's just round the corner. There's a Greggs on the way,' she added tentatively.

'Right.' He took a step back quickly and squinted up at the bedroom windows just in case. But it appeared that, genuinely, no one was home. 'Come on, then. Another stop. But no Greggs – I'm supposed to be on a bloody diet, remember?'

18

Okeke drove them into an industrial estate that looked as though it was little more than a warren of lock-up units with white transit vans parked outside, each with their own business logo cheaply stencilled on the side.

'Pond's Plumbing. Carly's Hair Supplies. Angie's Big Baps.' Boyd looked at her. 'Artisan baker, perhaps?'

She smiled. 'Good to see that those bras weren't burnt in vain, guv.'

'Ah, what's that?' He pointed at the unit at the end of the row. It backed onto what appeared to be a junkyard that was overspilling onto the land beyond.

There was a sign above the door: BEST MEDICINES DIRECT.

'I think we've got ourselves a winner,' he said.

Okeke parked up and they got out. In the distance he could hear a circular saw whining its way through lumber, and of course gulls. Always the bloody gulls.

'All right, then... Let's see if the mysterious Mr Rigby is here.'

Boyd wrapped his knuckles impatiently on the door. This

time there *was* a response. They could hear movement inside. Then finally a voice from behind the door.

'Who is it?'

Boyd cleared his throat and tried to sound less grouchy detective and more in-a-hurry delivery driver. 'DPD. Got a sign-for, mate.'

Something *snicked* behind the door and it creaked open. A large, pale face appeared, thick-rimmed glasses above a thick brush-like moustache.

'I'm not expecting anyth–' Rigby saw Boyd and Okeke and despite the lack of uniforms recognised them instantly as police. He pulled his head back in and tried to slam the door shut...

... on Boyd's extended foot.

'Ow!' he shouted more in resentment than pain.

Rigby stamped hard on his foot, and this time it *did* hurt. A lot.

'Ow!'

Okeke ducked back into the car and radioed for backup while Boyd held the door ajar and played a weird version of Stamping Wars with Rigby. 'Police! You idiot! Open!'

Rigby swung a kick at his shin and Boyd withdrew his foot before Rigby could have a second go and break the bloody bone. Instead Boyd pushed his arm and shoulder into the gap, angling his head as far back as he could, in case Rigby tried to swing a punch at his face.

'Rigby, it's the police!' he gasped.

A baseball bat poked out through the gap, nearly catching Boyd in the eye as Rigby tried to swing it down on him.

'For fuck's sake! I'm the fucking police, you stupid arsehole!' He pulled back, giving up on the door and jumping back, out of the bat's range.

The door slammed shut. 'Shit. Did I just hear you call for backup?' he called to Okeke.

'Yes, guv. They're on their way.'

'You stay here,' he ordered, and ran round the side of the unit towards the junkyard at the rear, just in time to see the back door swing open. Rigby appeared.

'Police!' Boyd shouted yet again.

Rigby glanced over his shoulder and bolted towards the junkyard. Boyd chased after him. Rigby was a big man, just as tall but carrying significantly more weight than Boyd. In a straight hundred-metre dash, he fancied his chances, but over what appeared to be an assault course of abandoned car chassis, mattresses and large drums of chemicals, that were presumably too expensive to dispense with in a legal manner, he suspected it was going to be a more evenly matched pursuit.

Rigby slid over the rust-flecked bonnet of an old Ford Gran Torino.

Christ, what is this... Starsky and Hutch?

Boyd followed suit and realised on the far side, as his feet landed on a bed of springs, that he was now inside the junkyard: a labyrinth of fly-tipped shite that presented the perfect opportunity for Rigby to jump out and take him.

'Rigby!' he shouted as he stepped cautiously forward. 'We've called in backup from just outside the entrance. You're not going to get away, mate. And you'd have to be really bloody stupid to assault a police officer!'

Again.

'So stop fucking around and come out where I can see you!'

There was, predictably, no response.

He sighed. 'Right, shithead,' he muttered. 'I'm coming to get you.'

He had a horrible flashback to playing hide-and-seek with Noah in a soft-play area. *'I'm coming to get you'* – followed by Noah's give-away cackle of excitement from beneath a jiggling pool of plastic balls.

Boyd reached down and picked up a length of tubular

metal. Chances were that it would bend like a McDonalds paper straw on impact, but it felt reassuring to have something baton-like to hold.

He could see to the far side of the junkyard and what appeared to be a high chain-link fence. He'd hear it rattle if Rigby tried to scale it.

And, so far, he hadn't. Which, somehow, he didn't find entirely reassuring.

'Rigby! This is stupid. We just want to have a chat with you...and we will, like it or not!' he added under his breath.

Silence. The circular saw in the distance whined to a halt. A flock of gulls circled high above the yard, curious to see how this little stand-off was going to play out. He'd hoped to hear the reassuring sound of approaching sirens by now, but then this wasn't London with several handy units nearby, waiting to be summoned.

The only sounds were his own heaving breath and the creak and clatter of debris stirred by the breeze.

This is ridiculous. He'd put himself in a dangerous position when, to be honest, he should just have shouted through the unit door that he'd be back later with a warrant.

'Mate. This isn't an arrest. I just want to ask –'

He heard a grunt to his left and turned to see Rigby charging straight at him, armed with a wooden stake.

Boyd had a nano second to duck as the jagged end of the wooden pole slid uselessly over his shoulder. Then Rigby slammed into him like a ten-ton truck.

They both went down onto a crash mat of brake discs, rusting bolts and shards of MDF, all partly disguised by tall grass and weeds that had promised, and failed to deliver, a soft landing. Boyd hit the ground with Rigby on top of him. Rigby's hands, very large fleshy ones, were around his neck.

What the actual fuck?

He could feel Rigby making a very real and deliberate

attempt to squeeze the life out of him. Boyd, however, wasn't some eight-stone, terrified weakling. He didn't waste time trying to peel Rigby's hands off. He cut straight to the chase and fumbled in the dirt for something big enough to brain the arsehole with.

The gods were smiling – kind of. He found something mushy and wet, grabbed a fistful and flung it straight into Rigby's face.

It took them both a second to realise what it was. Rigby recoiled in horror, gagging and loosening his grip with one hand to wipe the sloppy shit out of his eyes. Boyd seized the opportunity, shoved him hard and rolled over on top of him.

He used his shit-covered hand to grab Rigby's hair, lifted his head and smacked it back down, stunning him on whatever hard, unforgiving piece of junkyard tat was buried in the grass behind.

'Guv!'

It was Okeke.

'Over here!' She slid over the Gran Torino far more gracefully than either he or Rigby had and joined him armed with a baton and a pair of cuffs.

She threw her weight across Rigby's legs and handed Boyd the baton.

'Thanks.' He grunted and adjusted his grip, then held the baton across Rigby's throat in case he tried to sit up. But there was no real danger of that; the bang to his head had knocked the fight out of him.

'God, what the hell is that smell?' she asked, covering her nose with her free hand.

'Dog crap, I think,' said Boyd.

She shrank back, content to keep her weight down on Rigby's legs, well away from his stinky head and her superior officer.

The sirens and boots arrived a few minutes later, allowing Boyd the merciful opportunity to wipe his hand clean.

'My hand's going to stink for the rest of the day,' he muttered.

'Not just your hand, guv.' She pointed at a smear of crap on the elbow of his jacket.

'Oh, for...' He took his jacket off and lay it on the roof of their car.

Three patrol cars had arrived at the same time, like London buses. There were three uniformed officers dealing with Rigby and two hanging around like spare parts.

He pointed at them. 'You and you, come with me.' He led the way towards the rear door of the unit. 'Let's see what he's so twitchy about. Obviously don't touch anything, unless it's another twat about to jump me.'

The interior of the unit was small, about the size of a double garage. It was crammed with collapsed cardboard boxes and plastic sacks filled with thousands and thousands of capsule-shaped pills.

On a work bench there was a neatly stacked pile of flattened cardboard packaging. Boyd violated his own standing order and picked one of them up.

Placto-flourequine – 40mg x 80 capsules.
Coronavirus resistant. Take one daily. Store in a cool dry place.
Manufactured by Proctor and Geffin Pharma Ltd

Boyd shook his head. 'Well, there's a shocker. Fake meds. No wonder he ran.'

19

'You okay, sir?'

Okeke had caught Boyd sniffing his hand again. He'd washed it thoroughly in the industrial unit's small sink. Rigby had very thoughtfully installed a fragranced-soap dispenser in there, peach and mango. But, despite scrubbing until his skin felt raw, he was sure he could still smell the shit on his hand.

'Ugh.' He grimaced.

'The lads are going to run Rigby over to division HQ to process him. Do you want to go along and –'

Boyd interrupted. 'Nope, we'll carry on. We can have a chat with him later this afternoon when we get back.'

'You want to press on and check out Nix's house? Today?'

'Of course!' He studied his fingernails closely. 'We're up this neck of the woods, might as well continue with our plan.'

'I just thought...'

'What? I had a little wrestle with a scrote... and now I'll be needing counselling?'

'No.' She nodded towards the unit. 'The lock-up will need examining and –'

'Sutherland can pull someone from the main pool to be OIC for this. I suspect it's tangential at best and I don't want to get side-tracked into babysitting something else.'

'It might be important to the Nix case.'

'I'll send Minter along to keep an eye on things. It's all the more reason to check out Nix's house, then, isn't it? To see if there's anything we can find to throw at Rigby in the interview room.' Boyd paused for a moment. 'Oh, and thanks, by the way. For – you know – having my back.'

'Think that's part of the job, isn't it, guv? I'm sure I read that in a manual somewhere.'

One of the five officers came over. 'Are we taking him to Hastings, sir?'

'Yeah. That'd be good. Thanks,' Boyd confirmed.

'What's the arrest offence, sir?'

Boyd's eyebrows shot up. 'Really? Take your pick. Assaulting a police officer. Packaging, distributing and selling counterfeit medicines. Probably fraud, tax evasion, health and safety contraventions, to name a few. Let's go with the assault for now, shall we? And then we can add to that later on, once I've had a little chat with him.'

They watched the officers lead Rigby towards the waiting patrol car. Boyd found himself watching Rigby's feet. He had a distinctive, clumsy pigeon-toed walk.

'You thinking about that CCTV?' said Okeke.

'Uh-huh. It's not much to go on, is it?' They watched as he ducked down and was shoved into the car. 'I don't think it was him in that footage, do you?'

She shook her head.

Boyd waited until they'd secured him in the back, then turned to face Okeke.

'Right, then,' he said, brusque and business-like. 'Next house call.'

RYE WAS every bit as expensive-looking as Boyd had been expecting.

It looked like a village designed from the ground up by Thornton's or Cadbury's creative designers, and was the inspiration and muse, no doubt, for countless unimaginative water-colour artists. It was ridiculously pretty. He suspected this was how most mid-west Americans imagined how England looked – one large chocolate-box village in which little old ladies ran antique shops during the day and solved murders by night.

He tried to grade the property values as Okeke's satnav took them down the High Street. Holland Park price tags? Chelsea? SoHo even?

They drove through the other end of Rye and out into a winding leafy lane.

'Nearly there, guv. Keep an eye out – there should be a turning just up here on the right.'

The driveway was marked by a pair of moss-covered stone lions sitting, weather-beaten but proud, high up on their stone pillars. The gravel drive curved gently to the left, finally opening up to reveal Nix's house, an old flint-and-stone barn that had been completely renovated to within an inch of its life. The south-east facing gable wall was one big sheet of shimmering glass.

'Looks like something off *Grand Designs*!' Boyd commented. 'Obviously financial advice is the place to be.'

He was beginning to understand, and even empathise with, Jo Bambridge's bitterness. Her old home was stunning. The garden around it would have been equally impressive if it had been given some TLC over the last few months. The lawn was shaggy and punctuated by clusters of weeds that had seized the opportunity to bolt for the sky.

Boyd's attention was drawn to a dark blue Volvo SUV parked around the side of the barn.

Okeke saw it at the same time. 'Nix's?'

'Jo said it was still here,' said Boyd. He looked at her. 'If Nix and his girlfriend went to Eastbourne together, they could have taken hers?'

She shrugged as she parked their car beside it. 'There were no unaccounted-for cars in the car park.'

Boyd unclipped, climbed out and dropped down onto his hands and knees to look beneath the Volvo.

'What are you doing?' she asked.

'Checking for signs. Seeing if it's been parked here for a while,' he replied.

He could see nothing that confirmed with certainty that it had been sitting in the exact same spot for three months. The tires didn't look flat, but then that wasn't necessarily a given.

'Well?'

'Hard to say.' He got to his feet and made an old-man *oooff* noise.

Okeke chuckled. 'Really?'

'It's a habit I've got into. It's not an age thing.'

She laughed again. 'If you say so, guv.'

Boyd led the way to the front door. Around the stone step, a crop of nettles pushed their way up through the gravel and flanked the burgundy-painted front door. Boyd reached into his jacket pocket for his warrant card with one hand and banged the iron knocker with the other.

They waited in silence for a minute, then Boyd squatted down, lifted the letterbox and peered through.

He reached up and rapped the knocker again, then put his ear to the open flap and listened very carefully for any sounds inside. He looked through the opening, down at the wooden floor, expecting to see the pile of junk mail that Jo had mentioned, but there was none.

So someone had been home.

'Hello! Anyone in there?' he shouted. His voice reverberated around inside the house but provoked nothing in response.

'What do you reckon, guv?'

He stood up again. 'Let's go poke around the back.'

He led the way to the right of the front door, along gravel that seemed to crunch far more loudly than it needed to beneath his large feet. The grounds were surrounded by mature trees and beyond the perimeter there was more wood-land. It was truly isolated and perfectly private. The house was only half a mile outside Rye, but it could easily have been embedded deep within some rural wilderness.

Unlike Duke's Park Industrial Estate, it was eerily quiet without the distant and omni-present whisper of traffic. There was a breeze hissing through the bare branches of the skeletal winter trees, and the haunting sound of crows circling above them in the grey sky.

What is it with bloody crows? He hated that dead-of-winter sound they made. Maybe he'd watched too many horror movies featuring ominous cabins in the woods on Prime – with crows, of course, loudly making their point that some poor unsuspecting bastard was about to be sawn in half.

He reached the gable wall and peered through the plate glass at an expensively designed interior.

'All right for some,' huffed Okeke. 'It's like a bloody show home.'

'Save up all your police pennies and one day, in a thousand years' time, you too could have a place like this,' Boyd dead-panned, keeping his eyes on the view within.

Through the glass he could see carefully curated designer furniture and a slate floor that almost certainly would have had heating pipes beneath it. There were a few inexplicable shapes sitting on dark slate plinths, which he presumed, since they seemed to lack any apparent purpose, were objects d'art.

They pressed on to the rear of the barn and found an extension, turning the barn into an L shape and forming two sides of a little croquet lawn. The grass here, like the rest of the grounds, was overgrown.

The extension was one, long extravagant kitchen, which ended in an enormous sun lounge. Boyd made his way over to the French doors.

'You gonna try them?' asked Okeke.

'Of course.'

'That's entering without cause, isn't it, sir?'

'Well, I don't think so. Not really. Not a sunroom. I like to think of them as being more like a patio with a roof over the top.'

'Uh, I'm not sure that's a widely shared definition, guv.'

He tested one of the French doors. It was unlocked. He pushed it open.

'Guv?' cautioned Okeke.

'Do you hear someone inside?' he asked.

'Erm. No.' She looked up at him.

He raised a brow. 'I'll ask again. Do you hear or see something suspicious inside that gives you reasonable grounds to suspect that a trespasser or burglar might be on these premises?' He cocked his head. 'You don't hear that?'

She shook her head.

'Well, I thought I heard something.'

She sighed. 'What? Maybe. All right. Yes, guv.'

He pulled a face at her, pushed the door inwards and stepped inside. In order to satisfy his own conscience and tick all the appropriate boxes, he cupped his hands around his mouth and called out.

'Hello! This is the police! We're entering this property on suspicion that trespassing or a burglary is in progress!'

Of course, there was no response.

They crossed the wooden floor of the sunroom and stepped

over the threshold into the kitchen. There was a granite-topped central island large enough to put a small pool table on. It was cluttered with folders, printouts, dirty dishes and empty tin cans.

Okeke wandered over to a bowl that looked like it had contained baked beans. She pulled a biro from her jacket pocket and dabbed at the dark sauce. It was thick and treacly.

'Guv?'

'Yeah.'

'This isn't washing up from three months ago. Just saying.'

'Hello?' he called out again. 'Anyone home?'

He exchanged a glance over his shoulder with DC Okeke.

'Where are you going, sir?'

He waved at her to keep quiet. Then he tapped the side of his nose, not entirely sure what message that was meant to convey to her other than that he wasn't going to stand and chat with her about his next move.

20

He moved deeper into the kitchen.

The electricity was still switched on. He could hear the hum of the fridge freezer. Away from the glass walls of the sun lounge it was getting gloomier. The overcast sky and the mature trees that loomed close to the back of the property gave the muted light a dusk-like quality.

He found a switch, which, when flipped, lit up a row of concealed plinth lights. Very modern. *Very snazzy*, as his grandad used to say.

On the counter beside him was a plate with grease smears and a half-eaten slice of eggy bread on it. There was also a mug, half full with milky coffee. He lightly touched the side of it. Still warm, and there was no skin on it.

Someone had been here recently. Perhaps only minutes ago.

All right, sod this, he decided.

Experience – and, he liked to think, maturity – was getting the upper-hand over careless curiosity. Someone had been living in the house. Someone who presumably *wasn't* Nix or his girlfriend.

Thump.

He stopped dead in his tracks and waited to see whether the noise was a one-off.

Boyd's voice dropped down to a whisper and he gestured for Okeke to retreat to the sun lounge. 'Call for backup.'

Moments later he heard her speaking in hushed tones to a response operator on the other end of the line.

He heard it again. *Thump.* A definite footstep from somewhere further inside the house.

Shit.

It had been a bad day as far as being jumped by arseholes went, and those thumps sounded, to Boyd, like the sort of noise someone might make if they were attempting a stealthy exit. If he'd had a uniformed officer to hand, Boyd would have gladly taken their baton or pepper spray but, he realised with a sinking feeling, the situation was what it was. *Here we go again.* He reached for the greasy pan that was beside him, a skating rink of congealed white fat coating the bottom of it.

'Police!' he shouted loudly. 'I know someone's in here! You're best coming out where I can see you! I have a taser in my hand!'

He looked despondently down at the frying pan and inched his way towards the dimly lit end of the kitchen, towards a door on the right. It was half open and he guessed from what he'd been able to discern of the barn's interior through the plate-glass wall that it must lead to the dining room.

He pulled his phone out and activated the torch function. It wasn't pitch-black dark, just gloomy, but he didn't fancy stepping any further forward without a clear, illuminated look at exactly what he'd be walking into.

He gently pushed the door a little wider and aimed the torchlight inside.

It was a pretty luxurious dining room. The standard table,

chairs and chandelier. Several meaningless million-pound splatters on canvas hanging on the walls.

'Backup's on the way, guv!' Okeke called from the sun lounge.

'Hear that, shithead?' Boyd barked. 'Probably you best stop fucking around with me and step out where I can see you.'

Silence.

Bugger it, he thought. This was turning into the second, really dumb thing he'd done today.

He was about to back away from the open door into the relative safety of the already-explored kitchen when he heard the soft squeak of a trainer on a smooth floor.

Stupidly, that emboldened him. 'Look, mate. I can *hear you!*'

Boyd took a step forward into the dining room. He stretched his arm out ahead of him, panning the torchlight left, then very slowly to the right.

A white flickering blur came out of the gloom right at him. Whatever it was caught him a glancing blow off the side of his head. He went down sideways and onto his back.

His phone clattered to the floor and landed torch-side up, casting a foggy circle onto the high ceiling above. Someone leapt into the pool of light and right over Boyd like a graceful gazelle.

Instinctively he raised the pan and it struck something hard, making his arm go numb.

The 'gazelle' sprawled on the ground, winded. Boyd sat up and fumbled for his phone. He picked it up and swung it around, just in time to see the figure scrambling to their feet.

A pale-skinned figure, hoodie, jeans, trainers, lean, male – details he catalogued in the heartbeat he had before they disappeared through another door. He heard the slapping of soles on the ground, quickly receding into the distance.

'Front door!' he shouted.

He was on his feet now and through the door, standing in a

hallway with a wooden floor. Ahead of him he could see the figure, hood pulled up, wrestling to get the front door open, hissing and spitting curses under his breath.

'Police! Stop!' shouted Boyd.

The front door jerked open, filling the hallway with pitifully dull daylight, and banged and rattled in its frame as the man shot out onto the gravel. Boyd hurried after him, still slightly dazed from the blow to the side of his head. He bounced clumsily off one side of the door frame and nearly lost his footing as he lumbered outside onto the porch and onto a coarse bristle shoe-mat outside.

The man wrenched open the driver's door of the Volvo, jumped in and pulled it shut just as Boyd's body slammed into it. The engine roared as it started up and in the split second before the man found first gear Boyd looked down.

His tie was caught in the driver's door.

Time seemed to stand still.

He wrenched the knot down with both hands and backed his head out of the noose just as the car began to pull away, the front tyre kicking up a storm of sharp and stinging grit straight into his face as if he'd been peppered beyond lethal distance by a shotgun.

'Fuuuck!' he screamed, bringing forearm and hand straight up to protect his eyes from the rear tyre. Sharp gravel stones stabbed the bare skin of his wrist like shrapnel, stinging his scalp and forehead as they pinged off him at all angles.

He collapsed back onto the ground, still cowering behind his arms, as the car sped away.

He heard DC Okeke's feet pounding across the gravel towards him. She was talking fast – clearly still on the phone to Control.

'Dark blue Volvo SUV, registration number JHU... ends in a 6. A mile east of Rye.'

He felt her hand grasp his shoulder firmly and then she gasped.

'What?'

'Shit! Officer down. We need an ambulance!'

'I'm all right,' grunted Boyd, his face still contorted but ready to test his sight by un clenching his eyelids. 'Bastard tried to punch me in the face but missed.'

'No, guv... Your ear!'

'What about my ear?' He reached up and felt something wet and flappy, dangling by his neck.

'It looks like it's actually hanging off, guv. You're definitely going to need a paramedic to sew that back –'

Her face faded to grey, and he was out before she could finish her sentence.

21

They emerged from A&E at just after two in the afternoon.

Boyd was sporting a couple of stitches at the top of his left ear, with a large dressing that cupped his entire ear. He felt like he was wearing a bra on the side of his head. His forehead and cheeks were dotted with a constellation of little scabbed-over wounds where the gravel had caught him like shotgun pellets.

The biggest wound of all, though, had been to his machismo.

'I can't believe I fainted,' he grumbled at Okeke as she led him out of the hospital reception and headed across the car park towards their car. 'Again.'

'It was just shock, guv.' She gestured at his neck. 'I think you realised how close you came to being dragged off by that car.'

Maybe that was it – he was fully aware that if things had gone slightly differently Okeke and a family liaison officer would now be telling Emma that her father had been decapitated in the line of duty and that she and Ozzie were on their own. He felt exhausted now that the fight-or-flight cortisol had deserted his bloodstream. It left him feeling as though he'd run a marathon.

'And that knife was aimed at your head,' added Okeke. 'The man meant to kill.'

'Any news on the Volvo?' he asked, changing the subject.

She shook her head as she opened the door to their car. 'Nothing yet. It's a high-priority alert on ANPR. If he's still driving around, he'll be spotted soon enough.'

Boyd opened the passenger-side door, slumped down into the seat and reached for the seat belt. 'If he's smart, he'll have dumped it and torched the – FUCK'S-SAKE!'

'Sir?'

'Bloody seat belt nearly pulled my damn ear off!' Boyd yelled, clasping his left ear.

'Let me see.'

He turned his head around so she could inspect the dressing. 'No, guv, it's fine. You just bumped it. Here, pass me your seat belt.'

He gave her the clip and she eased the belt carefully around him.

'Bloody thing.'

'Shhh. Don't be such a baby,' she said as she clicked him in.

'You need to work on your bedside manner,' he muttered. 'Anyway, have we got Sully and his bunny men over in Rye yet?'

She started up the car. 'CSI's already in. The house has been secured.'

'Good. Right then, I want to talk to Rigby.'

'Sutherland said I was to take you home.'

'I don't care. Take me to the bloody station!'

AIDEN RIGBY WAS ALREADY in the interview room accompanied by two custody officers, who both looked more than a little relieved as Boyd entered the small room.

He took the seat directly opposite Rigby; Okeke sat down beside him.

Rigby smirked. 'Dog bite your ear off, did it?'

Ignoring him, Boyd silently settled his notes on the table, then turned the tape recorder on.

'The time is 14.55. Today's date is the ninth of February. Interviewee is Aiden Rigby. Interviewing officers are DCI William Boyd and DC Samantha Okeke. The interviewee has been read his rights and charged with assaulting a police officer. He has no legal counsel present at this interview.'

Boyd looked Rigby in the eye. 'I'm not going to discuss your little fake pharmaceutical business, since that's another inquiry and another officer's case. I am, though, going to ask you about Gerald Nix.'

Rigby's smirk vanished. Boyd wished, not for the first time, that these interviews included close-up video of the face. The sudden change in Rigby's expression was worth a thousand words. On the interview tape, however, it was nothing but a pause in conversation.

'For the record,' said Boyd, 'Mr Rigby has changed from looking very smug to looking extremely wary.'

Okeke glanced sideways at him with an expression that clearly said, *Can you even do that?*

Rigby was evidently of the same opinion. 'Fuck off, you can't say something like that.'

'I can make any observations I want.'

'Fuck off,' said Rigby again. 'This is my normal face when I have to deal with police arseholes.'

Boyd steepled his fingers in front of him. 'Now, tell me about your relationship with Gerald Nix.'

'No comment.'

Boyd sighed inwardly. *Great. One of those.*

'Did you have a business relationship with Mr Nix?'

'I heard he's dead,' said Rigby. He smiled. 'Got cut up on his little boat and dumped for all the little fishes in the British Channel to gobble up.'

British Channel – that's what some of the more bellicose types liked to call it these days. As if leaving Europe had come with the right to claim as much of the surrounding sea as they wanted.

Boyd pressed on. 'You assaulted Gerald Nix in the Golden Dog pub in Rye a couple of years ago. Can you tell me why?'

'No comment.'

'Did you have a working relationship with Mr Nix? He was advising you on financial matters, wasn't he?'

Rigby snorted. 'Thieving fucking arsehole.'

'Why was he a thieving fucking arsehole? What did he do to you?'

For a moment it looked as though Rigby was going to take the bait. But then he pursed his lips and shook his head. 'No comment.'

Boyd tried a different tack. 'You were charged and prosecuted with defrauding vulnerable pensioners out of a lot of money four years ago. You made quite a bit, didn't you?'

'No comment.'

'Did Nix invest it for you? Launder it? Hide it for you?'

'No comment.'

'Did he hide it *from you*?'

Rigby's glare hardened.

'All that money, Rigby. You got charged, you served time... and now you've nothing to show for it. You've had to start from scratch with your hokey little pill business. That's gotta piss you off.'

'Fuck off.'

At least that was refreshing change from 'no comment'.

'Is that why you kidnapped Mr Nix?'

Rigby sat back in his chair. 'I didn't fuckin' kidnap him.'

'Is that why you took him out to sea and tortured him? To find out where he'd stashed your money?'

'Fuck off. No comment.'

'You didn't get what you wanted, though, did you? Is that why you killed him and his girlfriend? Chopped them up –'

'I didn't fucking do it!'

'Then tried to sink the boat to cover your tracks?'

'I said... I DIDN'T FUCKIN' DO IT!'

Boyd studied the man in front of him. Anger was a very telling emotion. It was hard to fake it well but, with a bit of practice, indignant outrage was something a seasoned bullshit artist could pull off. Particularly in an interview room.

'Is that why you sent someone round to Nix's house? To go through his papers? To see if you could find out where your money was stashed?'

'Why the fuck would I do that?'

'You knew his house was empty.'

Rigby closed his eyes. 'I'm glad the lying little wanker is dead. He got what he deserved. But it wasn't me.' He opened his eyes again, calmer now. He even managed a cool smile. 'You've got nothing, have you?' He laughed.

'What's so funny?'

Rigby leant forward, still smiling. 'No. Fucking. Comment.'

DSI SUTHERLAND finally caught up with Boyd and Okeke coming up the stairwell from the interview room.

'Ah, Boyd, there you are.'

'Sir.'

'Look. Chief Super said she insists you clock off early today. You've had two run-ins this morning and frankly you really do look a bit shit.'

Boyd was aware that his shirt was smudged with dirt, the front dotted with his own blood. 'I'll get changed, sir.'

'No, you'll take the afternoon off, Boyd,' Sutherland replied. 'There's nothing more you can do today. CSI are over at Nix's house and I've put DI Grove as officer in charge on Aiden Rigby's little pharmacy business. So, really, this afternoon you're free to go home and put your feet up.'

He had a point. Sully's report on Nix's house was the next step in the inquiry. Boyd would only be kicking his heels in the incident room until it came in. And the missing Volvo? Chances were that it was going to turn up smouldering away in a field within the next twenty-four hours.

'Go on,' said Sutherland, patting his arm. He looked at the bandaging over the ear. 'You've had a hell of clobbering this morning. Sully won't want you blundering around over in Rye. The uniforms are on the Volvo, and Rigby isn't going anywhere. For Christ's sake, go home and recover.'

He turned to Okeke. 'Can you take him home, Okeke? *Please?*'

She drove him back along the seafront.

'He's right. You should get some rest this afternoon,' she said. 'Take it easy.'

'I'm not a senior citizen who just had their bag snatched, thanks,' he grumbled.

Okeke raised a brow at him. 'But you're a cat that's just lost two of its lives.'

'Really? Not the nine-lives metaphor please.'

'Nearly stabbed in the face? Almost dragged by a car? Both could have been fatal. Once the adrenalin wears off and you think about that, it's going to hit you, guv.'

She was probably right.

They drove in silence. It had been stupidly reckless of him to push further into the house when he knew backup was already on the way. He and Okeke should have gone back outside, watched the doors and windows, and waited for the cavalry to arrive. If he'd been even a little bit smarter, he would have had DC Okeke park the car in such a way as to block that Volvo in.

What an idiot.

He stirred from his thoughts as she turned right onto Ashburnham Road and started up the long hill.

'Nice part of Hastings, this,' she said. 'Lucky you.'

'That's what trading down from London gets you,' he muttered. 'Where are you based?'

'St Leonards. In a not such a nice part. Which number, sir?'

He couldn't remember. Instead he pointed to his house.

Her mouth dropped. 'You own *that*?'

'*Half* of it. The other half is owned by a lady pirate with her own parrot. Don't ask.'

She didn't ask and he didn't explain. Apparently quirky individuals were common enough in Hastings that there was no need to question him further. She parked outside the low wall in front of his small front garden.

'Thanks for the lift.' Then he raised his eyebrows. 'You want a brew?'

She sighed. 'Unlike you, guv, I'm still on the clock. Sutherland wants me to head straight back and update him on what happened this morning.'

Boyd raised a finger. 'Just remember to say... we heard a noise inside *before* we enter –'

'Yes, sir.' She leant over towards him. 'And you take it easy this afternoon, okay?'

'All right, Mum. Not that I've got much bloody choice.'

22

'You're back early.'

Emma's eyes rounded as she stared at the bulbous dressing on the side of Boyd's head and the scabs peppering his face. 'Dad! *What's happened?*'

'I had a bit of a scrap with a scrote. It's really not as bad as it looks,' he said, trying and, from the look on her face, failing to dismiss her concern.

'Ohmygod... are you all right? Come on – you should be sitting down!'

'It's just some stitches –' he pointed to the dressing – 'and a couple of scrapes.'

'Shit.' She took his coat and led him gently to the lounge. 'This was meant to be an easy, stress-free first week back! So much for that!'

'Well, at least it's not been a boring one, eh.'

She looked at the dressing. 'Stitches?'

'Just a couple. It's nothing serious.'

'God. I thought Hastings was going to be peaceful and quiet compared to London!'

'Well, Ems, everywhere has a troublemaker or two. You'd do

well to remember that when you're out and about on the town, you know...' He smiled. But she wasn't going to let it drop.

'Dad, how the hell did you get injured? You're supposed to be office-based.'

He glanced around the room, looking for distraction and noticed she'd got a couple of logs crackling away in the fireplace. 'Ooh, real fire! This is nice!'

'Yeah, I got a bag of logs for a couple of pounds from the Tesco Metro. Dad?'

Ozzie had commandeered the spot right in front of the fire and was tucked up into a dozy circle of contented dog.

'He seems much more relaxed today.'

'I think he likes the fire. Dad...?'

He looked at her.

'No more getting your hands dirty please?'

'It wasn't on purpose, Ems. I was –'

'No more.' He could hear emotion in his daughter's voice.

'Okay,' he replied. 'That's the plan.'

She nodded and brushed her hand across her eyes. 'Cuppa?'

'Oh yes, a cuppa would be bloody lovely. Have we got anything to go with it?'

'We've got some mini Bakewells. Fancy one?'

'Perfect.'

He settled back into his chair as she disappeared into the kitchen.

EMMA REGARDED him sternly from across the dinner table that evening. 'I just can't believe first week back and you come home looking like this.'

He shrugged. 'Some berk with a saucepan got spooked and here we are. Not the most glamorous fight I've been in...'

He hadn't mentioned the knife. Nor would he. He'd told her the lip of the pan had caught his ear, hence the dressing. He certainly hadn't mentioned being nearly decapitated by his own tie and a Volvo.

'This is just normal old-fashioned rough-and-tumble. I had plenty of injuries like these when I was in uniform. You probably wouldn't remember.'

'Was this about the yacht case?'

'I was following a lead and I stumbled across some other incidental stuff.'

Rigby had been an unexpected bonus lead from Jo Bambridge, but maybe his judgement had been a little off-kilter after taking the big bastard down. He'd been feeling a little kick-arse, in a bit of a Dirty Harry mood after that, which was almost certainly why he'd been idiotic enough to go deeper into that house alone when he should have pulled back and waited for assistance to arrive.

'Are you going in to work tomorrow?' Her tone indicated there was a right and a *wrong* answer to be had.

'I have to, Ems.'

She clenched her teeth and tensed her jaw. It was the exact same face she used to pull when she was younger and absolutely refused to eat her greens. He fought the urge to smile.

'What about you?' he asked.

'What do you mean?'

'I mean, what are your plans?'

She gave in with a sigh. 'Well, I thought I'd make a start on decorating some of the rooms. The wallpaper's doing my head in.'

He nodded in agreement. The wallpaper in some of the rooms was peeling off at the corners, but far more pressing, in his opinion, was replacing the depressing faded patterns. They gave the house, particularly the bedrooms upstairs, a creepy Bates Motel vibe.

He scooped up another forkful of lentil bake. '*Plans*, Emma. I actually meant longer term. Not just tomorrow.'

'Longer term?'

Boyd smiled. 'You've been a super-star, Emma. Sorting out everything. The move. The sale...' He looked down at Ozzie, whose sole focus was the laden fork hovering in front of his mouth. 'The dog. You've got me focusing back on life again.'

'Well, you just needed my boot up your arse, that's all,' she said with a grin.

'And a great job you did. But now... it's my turn.'

'I'm fine, Dad. Don't you worry about me.'

'But –'

'I'm fine,' she said more firmly. 'I'll get a job somewhere round here. Soon. I promise, I'm *not* going to spend the rest of my life being your housekeeper. Relax.'

'Okay.'

'First, I just want to brighten it all up a bit. Make it nice. Then I'll get myself sorted.'

'You could still go to university.'

'I know.'

'Or college.'

'I know.'

'Or...'

'Dad?'

He looked up from his plate. 'Hmm?'

'I know,' she said. 'One thing at a time, hey?'

~

No one makes pillows that cater for bra-cup-shaped ear dressings.

Now *there* was a gap in the market worth pitching to the Dragons. Pillows with a hole in the middle that allowed an ear to stick through – perfect for those with one ear hanging off, or prone to sleeping with headphones on.

Boyd was an on-the-side sleeper: knees drawn up and his arms stretched out straight in front of him like a dog's front paws. Always on his left side. Of course it had to be that side.

He turned and lay on his back, staring up at the cracks in the ceiling rose and watching bare branch shadows wave down at him like cheery skeletons.

Billy... Only Julia and his parents had ever called him that. 'Billy Boyd' sounded like piss-taking from any other mouth. But Julia'd said it with love.

Billy ... Em's too young to be parenting you, baby.

Yes, that was exactly what Em was doing. Looking after him, afraid to leave him alone in case he began to spiral down.

Billy ...

He liked Julia haunting his mind. It happened so rarely, but, when it did, he could almost hear her voice as if she were there beside him, almost smell her presence – the pine-like smell of rosin from her cello strings, that brand of roll-on that he sometimes used to borrow when his ran out...

Let her go.

'I'm trying but she *won't* go,' he muttered. Emma was stubborn. Like him. Maybe even more so. Add his overwhelming, fatherly love into the mix and he'd lose a battle of wills against her every bloody time.

You have to push her away then, Billy. Otherwise she'll never start her own life.

'I know.'

Show her you're stronger now.

He would. He was better than he'd been six months ago – and a different person to this time last year even... But he was mourning a partner and a child. The loss of fifty per cent of his world...

As was she. And on top of that she had him to look after and worry about. He felt the familiar sense of shame.

She deserves to begin a new life.

That she did.

Sleep on that, love.

The subtle scent, the whisper of her voice faded. Never truly there in the first place but comforting all the same.

'All right,' he said, nodding. 'I'll do that.'

23

'It's not *foundation*,' said Boyd. 'It's *not* foundation.'

Minter leaned over Boyd's desk and peered more closely at him.

'It *looks* like foundation, boss.' He squinted. 'Yes, it definitely looks like lady's foundation.'

'It's a medical... *ointment*,' he replied irritably. He was damned if he was going to admit to Emma dabbing some concealer over the scabs on his face that morning. She had assured him you couldn't tell. He'd be having words when he got home – that was for sure.

'Whatever you say, boss,' Minter said with an irritating wink. 'You know, whatever floats your boat. It's nothing to be ashamed of. We're all very inclusive here, aren't we, team?'

Boyd ignored the stifled guffaws and glanced down at the blue folder Minter was still holding. 'SOC examiner's report on the Nix house, I hope?'

'Indeed it is, boss.' He handed it over. 'Sully told me to tell you it's still nice and warm from his photocopier.'

Boyd opened the cover and started to scan through the

contents. After a few moments he became aware that the detective sergeant was still lingering.

'What now?' Boyd said with a sigh, still not entirely sure if he was irritated or amused.

'Also,' said Minter, 'there was a call from a Mrs Nix. She wanted to know if there were any further developments on the case.'

'Right, thanks. I'll call her later.'

He returned to the contents of the SOC report. As he read through Sully's observations of the Nix house, peering closely at the evidence photos and location images, he felt as though he was beginning to get a better understanding of Gerald Nix.

The house was thoroughly stamped with his masculine personality. Any sign that he'd shared, or ever shared, this place with a woman had been wiped clean. Purged. Nothing current and nothing that even nodded to the twenty-odd years he'd lived with Jo.

There was a picture of Nix holding a certificate for something or other on the wall in his study. He had dark hair, wore glasses and had what a casting agent would call a weak chin. He had a Bill Gates-ish look to him – slightly nerdy and slightly gawky, but then appearances, as Boyd well knew, meant nothing. Ted Bundy, for Christ's sake, had looked like the kind of lovely young man you'd want to bring home to meet your nan.

The Nix lounge was large, open-plan. It was all modern leather-and-chrome furniture with, of course, several pieces of expensive 'art', no doubt curated and sourced on his behalf by some interior designer. There was an expensive Bose sound system and a large TV screen secured to a wall.

The kitchen was *used*. But that was because whoever'd been lurking in that house, the guy who'd jumped Boyd, had been making himself at home – for several days, it seemed. The pantry and freezer had cleared of ready meals, the dirty packaging piled up on the side.

Upstairs there was a master bedroom and two guest bedrooms, all en suite. The master was, again, very masculine, very minimalist. A wardrobe that ran along the entirety of one wall was hidden by sliding, mirrored doors.

Boyd presumed that Mr Nix enjoyed getting a good look at himself in bed.

Speaking of which...

There was no sign of his alleged trophy girlfriend – this Zophie, if that was even her proper name. Jo had seemed quite certain that the young woman had moved in with Nix, spraying her 'this is mine' pheromones all over the house that she'd called 'home' for so many years, like a feral cat. At least that's what Jo had said.

However, the photographs gave little evidence of that. If this young woman *had* moved in, she'd done it very minimally. The only evidence that was a few female toiletries in the bathroom and some clothes in a couple of wheeled suitcases.

She also appeared to have been sleeping in a guest bedroom. *So,* Boyd asked himself, *what does that suggest?* That Nix preferred his own room, his own space, but a little action down the hallway to call upon when the mood took him? Or perhaps she was calling the shots?

Maybe he was being too cynical here. There was always the boring alternative that she'd only partially moved in and they were just taking their time. One step at a time and all that.

In terms of clues about the nature of Nix's departure from his home, there were no apparent signs of a struggle, other than those caused by Boyd yesterday. Nothing broken or dislodged, no scuff marks or drag marks anywhere. But then, if the mysterious guest who'd been making himself at home there had been ransacking the house, pulling things out, looking for spoils, any potential evidence would probably be long gone.

Nix's study was very much the financial man's home office. A huge rosewood desk with a leather chesterfield armchair, neither of which would have looked out of place in the White House, sat next to a fully stocked, faux-cartographer's globe drinks cabinet. The only thing missing seemed to be Nix's computer. A rat's nest of detached cables splayed out from beneath the desk, suggesting Sully's team had taken it before the photos were taken. Boyd checked the addendum and saw that DC Warren, his exhibits officer, had dutifully logged Nix's computer as being bagged and tagged for forensic analysis.

Boyd found some margin-space in which to scribble.

Motive/narrative?

1. Nix does a runner with gf – why? Avoid debts? Liabilities?

2. Nix and gf forced onto boat – Why? Kidnapping? Extortion?

There was definitely a third party in the CCTV footage. Just a pair of legs, but that pair of legs that was very much with the other two. Another thought occurred to Boyd.

3. Jo Bambridge – revenge? The 3rd person a hitman?

Not that Jo Bambridge seemed to be the type to be well-acquainted with Sussex's criminal underworld, but that didn't mean she couldn't have found someone. And, to be fair, she had reason to want revenge.

4. Rigby. Was he somehow caught up in this?

Maybe he'd decided to get his money back from Nix. Or hired someone else to do it.

'KIDNAPPING?' DSI Sutherland repeated the word slowly like it was a charming new colloquialism he'd never heard before.

'The CCTV footage suggests that Nix and his lady friend could have been forced onto his yacht. There were definitely three of them, and enough people pissed off with him to make it a real possibility.'

Sutherland pursed his lips. 'You think maybe Rigby had

someone take them out to sea and torture Nix to find where his money was. Then murdered him and the girl.'

'It's an option.'

'Hmmm.' Sutherland absently tapped his cheek with an outstretched finger. 'You see, Chief Superintendent Hatcher has a theory that Nix and his lady friend may have encountered another vessel, possibly a migrant dinghy. Sully's SOC report from the boat mentioned multiple prints all over the deck.'

'Has she read the Nix house report?' Boyd asked, pointing to the folder on Sutherland's desk.

'She's read both reports. She's very *on it*, Boyd. This has the potential to get very political, Boyd. Which is why she wants to be kept in the loop.'

Boyd made a face. 'There's too much about Nix that stinks for this to be just some random encounter in the Channel with a boatload of migrants.'

'The Channel's a busy place. Chief Super thinks it's likely that the *Magpie* might have encountered and attempted to assist a struggling migrant vessel, and then ended up being overrun by them.'

'And what? Got tortured and butchered by the very people they'd just rescued? And then the killers hopped back into their shitty dinghy and carried on their merry way? D'you really think that's likely?'

Sutherland shrugged. 'A struggle ensued aboard. The cabin door was clearly smashed in. Perhaps Nix was trying to fend them off for fear he was about to be swarmed. Got badly wounded or killed in the process. Whoever did that would have needed to get rid of the evidence.'

Swarmed, that word again. Like migrants weren't people but some malevolent force of nature. As if they were creatures, fit only to be culled. Boyd took a deep breath and willed himself to stay calm.

'Sir, as you can clearly see from the ridiculous-looking

dressing on the side of my head, I was jumped and very nearly killed at Nix's house.'

'Yes. I know. Which begs the question, should you even be back at work?'

'Let me finish, sir – it's one hell of a coincidence, wouldn't you say? That somebody was there, in Nix's house going through his things, with him missing and the boat floating in the Channel in the state it was in?'

Sutherland shrugged. 'His house has been sitting empty for, what, three months?'

Boyd nodded.

'Right. Well, it's not beyond the realms of possibility that some local opportunist noticed that and decided to take advantage of it.'

Boyd took in another deep breath. He couldn't believe what he was actually hearing. 'Yes. I suppose that's a possibility. But we do have two people with clear motives: Rigby and Bambridge. It makes sense to rule those out before we start going down the road of a random –'

'Boyd,' Sutherland cut in. 'Her Madge has made it very clear to me, and so now I have to make it very clear to you, that she believes Nix and his passengers had an encounter out in the middle of the Channel, and that encounter may have been chance, or it may have been intentional.'

'Smuggling?'

'Or migrant trafficking.' Sutherland shrugged. 'There's good money to be made there.'

'And that's what the Chief Super believes?'

Sutherland nodded.

Boyd pressed on with his questions. 'Why is she steering this investigation?'

'She's not *steering* it, Boyd. She's just offering a fresh pair of eyes, that's all.'

'She's interfering.'

'Look, Boyd – she stuck her neck out to keep this in-house rather than hand it over to Border Force.'

Bloody Border Force. In the space of ten years they'd gone from Theresa May's cobbled-together version of Thunderbirds to a big brute of an agency. The Home Office had been steadily expanding, and it had grown even larger in the wake of Brexit. With their increased remit, they could easily have taken this case.

Boyd frowned. 'And why did she do that?' he asked.

Sutherland looked decidedly uncomfortable. 'Well, that's an operational matter.'

'And what exactly does that mean, sir?'

The Detective Superintendent was becoming pink-faced. 'This is policy-level stuff, Boyd. Which is above your pay grade and mine. She has a direction she wants you to focus on, and if you're going to be difficult about it, I can juggle DCI Flack's workload and he can take over. That's the long and short of it.'

Boyd got the feeling that Sutherland wasn't entirely happy with the position he found himself in. He wondered whether Her Madge had had taut words with him in turn.

'Sir?'

'Yes, Boyd.'

'Can I ask you about Nix's home computer? It says in the report that we logged it, but it's not in the station. Do you know where it is?'

Sutherland looked surprised. 'The digital forensics team here should have it.'

'Indeed they should. But they don't.' Boyd grabbed the file and flipped to the back of the SOC report. 'DC Warren signed for it to go to them, but they didn't receive it.'

'Hmmm...' Sutherland seemed genuinely puzzled. 'That's odd.'

'Well, yes. In fact, I'd go as far as to call it piss-poor evidence logging,' said Boyd. 'Unless, of course, somebody else asked for it to be redirected.'

Sutherland's expression hardened.

'Keep your mind on the case, Boyd. It'll turn up. Meanwhile, you take a long hard look at that migrant angle. All right?' said Sutherland, as he picked up his cold mug of coffee and leant back in his squeaky chair.

The meeting was over.

24

The table in the far corner of the canteen, away from the noisy serving counter and surrounded by comfy padded seats, seemed like a good enough place for an out-of-office meeting.

Boyd had gathered Minter, Okeke and Sully around the table and had even been generous enough to spring for a round of coffees and Danish pastries.

'I didn't know Apple airBuds came in that size.' Sully nodded at the dressing over his ear.

'Yeah, hilarious.' Boyd rolled his eyes. 'On any other day I'd be laughing my socks off.' He tore a sachet of sugar in half over his coffee and stirred it into the frothy milk. 'It appears,' he said, gesturing for them to speak quietly, 'that further up the chain of command they want us to lean towards an encounter with belligerent migrants at sea, alongside –' he held a hand up to Okeke, who was about to butt in – 'an unrelated random squatting-cum-assault-of-police-officer as the explanation for this case. Which, I'm sorry –' he looked at them in turn – 'strikes me as a load of old bollocks.'

'*What?* Is that coming from Sutherland or Hatcher?' asked Sully.

'It's coming through Sutherland from Hatcher,' Boyd replied. 'God knows why she wants to push us in that direction. I suspect it could be some sort of turf-war thing.'

'You're pushing your luck, aren't you, Boyd?' said Sully. 'You've been here at Hastings for all of two minutes and already you're a squeaky wheel.'

'Trust me when I say I'd much prefer to have a straightforward case dumped on me for my first effort.'

'There's too much "coincidence" in Her Madge's explanation,' said Minter. 'And, anyway, where does she think they disappeared to? This dinghy full of blood-soaked, murdering migrants?'

'Exactly.' Boyd scratched at his increasingly itchy beard. He really could do with finding his damned shaver. 'So... anyway, she wants us to go with this "migrants did it" thing. Okay, it's a theory. A bloody stupid one, if you ask me. But, fine, we'll enter it in the action log as an active line of inquiry. Meanwhile, I think we need to follow through on the Nix house... and concentrate on any leads we get from that.' He looked back at Sully. 'The scrote that jumped me... have you had anything back on the DNA swabs yet?'

'There's no match with anything on the boat, I'm afraid. We got a match for Gerald Nix and his girlfriend from some samples in the house. But passenger number three remains a mystery.'

'Well, it's good to have that confirmed at least,' said Boyd. 'So, we have several things going on here: Nix, who seems to have been a bit of a shit, to put it mildly, merrily making enemies. We've got Rigby with a ton of money that Nix seems to have hidden away from him. And we have Jo Bambridge, whose home and business that she helped build up were whipped out from under her feet by some new, younger model.'

'That's not entirely fair,' said Okeke. 'It was Nix who took everything from Jo, not this woman.'

'Right. Yes. Sorry, that's true.'

'And, let's not forget, this mystery woman has become collateral damage in all this. Probably dead in a possible revenge act that isn't actually anything to do with her.'

Boyd raised a hand in an admission of guilt. 'The point is,' he continued, 'the answers to this will almost certainly be on Nix's computer, which, between his house and this station, seems to have gone AWOL.'

'DC Warren signed it over to one of my team,' Sully interjected. 'Karl, I'm pretty sure.'

Boyd shook his head. 'Well, can you ask Karl where the hell it's gone?'

'I'll do it right now.' Sully got up from the table and headed out of the canteen with his phone to his ear.

Boyd turned to Minter. 'Can you go and have a chat with DI Grove? He's been given the Rigby pill factory to look into. Then maybe you and O'Neil can have another go at Rigby to see if there's anything else we can get from him about his dealings with Nix.'

Minter rubbed his hands together gleefully. 'Okay, boss. I'm on it.'

'And, Okeke, I want you to set up another interview with Jo Bambridge.'

'You want me to bring her in, guv?'

'No. Let's not put her on the defensive. Just make it sound like a follow-up chat. Like a family liaison visit or something. She was married to him for over twenty years – we don't want to go in too hard.'

'All right.'

'And see if you can find anything else out from Jo about this other woman. This Zophie. Just probe her a bit and see what gives.

'You want me to see if there's any meat on the bone for the revenge motive?'

'Exactly. And maybe chat woman-to-woman. Without my ugly mug around, she might open up a little more.'

'Gotcha.'

Sully returned to the table, pocketing his phone as he sat down. 'Border Force has got Nix's computer.'

'Why the hell have *they* got it?' Boyd could feel his temper rising. This didn't sit right with what Sutherland had told him about Her Madge wanting to keep this case in-house. Had someone overruled her?

Sully shrugged. 'All I know is what Karl told me. The Chief Super asked him, in person, to redirect it to them to look at. Border Force sent someone to collect it from the station while you were being sewn up in hospital.'

'For fuck's sake!' Boyd exploded. 'I go to A&E for a couple of hours and while my back's turned –' He stopped, shook his head and sighed. 'Right. Fine,' he said, getting up.

'Where are you going, guv?' asked Okeke.

Boyd glanced at the polystyrene ceiling tiles above.

'I think it's about time I had a little chat with Her Madge.'

25

'So they met on the internet?'

Okeke had struck lucky. Jo Bambridge was home in between work shifts. She was due back on the shop floor in a couple of hours.

'He found her on one of those sites where dirty old men look for flirty young tarts. He always had an eye for the younger ones. Don't all men when they reach that age? They fool themselves they can still attract something half their age,' said Jo. She squeezed the teabag against the side of the mug, then fished it out. 'Sugar?'

'No thank you,' replied Okeke, then she added, 'Men *are* fools. It's in their genes.'

Jo snorted. 'And that's where it should flipping well stay.'

Okeke laughed at her unintended pun. It was a good job Boyd wasn't there – he'd have never let her live that one down.

Jo handed Okeke her tea and led her back into the small lounge. They both sat down on the sofa, cups and saucers carefully balanced on their knees.

'When do you think Gerald first started talking to... is it Zophie?' asked Okeke.

'Zophie with a "Z".' Jo rolled her eyes. 'I remember thinking how pretentious that was. Pathetic.' She stirred her tea absently. 'I don't know. I don't imagine it was too long before I caught him out, because girls like that don't hang about, do they? Once they realise they've struck gold, they go in for the kill.'

'You make that sound like he's not to blame.'

'Of course it's his fault. He...' Her voice faltered. 'He basically cashed in twenty-two years of my life for a better-looking offer. I mean, I suppose I should be grateful to her for showing me what a nasty selfish piece of shit he is while I'm still able to go out there, get a job and help myself – to think I could have been turfed out of my home in my fifties or sixties.'

Okeke nodded along. 'You're still young, Jo.'

She managed half a smile. 'I'm not young.'

Okeke looked down at her notepad. 'So you separated eighteen months ago?'

'Nineteen.'

'Remind me how it happened?'

'You mean how I discovered it was going on?'

Okeke nodded.

'It was quite by accident. We were both at work.'

Okeke flipped back a couple of pages. 'That's the office you had on the High Street. In Rye was it?'

'Yes. I was at my desk; he was at his. It was a quiet morning – no appointments, no walk-in queries. He went out to grab a coffee from the Costa down the road. I got up to put a letter for him to sign in his in-tray. My hand nudged the mouse, the screen flicked on... and there it was...' She stopped for a moment, steadying her voice and clenching her lips together tightly.

'I know this isn't easy...'

'No. Look, I'm fine.' She sucked in a deep breath, then continued. 'I saw a pornographic image. A selfie. At first I just thought he was just being a dirty sod, downloading a bit of porn at work, filling in some boring time with, you know, that kind of thing. But then a message pinged up on his screen.' She took a sip of her tea. *'What do you think... Gerry?* That's what it said. And that's when I realised he wasn't just surfing porn but chatting someone up.'

Okeke nodded sympathetically. 'My man would lose his balls if I caught him doing that.'

'I clicked on the message... which, of course, took me to the chat they'd been having *all that morning...'* She laughed bitterly. 'And there was me thinking he'd been typing up another investment report for someone.' She looked at Okeke, her eyes glistening. 'They'd been exchanging messages for weeks. Talking about getting together, talking about *me.'*

'Saying what?'

'Oh...' She shook her head, as the threatened tears started to fall. 'That he found me unattractive. Uninteresting. *A dried-up old prune*, I think was the phrase he used.' She dabbed at her face. 'That's the second bloody time I've done this. I don't constantly cry about this, you know. I've honestly moved on from that bastard...'

'But it still hurts,' said Okeke gently. 'The betrayal.'

'Exactly. I was hurt, and I was conned.'

Their marriage had had another dimension to it. They were business partners as well. Twice the damage done.

'I'm not a weak woman, you know?' said Jo.

'Nor do you come across that way,' said Okeke. 'Having a cry about it – that's not weakness. That's how we vent, right? Men smack their fists into punch bags and laundry baskets. We do this.'

Jo nodded.

'So, go on... When he came back from his trip to Costa, what happened then?'

'We had a big shouting match right there in our office, in full view of the High Street. People walking past and looking in at us. If I hadn't been so angry and upset, I'd have been mortified at the idea of us screaming like that in full view of everyone.' She rummaged around in her sleeve for a tissue and dabbed at her cheeks. 'I left the office. I went home. I packed a bag and left.'

'You moved out?'

Jo nodded.

'And afterwards?' asked Okeke.

'There was no afterwards. That's the thing. He didn't try and call me to explain himself, to apologise. He didn't ask me to come back. I reckon he was rubbing his hands with glee. Like, "well, that was easy." I ended up calling him a week later. And he never answered. Eventually he sent me a text saying it was all over. That he'd found someone else. He said he was going to put together a document in which we'd agree the terms of the separation and our divorce.'

'And then you didn't hear from him. Is that right?'

'Yes. The divorce papers never came through. I left him voicemails and emails – he ignored them all. So last October I got a solicitor to write to him, several times over a couple of months. Gerald ignored her too.'

'And so you eventually went round to see him?' Okeke prompted.

'That's right. It's still officially *our* house. It was locked up – he'd changed the locks, so I couldn't get in. I could see he wasn't there. There was post built up in the hallway. I panicked that he could have disappeared with the money, and then I drove to the marina to find our yacht was missing.'

'And that's when you called the police to register a missing person?'

She nodded. 'And now he's dead, isn't he?'

'That's not confirmed, Jo. And I really can't comment further on the investigation yet. We're still gathering information.'

'The local paper said the boat had probably been swamped by migrants. That he'd encountered one of those overloaded little boats and that things got out of hand.'

'Well, that's the press for you, Jo. They'll write anything that sells papers.'

'Quite. It's utter, utter rubbish. There's no way that's true.'

Okeke looked at her; Jo seemed very certain. 'Why do you say that?'

'He hated them. Migrants. Said they were all vermin. They're the last people Gerald would have stopped to help.'

Boyd eventually received an email from Chief Superintendent Hatcher saying that she had a slot available to chat with him the next morning. He'd been very careful not to include mention of Nix's missing computer in his message, just that he wanted to update her on progress in the case so far.

That way, when he asked her about it directly, he'd get an unrehearsed answer.

He hung on in the office, waiting to hear back from either Minter or Okeke, but come five o'clock he decided that he could get their updates tomorrow morning. He grabbed his jacket and anorak, and threw a cursory nod to O'Neal and Warren, who were both clearly waiting for him to go so that they could clock off too.

He walked back home through misty rain that didn't even have the decency to form proper drops. By the time he got back it was fully dark and six o'clock.

26

Emma met him at the front door. 'I thought we could try some pub grub tonight. What do you think?'

She had her coat on already and Ozzie was on a lead – good to go. Boyd realised his ever-patient daughter must have been going a little stir-crazy, stuck at home all day with their uncertain rescue dog. She wasn't ready to walk Ozzie on her own because she had no idea how he'd react if he saw another dog.

After the fifty-minute walk back from work, Boyd had rather fancied lighting a fire in the grate, putting his feet up, pouring a glass of red and watching the flames dance while Emma watched her way through the early evening soaps.

But seeing her now, standing there in the hallway, lead in one hand, car keys in the other, coat on and a desperate beseeching expression on her face... he just couldn't bring himself to say no.

'Lovely. You got a particular pub in mind?'

'Yup. Just down the hill. I'll drive, though,' she said quickly. 'Save you walking any more. Your legs must be knackered with all this exercise!' She held out a hand through the open door. 'Anyway, I think it's starting to rain.'

EMMA PARKED the car in Pelham Place – the town's main seafront car park. The crazy golf course beside it looked rather forlorn in the spitting rain. A man and his two small kids were on the last hole and looked keen to get this dumb idea over and done with.

They walked Ozzie along the beach, past the deserted Flamingo arcade, all the way up to the Rock-a-Nore breakwater wall. Emma wanted Ozzie to go to the toilet before taking him into the pub.

'So this pub takes dogs in, then?'

'Yes, I checked on Tripadvisor, Dad – dog's welcome. Dog poo... not.'

Ozzie delivered, and Emma bagged it up and dropped the package into a bin. 'Finally.'

She led them into George Street. Okeke had been right, Boyd mused: George Street did look a little like something J. K. Rowling might have dreamt up – a mixture of black wooden and white-washed wattle buildings that tilted precariously towards each other across the narrow street, almost as though they were leaning into a whispered conversation, mixed with the faded grandeur of the Edwardian stone and Victorian brick. The street lamps were on, forgotten Christmas lights drooped across the narrow pedestrian-only cobbled road, glistening like junk jewellery. Either side of them, old pubs and revamped vodka bars jostled for attention alongside antique stores and knick-knack boutiques, all spilling their warm light across the cobbles in a come-hither invitation to passers-by.

'Very nice,' he said appreciatively, puffing out a cloud of

breath as Ozzie snuffled at a ball of discarded chip paper at his feet.

'You'll love this pub, Dad. It's got character.'

She led him to a place called Ye Olde Pump House with an old doorway so low he had to duck to get through. Inside, the warm fug immediately hit them and Boyd quickly shed his coat.

A jukebox was playing the WaterBoys – 'The Whole of the Moon' – the fireplace was crackling with freshly poked, turned logs and the whole place reeked, very pleasantly, of wood smoke and varnish.

Emma spoke to a young man behind the bar who replied, 'Anywhere you like. I'll just get you some menus.'

They found a quiet alcove at the front beside a lead-lined bay window that looked out onto the street. Boyd sat down on a threadbare red velvet bench. Ozzie remained on all fours, staring at him.

'This your first pub, eh, boy?'

Ozzie's eyes flicked sideways to Emma for advice on how to respond. 'Probably,' she replied for him. 'He's spent most of his life tied up in sheds and backyards, though he did live on the streets for a bit, so you never know.'

She'd told her dad all this before. She'd read out Ozzie's backstory from the Spaniel Aid website. There'd been something about him being kept in a garage for two years before being adopted and rejected a number of times. He'd had no chip in him, so they had no real idea of his age; it was all guesswork.

'That's so sad, isn't it?' she'd said at the time. 'The vet thinks he's about nine, and we'll never know what he's experienced in all those years.'

Ozzie finally seemed to understand he wasn't going to be invited to sit up at the table with his new family and instead curled up beneath it and let out a sigh.

The young barman came over with menus and cutlery ,and set them out on the table. 'Chef's special tonight is –' he started, then stopped mid-sentence as he stared at Boyd's face. 'Ohmygod!' He grinned beneath a floppy black fringe. 'You're the guy!'

'The guy?'

'The guy!'

This exchange was beginning to sound like a crap version of *Breaking Bad*.

The young man laughed. 'The bleeped copper?'

Boyd looked around the pub – the general idea, in the force, was to be discreet about your job. Luckily it was virtually empty.

'Yeah,' said the lad. 'It's you, isn't it? The guy who got swear-bleeped by BBC Southeast?'

Emma snorted with laughter. 'Yup. That's him.'

The barman glanced at the dressing over Boyd's ear. 'What happened to you, then?'

'I had a fight with a lawnmower,' Boyd deadpanned.

The young man grinned and winked. 'Lawn Enforcement, eh?'

Boyd couldn't help a chuckle. To be fair, the lad was quick and funny. Still, he was bloody starving. And he knew exactly what he wanted.

Boyd ordered cod and chips. The bastard seagull buggering off with his lunch had left him feeling cheated. But, he was out of luck again. The young man came back five minutes later and apologetically reported that they'd been let down by their usual supplier today. Boyd wondered whether the same bloody bird was somehow to blame. He ordered a cheeseburger instead and settled back.

'I don't think I actually thanked you properly yet, Ems,' he said after the young man had deposited their drinks in front of them.

'For what?'

'All the help. Getting us down here.'

'*Pfft*,' she replied.

'And for the last two years,' he added.

She frowned as though it was a stupid conversation for them to be having. 'I think we both needed to get out of the old house. It wasn't good for either of us there.'

'I could have been more helpful, though.'

She shook her head, her frown deepening. 'No. You couldn't.' She took a sip of her drink. 'You were broken, Dad.'

'And so were you.'

'But you *saw* it. You spoke to Mum –' She stopped, sipped again. Then continued: 'I didn't have to process *that* on top of everything. You needed me to step up... or we'd both be back there still.'

She was right. Without her, they wouldn't have moved forward at all. Putting the London house on the market, finding a buyer and then the new house in Hastings had taken eighteen months. Much of that time Boyd had been barely able to function. She'd done all the thinking and doing for him.

'Anyway, it's all sorted now,' she said with a smile. 'We're here. And I love it already.'

Boyd returned her smile. *Stay positive.* 'So, what's so good? What do you love about it?'

'Err... not having to take the Tube to work every day. Having a view of the sea. Having room for a dog... and places to walk him. The ambience at this end of town, the quirkiness... everything really!'

Emma had left behind school friends she'd known since reception, as well as a boyfriend – although Boyd suspected she'd been looking for an exit there for some time – and she'd only just begun to build a social life that took advantage of the best bits of London living: the music venues, wine bars.

Boyd couldn't help but ask, 'It's not too, I dunno, *too quiet* for you, though?'

'You're kidding? It's what I need. All that constant –' she shook her head as she tried to pluck the right word from it – '*city*. The noise. The hassle. The cost. The shitty manners.' She rolled her eyes. 'And those red-eye shifts were awful.' Emma had spent the last year working in a hotel, doing the kind of work and hours that most Brits turned their noses up at.

She was being sincere, he could tell; she wasn't just saying what she thought he wanted to hear. After what had happened to her mother and brother, followed by practically a whole year of Covid lockdown and having to deal with him on top of that, London probably didn't have a whole load of great memories for her.

Still, Emma was young. Only twenty-two. University and her design degree had been put on indefinite hold after what had happened. Her independence had been postponed for over two years now because – and she'd never admit this, not to him, anyway – she was too afraid to leave her broken father at home on his own.

And all the while she was shouldering her own burden of grief.

Boyd desperately wanted her gone – that sounded bad. Gone, for all the right reasons. Gone – to begin her university degree, to capture her life in snatched selfies on a Facebook page, to hear her night-out stories in hasty, noisy phone calls home. He didn't want her stuck in a creaking old Edwardian half-a-mansion overlooking a crusty old fishing town. Although, he admitted, he'd miss her so much.

'I know you worry about me, Dad,' Emma continued. 'That I'm missing out on things and that I'm just here for you. Well, I'm not. I'm here for me too. I can't... I couldn't face leaving home. Not last year.'

'What about now?'

She shrugged. 'Now?' It took her a few moments to come up

with an answer. 'I think I'm in a better place now. I think you are too.'

He nodded. 'A better place. Though, that's a pretty low bar to jump.' He smiled ruefully.

She smiled back. 'Onwards and upwards, eh?'

'Onwards and upwards,' he echoed, raising his glass. 'So,' he continued, 'university?'

'I dunno, maybe, at some point. I was thinking of getting a job soon. You know, once we've sorted the house out and made it look a little less gloomy.'

'Well, you know, we've got spare money,' said Boyd. 'There's no need for a student loan. You could –'

'I don't know, Dad. Maybe I'm not quite ready to think long term yet. A job will do me just fine for now.'

'Doing what?'

'Not policing, thank you.' She absently reached down and stroked Ozzie's rump. 'Maybe in something like hotel management. I've got London-based five-star experience. I've got decent A-level grades. I'll get a decent reference from the Wharton.'

'It's mostly grubby bedsits down here.'

'No, there's hotels too, Dad. It's a town that's slowly coming back. The whole staycation thing is exploding. I'll get a job in the next month. No probs.'

Boyd felt an overpowering urge to reach out and hug her tightly right there in the pub. *You, Emma, are the most level-headed, most resilient person I've ever known*, he wanted to say to her, but he didn't. She tended to cringe every time he tried to praise her. Daddy's Little Princess syndrome didn't sit too well with her. She was every bit the strong woman Julia was and a probably a little bit more.

'A big-city girl like me?' She grinned with a dash of casual bravado. 'I'll do just fine here, Dad.'

He suspected she'd do fine anywhere.

The barman came back with their meals. He set them down on the table and asked if they needed anything else.

'We're good, thanks,' said Boyd.

Instead of turning and heading back to whatever task he had next, the young man lingered. Boyd looked up at him. 'Can I help you?'

He pulled his phone out of his back pocket. 'Look... uh... Do you mind if I grab a selfie?'

'What?'

The barman shrugged. 'You're kind of, like, a local celebrity, mate. Sort of a Hastings meme. You're the Bleeped Copper.' He tapped his iPhone screen. 'Can I?'

Boyd waved him away in horror, while Emma laughed.

'No, you bloody can't!'

27

Sea Breeze Campsite was a caravan and camping park that had enjoyed a good fifty years of business before it finally went under in the shitty wipe-out year that was 2021.

The combination of gradual decay, lack of investment, the years of austerity and the final straw – the year of Covid – were the reasons for its inevitable demise. The seven-acre camp site with one hundred and seventeen trailers and fifty-three vacant hard stands, for those visitors with their own camper vans or caravans, had had a good innings, but time had eventually been called.

The business had gone bankrupt, its thirteen staff laid off, and a firm of accountants were brought in to determine what money, if any, could be made from selling off the trailers and land.

It hadn't been a quick process, and eleven months on not much had happened, other than the once-tidy lawns around each plot had become islands of tall grass, hiding the wheels and stands of the trailers, and various weeds had begun taking advantage of the cracks and potholes in the tarmac drives and cycle paths.

Sea Breeze Campsite was a ghost town now.

The accountants overseeing the bankrupt camp had hired a permanent security guard to reside there for the first six months, but eventually they'd given up on that. There was nothing of much value to watch over once the camp's office huts, grocery shop and licensed clubhouse had been stripped of their tills, computers and vending machines.

It had become the place of choice for errant teenagers to hang out, smoke and get trashed. A number of the trailers had been broken into and were surrounded by a constellation of crushed beer cans, broken alcopop bottles, empty capsules of nitrous oxide and used condoms.

Right now, though, at this precise moment, Sea Breeze Campsite stood empty and alone, save for a few feral cats and opportunist foxes.

And one solitary human occupant.

Here, lived a man on his own. Living by candlelight.

Living off of an ever-decreasing stash of money. Living a cat's ninth life that was also, he suspected, counting quickly down.

His nights were disturbed, sometimes by foxes squaring up to each other, and occasionally by kids messing around where they shouldn't.

He spent the nights watching and waiting.

The days were when he felt safest sleeping.

28

'Ah, yes, the update on the Nix case. Do come in!'

Boyd stepped into Chief Superintendent Hatcher's office.

'DCI Boyd, I'm so sorry I haven't had the chance to personally welcome you on board our Division before now. How're you finding things? Settling in okay?'

Her black rimmed glasses were worn halfway down her nose and her dark hair was cut into a wavy bob, one side tucked away behind her left ear, the other side flapping like a bat's wing.

'I'm settling in fine, thanks, ma'am,' he replied.

'It's been a busy first few days for you. I'm sorry we had to throw you straight in at the deep end,' she said, studying him over the top of her glasses.

'That's all right. It's done me good to hit the ground running, I think.'

She gestured at one of the two seats in front of her desk. 'Come, sit down. Do you want a tea? Coffee?'

He wasn't sure how long this was going to take, and there was nothing worse than having the business end of your chat over and done with before the coffee turned up and then having to make small talk until it was gone. Particularly with the Chief Super. Any Chief Super.

'I'm fine, thanks, ma'am. I've just had one.'

He took a seat.

'How are you finding it here?' she began.

'Well, I know my team's names now, where the canteen is and the nearest toilet,' he quipped. 'That's not bad progress for a first week, right?'

She laughed. 'That's good work.'

Her Madge was younger than he thought she'd be. With that nickname he'd been expecting – obviously not Margaret Thatcher – but another mature grey-haired iron lady with flinty eyes.

Actually, Hatcher could have been anywhere from forty to fifty-five. Young for such a rank. Possibly younger than him. Which made for an odd, slightly unsettling dynamic. He was used to grizzly Old Sweats in the ranks above him.

She glanced at the dressing over his ear. 'I hope that looks worse than it is,' she said. 'I heard you'd been in the wars.'

'It's just a few stitches. But because it protrudes –' *obviously it protrudes it's an ear, idiot* – 'the A & E nurse made me wear this dome-thing to protect it.'

'A bra cup?' She widened her eyes comically.

He laughed politely, as if it was the first time he'd heard that particular description. 'It does look a bit like that.'

'Very vogue,' she said, smiling. She didn't comment about the scabs on his face – the foundation dabbed on this morning had been a little more refined and a bit less of a Donald Trump job.

Hatcher tapped the keyboard of her open laptop and in the reflection of her glasses he saw something on the screen had changed. 'How are you finding Hastings?' she asked.

'Nice. It's a welcome change from London. It's all a bit messy and chaotic there now.'

'All the upheaval? I know. Brexit has created a completely different eco-system in this country. There've been winners and losers right across the board.'

He nodded.

'Everyone's running about like headless chickens, investors either fleeing for the hills or scrambling for the bargains. Things will eventually settle down.'

Boyd cleared his throat. He was here for a reason, and discussing the state of the nation wasn't it. 'Ma'am?'

'Yes?' She looked up from her laptop.

'The Nix case.'

'Yes. Now, how's that coming along?'

After his chat with Sutherland, he was sure she was right up to speed. But he played along. 'Slowly. Because the forensics on the yacht were pretty messy and compromised, exposed to the weather for maybe three months, we're exploring avenues via the forensics taken from Nix's house.'

She nodded at his bandaged ear. 'And that's where you got that injury?'

'Right.'

A frown flitted across her forehead. 'You know, I do wonder whether throwing this one at you so soon was a good idea.'

'No, it's fine, ma'am. To be honest, getting back into the swing of things, being on a team again, I think it's what I've needed for some time.' He nodded. 'This is good for me.'

'Well, I'm sure you can understand my concern,' she replied. 'From what I heard, you rugby-tackled one chap at a junkyard and were then swiftly ambushed inside a house by a burglar. Call me old-fashioned, but I think it's conventional for a DCI to be more HQ-based.'

A burglar. He was pretty sure that neither of them believed that one. He kept his face neutral.

'Yes, quite right, ma'am. It's just... how things shook out.'

'DSI Sutherland and I have been chatting and he says if you need a recovery day or two, DS Minter's perfectly capable of running things. And, if you need longer, DCI Flack could supervise your case as well as his?'

Boyd suspected she was aware that he didn't share her migrant theory. Did she want him out of the way for a bit so he couldn't stir the pot?

'No, thanks. I'm okay. I'm fine, ma'am.'

She nodded. 'Well, the offer's there.'

'Thank you. Anyway, the Nix case...' He sat forward in his chair, which groaned audibly under his weight. 'I was informed that Gerald Nix's personal computer has been redirected to Border Force.'

Here we go.

Her face flexed for a moment, then in a smooth motion, her gaze met his and she clasped her hands together in front of her chin. He knew it had been done on her orders. She was either going to fake ignorance or acknowledge the instruction. Lie or level.

If she went with the former, he was going to have to tread *very* carefully.

She nodded slowly. 'Yes, I know about that.'

Inwardly he let out a sigh. 'Do you know why that was, ma'am? We could really do with it here. We need to get going with our investigation into Mr Nix's online activities.'

She pushed her glasses up her nose. 'Do you think he's guilty of anything, Boyd?'

'All options are on the table at the moment, ma'am. But it may help us to identify who else was on the boat with him at the very least.'

'A partner and someone else, wasn't it?'

'His partner, yes. We don't really know much about her yet.'

'So do you think we're definitely looking at murder then, or do you think missing persons is still on the table?'

'There was a fair bit of blood down below and in the cockpit.'

She'd read the reports, according to Sutherland. Why was she being so resistant to the possibility that a murder or two had occurred on the boat?

'I mean,' he continued, 'since we don't have bodies, it's always possible both Nix and his partner are still alive, but... I think it's very unlikely.'

She tapped her finger on the edge of her laptop thoughtfully. 'And the other person? Do we have any idea who that was?'

'Well, they, by elimination, are a person of interest.'

'The person who attacked you –'

'Isn't him. The forensics on the boat didn't match.'

'Hmmm.'

He absently fiddled with his tie. 'Ma'am?'

'Yes?'

'Ma'am, can I ask why Border Force have taken possession of his computer?'

Hatcher tucked the loose bat wing of dark hair back behind her ear and paused to think. 'They have an interest in Nix,' she replied slowly.

'Such as?'

Her face hardened ever so slightly. 'If they have their reasons, Boyd, they have their reasons.'

'Well, that computer *may* have – probably *does* have – a direct bearing on my case.'

'DCI Boyd, I appreciate that you're trying to do the best job you can here. But Border Force answers directly to the Home Office. As an agency, they outrank us. If they want the computer, they have the computer.'

'The thing is, ma'am, Nix may have had some dodgy dealings with Aiden Rigby.'

'That's the chap who was brought in yesterday?'

'Yes. He's got form for fraud, scams, that sort of thing. He had Nix hide a tidy sum of money away for safe keeping. So it's possible – in fact it's quite likely – that Nix has got a digital paper trail on that computer that implicates them both in laundering and hiding criminal money.'

Her body stiffened ever so slightly. 'Boyd,' she said sharply, 'I'll tell you what I know. Border Force believe Mr Nix may have been involved in trafficking migrants with his yacht. They think he was making money rendezvousing with high-fee-paying migrants in the Channel. They believe that something went wrong this time, perhaps a disagreement about the price – who knows? But it went wrong for him.' She settled back in her seat. 'That's *all* I can tell you.'

'What about the man who jumped me in the Nix home? That wasn't just a random coincidence!'

'Now listen.' Her voice lowered in tone. Indeed, it was almost Thatcher-like. 'They have more information than we do. They have an investigation already running on Gerald Nix –'

She stopped talking and glared across the desk at him.

He said nothing. Boss Interview 101 – once they start glaring, you shut up.

They played ten seconds' worth of Who Blinks First?

'Ma,am,' Boyd said in a conciliatory tone. 'Migrants or no migrants, I really can't get much further without that computer.'

'Don't turn this into something it isn't,' she snapped. 'The focus of this investigation, Boyd, is *what happened on that boat with those migrants!*' She took a deep breath and continued in a slightly softer tone. 'Border Force have a more complete picture than we do. And we're not going to waste valuable resources wrestling with them, second-guessing where they're going with it. We do know, however, that a violent exchange occurred on board that yacht and we have signs, as far as I'm concerned, of a boat impact, with scuff marks, footprints and fingerprints that suggests it was boarded by someone.'

'Uh, that's –'

'And... trafficking is the way Border Force are leaning. So, we're not going to have two departments touting two different theories, understood?' The lines on her forehead smoothed out as though they'd never been there. 'Is that clear? If that's all...'

Boyd nodded as he stood up to leave. 'Yes, ma'am. Perfectly.'

Clear as bloody mud, he thought. *What the fuck is going on here? And what are you up to?*

29

'Battered sausage and chips please.'

Boyd took his boxed lunch away from the seating area outside the café and away from the feathered thugs perched on the nearby safety rails, watching and waiting for an opportunity to strike. He walked the length of the pier, past the Bier Garden to where Perspex windbreaks offered him some shelter from the chilly sea breeze.

He found an empty bench with a view out across the Channel. The sea was grey and choppy today, throwing suds and spray up into the air, almost reaching the pier's decking.

He drizzled zigzag ketchup lines across the chips and speared the first of them with his wooden fork. More than once recently, Emma had voiced that he was putting weight on around his middle. Not the usual up-down amount, but a steady growing gut tyre that was in danger of taking him over the line from dad bod to fat plod.

But dammit. These chips were good.

His mind turned to the press conference he was supposed to be giving later this afternoon. Apparently one of the red tops had run the yacht story on their third page this morning. On a *slow* news day, Nix's boat might have made page one, but this morning another member of the cabinet had been caught with his trousers down – literally – and salacious details of that had trumped migrant fearmongering.

All the same, the third-page headline had been unhelpfully large and eye-catching.

So this afternoon's Punch and Judy show was going to be about tamping down that nonsense while at the same time gently airing Hatcher's suggestion that Nix *might* have got his hands dirty in the trafficking business.

What Boyd didn't get was why Hatcher cared one way or the other. Maybe she just wanted to stay on the right side of Border Force? These days they seemed to be the one government body whose budget actually increased year on year. Maybe Her Madge saw a sunnier future working for them than Sussex Police? Paving the way, perhaps?

He managed to finish his sausage and chips without being mugged by gulls and made his way back along the pier. On his way past the café he spotted Minter and Okeke inside, standing in the queue. Minter was saying something that was making her laugh heartily. She was almost doubled over and waving a hand for him to stop so she could catch her breath.

Boyd almost managed to pass by without being spotted.

Okeke caught his eye and straightened up, the smile still on her face as she waved to him and beckoned him to join them. He raised his arm and mouthed *Sorry*, as he shook his head and continued in the direction of the station.

'The Chief Super's a little concerned about you doing the press conference, Boyd,' said Sutherland.

'Why?' Boyd asked.

Sutherland lifted his chin and gazed down his nose at the

side of Boyd's head. 'That silly dressing on your head. She thinks it'll be a visual distraction.'

'Oh, for fu– *really*?'

'She's worried that all people will see is a damn bra cup strapped to your head.' Sutherland pressed his lips and tried to look apologetic. 'Her words, Boyd, not mine.'

'Of course she is,' muttered Boyd. He suspected it had more to do with what he might say rather than how ridiculous he might look.

'How do you feel about DS Minter standing in for you today?'

'I'm not sure, sir. Has he done one before?'

'Not really, no. But he's a good lad. I'm sure he'll be fine.'

Boyd suspected it was going to be a packed house, thanks to the tabloid's wonderfully antagonising headline. Although God knows he would be more than happy to pass that particular buck, it would be a hell of an ask to throw Minter straight into something like that. 'Does he know?' Boyd asked.

'Not yet. I thought it best to run it past you first.' Sutherland's pale round snowman head bobbed up and down. 'Out of courtesy.' He coughed out an awkward laugh. 'Not that you get to decide, of course.'

'Well, if he's not done one of these before, it's probably not a great idea to start him on one that's got this kind of attention,' said Boyd.

Sutherland screwed up his face. 'The Chief Super thinks it'll be good for him. And she really, *really* wants someone other than you to do it. Come on, Boyd. She's right. That's thing's distracting. Do you want to brief Minter, or shall I?'

Boyd shrugged and sighed. 'I'll talk to him.'

'*What?*' said Minter. His handsome, chiselled face suddenly had a pitiful lamb-about-to-be-slaughtered quality to it. '*This* afternoon?'

Boyd looked at his watch. 'In just under two hours' time. I can't do it cos those hacks are just going to question-bomb me about this.' He gestured to his ear. 'Right, we need to work out what you're going to say.'

'Fuck me. Really?'

'That would be a poor way to start,' said Boyd, trying to raise a smile. 'Look, I'll type up the statement for you to read out. If you read it in the monotone way most of us do, they'll barely even notice you speaking.'

Minter... Muscly Minter with his barely concealed tattoos and bulging pecs suddenly looked like a toddler staring down his first day at reception.

'C'mon, mate – that was meant to be funny,' said Boyd, trying to be jovial.

'Oh, right.' Minter was starting to look a bit green at the edges.

Boyd felt sorry for him. He gently dropped a fist on Minter's shoulder like he was a best man offering wedding day advice. 'You'll do fine. The press lights usually wash everyone out. You won't really see them. And you just read what's there.'

'Just the statement, sir?'

'They'll ask questions at the end. Usually all at the same time. Just pretend to pick one of them out of the noise and answer it with a bland "It's early days yet". Plus, it'll be the end of the day – they're all going to want to get home straight after. Then you can go home and have a beer.'

Minter's face had gone so pale he actually looked like he was about to throw up his fish-and-chip lunch on the incident room's floor.

'You all right?'

'Ah... it's... okay, guv. I just... I've just never been very good with public speaking.'

'The British curse.' Boyd smiled.

'Huh?'

'The mortal fear of embarrassment. Us awfully polite Brits are castrated by it.'

He remembered reading an article about the Fear. Apparently a number of Fortune 500 CEO's had been quizzed about the stresses of their jobs and the things they found hardest and easiest to do. For British CEOs, laying workers off had turned out to be surprisingly low on their list, but right at the top was making the end of year speech at the work's Christmas Do.

'You'll be fine,' he said again, reassuringly. 'Right then, I'd better get the statement typed up.'

Boyd returned to his desk and was about to sit down when he noticed that Minter had followed in his wake. 'Yes?'

'Do you want me to help you, sir?' he asked.

'Nope. It's okay. You go and get yourself ready for your big date.' Boyd flapped his hand. 'Go on and let me get on with this. You'll be fine.'

30

'Following a number of lines of inquiry, which include the possibility of an act of murder, at sea some three months ago...'

DS Minter took a deep breath and looked up from his sheet of paper. Boyd was standing a few feet behind him, trying to hide his dressing by turning his head to the left as if staring at something far more interesting than the speaker in front of him.

The detective sergeant had done well so far. Slow, steady, monotone and dull-as-hell with frankly no more information than Boyd had given out at the press briefing earlier that week.

Now, however, it was time for questions. The trickier off-script bit.

'All right,' said Minter gruffly, looking round the room. 'I'll take a couple of questions.'

As Boyd had anticipated, the room was packed this time. The tabloid headline had done a fantastic job of prodding every news editor in the country into sending someone to Hastings to catch up on it.

'Do you know if the murderers were migrants travelling from Calais?'

Migrants – bingo. Boyd mentally ticked the first box.

Minter cleared his throat. 'At this, uh, stage in the investigation... we are not ruling anything in or, uh, indeed, committing to have anything ruled in or out. Even.'

Boyd resisted the urge to face-palm and instead clamped his jaw shut and carried on studying the very interesting wall to his left.

'There are suggestions that Mr Nix was attempting to provide assistance to a migrant dinghy when they were swarmed. Can you comment on that?'

Swarmed – bingo again.

'At this... stage in the investigation...'

Oh, for fuck's sake, don't say the exact same thing again!

'... we have not ruled out any line of inquiry... at this stage.'

Better. Jesus.

'Chris Simmons, BBC. Are you certain Mr Nix and his passengers are dead? Is this still a missing persons inquiry or has it become a murder inquiry?'

Minter absentmindedly scratched the side of his head, a worried expression on his face, and Boyd wondered what that was going to look like on the six o'clock news this evening. Some of the cameras flashed.

Great. That's tomorrow's print image, then.

'Well, we're uh... we're not assuming they're dead, but...' Minter glanced back over his shoulder at Boyd for help.

Boyd flashed his eyes angrily at him. *Turn back around, you muppet!*

He did so. 'Uh... since the murders happened three months ago, we're –'

'So you ARE confirming they're dead?'

'No. I said we are *not* assuming that, but... you know...'

'You just said "the murders",' replied Simmons.

'*Oh for Christ's sake,*' muttered Boyd. He took a step forward and joined Minter at the lectern. 'The forensic evidence suggests that there was a violent altercation aboard the boat, which may – I'll stress that word... *may* – indeed be a murder, but at this stage we can't say for certain.'

Boyd saw a ripple of camera lenses glinting as they swung ever so fractionally to zero in on him. *You buggers all getting a clear shot of my ear, are you?*

He continued, 'Now, there *is* evidence that the boat was sabotaged in a bid to make it sink – obviously to eliminate the crime scene and any forensic evidence.'

'We heard reports that this was impact damage from another boat?' said the BBC journalist. 'That could suggest a migrant boat encounter? An act of assistance that went wrong, perhaps?'

'No. Not necessarily.'

'Are there any indications that Mr Nix might have been involved in drug smuggling or even migrant trafficking?' called out someone in the audience

Boyd's honest answer to that was there was no evidence to suggest he was involved in that. None whatsoever. But it was Her Madge's go-to theory and now some twat had just forced him to back it or sack it.

He felt like a bloody deer caught in the headlights of a container truck.

'It... Well, it can't be ruled out,' Boyd answered. 'But, as far as I'm *aware*, there's no evidence to suggest that's the case.'

Shit. He'd done it now.

'Do you have a more likely working theory?' asked someone else.

Boyd was dimly aware he was standing in the full blinding glare of a dozen or so LED lamps on stands, probably looking pasty-faced and like roadkill to boot... with a sodding bra cup stuck to the side of his head. Well, at least it would keep Minter's face out of tomorrow's papers.

'A kidnapping gone wrong,' he said finally. 'That's what I believe we're most likely dealing with.'

And I, he thought ruefully, *will most likely be dealing with Her Sodding Madge as soon as I get back to the office.*

Thank fuck it's Friday.

31

oyd was nursing a very sore head.

Last night he and Emma had ordered a Chinese, watched *Bake Off* and opened a bottle of red. And once again he'd finished it off after she'd gone to bed. If that wasn't bad enough, he'd gone on to open a second one.

He'd poured a big glass, turned the lights out in the lounge and sat there, his eyes adjusting to the amber glow from the street lamp outside, and watched the winter rain spatter against the tall windows for what had turned into a couple of hours.

This morning a lazy mist was lingering along the beach, turning the hill line, the tall seafront townhouses and the pier into a monochrome shadow theatre of haunting grey silhouettes.

Ozzie was enjoying himself, at least. He'd thrown his anchors down and was stubbornly holding ground as he investigated a tangled clump of seaweed and plastic that the silent tide had left behind.

Boyd had had a day and a night to review how things had gone down on the Friday.

Not that well, was his verdict. DSI Sutherland had pulled

him aside just as he was getting ready to pick up his coat and head home for the weekend.

'I think we know how this conversation goes, right?' Sutherland had said.

'The Chief Super's not happy?'

'Not happy? She's incandescent. She said you directly disobeyed an order!'

'DS Minter was struggling. I stepped in to help.'

'That's not what she's furious about, Boyd. You floated a bloody kidnapping theory – without any evidence, without any warning –'

'There's more evidence for that than this ludicrous idea that migrants attacked the boat and killed Nix,' Boyd had countered.

'You check with me first before you announce a new theory. Especially in front of a room full of bloody journalists!'

'I floated the idea to the Chief Super.'

'I know. And she told you that Border Force have an ongoing investigation into Nix. Your blurted-out speculation may have had a detrimental impact on their case. I don't know how you did things in the Met, Boyd, but you're here now and you answer to us.'

'So what the hell was I meant to say?' he'd pushed, obstinately.

'You say what the Chief Super tells you to say. Look –' Sutherland suddenly softened his tone, obviously trying to turn the bollocking into something more like a piece of big-brotherly advice – 'the Chief Super wants you to take a week off. Minter's senior enough and experienced enough to oversee the investigation in the short term, and he's got DSI Flack on hand if he needs help.'

'So I'm suspended?'

Sutherland had shaken his head. 'This is sick leave. You've got a face that looks like you've been attacked by a feral cat – and the ear, the concussion...'

'No concussion, sir.'

'The PTSD.'

'I don't have any –'

'*Boyd!*' he'd snapped, his little apple-shaped cheeks suddenly blotching pink. '*Take the fucking week off.*'

It hadn't been the most auspicious end to Boyd's first week in Sussex Police.

He had a nagging feeling about this kidnapping theory, though. That's what it was beginning to look like and smell like to him – a kidnapping, or some sort of botched attempt. And, at the moment, the most likely candidate in Boyd's eyes, was Aiden Rigby, whether he'd been physically involved or not.

And there was something else niggling away at the back of his mind.

The girl. Zophie. They had virtually zero to go on, but, based purely on Jo's descriptions, he was beginning to form a picture.

Boyd recalled a nature show he'd watched on TV last year. (There'd been a *lot* of that last year – daytime-telly watching). It was one of those programmes with David Attenborough and his whispery voice-over. It had been about symbiotic relationships between animals. How evolution had produced these weird double acts of co-operating species that figuratively *scratched each other's backs*. There'd been the mutually beneficial ones, such as sharks with little fish that cleaned their teeth by eating the shreds of meat caught between them. Then there'd been the more parasitic relationships, where one species didn't co-operate with another but coerced it, or, more accurately, hijacked it. One particular example that he could distinctly remember was that of the emerald wasp and the cockroach. The wasp would sting the cockroach in the back of its head with a hormone that would turn the cockroach into a lethargic, completely compliant slave.

Was this mysterious Zophie... an emerald wasp? Maybe this

was her MO: trawling for older men with money. Men who thought with their peckers. And she'd stung Nix – sucked him dry of money, then, like the wasp with the roach, she'd steered him out into the middle of nowhere to finish him off.

But her blood was in that boat too.

And there'd been the third person.

'Excuse me?'

Boyd was jerked from his wool-gathering by a voice coming out of the cool grey mist. He turned round to see a woman in a parka. She was holding out a small black plastic bag.

'Huh? Is that for me?' he asked, not quite with it.

'In a manner of speaking,' she said gruffly, and thrust the bag towards him.

He took it, grabbing the saggy bottom. It was warm. 'Thanks. *What the –?*'

She pulled a face. 'Uh... you might want to hold it from the top, like I was doing.' She pointed at Ozzie who was busy investigating the Case of the Discarded Chocolate Wrapper. 'Your chap was busy over there on the shingle.'

Busy?

'Oh,' he said, finally catching up. He quickly switched to holding the little bag from the top. 'Yuck.'

'Look, I don't want to be that naggy person,' she said, 'but kids play on this beach, even in the winter.'

'Right. I'm a bit new to this. It won't happen again.'

She handed him a tight roll of black plastic. 'Poo bags. For all emergencies. Always good to have them on you.'

'Ah, thanks,' he said, taking them.

'No problem.' She turned away and called out, 'Mia, come on!' Then she headed up the sloping shingle towards the car park with her dog, a smaller, sleeker version of Ozzie.

'Shit,' he muttered, looking down at Ozzie. 'Well, that was embarrassing, wasn't it?'

THEY HEADED BACK the way they'd come, the beach all to themselves and swathed in an ethereal pale mist as the morning sun tried its best to break through. The tide lapped to his right, a soft splash followed by a withdrawing hiss across the shingle, regular as a heartbeat.

As he made his way diagonally eastwards and up the beach, he spotted a figure to his left, standing on the steep hump of shingle that led up to the promenade path. A solitary figure looking in his direction. A man wearing a hoodie. Staring straight at him, no doubt enjoying the drama of poo-gate.

For fuck's sake. My dog shat on the beach, he thought. *Gimme a break for Christ's sake.*

The sea would have washed it away anyway, he reasoned. He bent down to give Ozzie a reassuring pat, and they headed home.

32

'Sorry about the roast, Dad.' Emma grimaced apologetically.

'Don't be silly!' Boyd, who'd been surreptitiously feeding Ozzie under the table, feigned what he hoped was disbelief. 'It was lovely.'

'No it wasn't, Dad! The spuds were awful and the chicken was pink in the middle.'

Emma had had to microwave their plated meals to make sure the chicken didn't kill them both. The end result was that the roast potatoes were waxy little bags stuffed with dry mash, the greens looked like they'd been boiled in a school kitchen all day long, and the chicken was the lifeless grey of a pathologist's cadaver.

'It's a new cooker for us to get our heads around, Ems,' he said reassuringly.

'It's gas. I've never worked with a gas oven before.'

'Well, there you are. It's not your fault, love.' He smiled over at her.

He could see that she'd made an extra-special effort today – for their first proper Sunday lunch in the house. She'd spread out the red tablecloth that Boyd recognised as one of the ones Julia used to lay out for Christmas and Boxing Day meals. The nice cutlery was out. She'd placed a candle in the middle of the table, and she'd got Aretha Franklin on Spotify, piping some life into the tired old creaking bones of the house.

'I'll get it right next Sunday,' she said, smiling back at him.

They gathered up the plates and headed into the tiny kitchen. Ozzie followed, just in case there were any further scraps to be had.

'It's my turn next Sunday, Em. How about we score each other's roasts?'

She grinned. 'Okay – but I have to say, even after today, I fancy my chances!'

'Well,' he said, laughing, 'your effort today gets a less than stellar seven out of ten.'

'Hmmm.' She pressed her lips. 'Higher than I thought.'

'Yeah,' he agreed. 'Too generous. Let's call it six.'

'Hey!' she exclaimed, swatting him on the arm.

He put the two-minute chocolate sponges in the microwave and turned the kettle on for their instant custard.

'I'm okay, you know,' he said, as they went back to sit down in the dining room to wait for Chef Mike's ping.

'Huh?'

He gestured at the table, the candle. 'All this. It's lovely and I appreciate it – really, I do – but I hope you didn't do it just for me. Cos I'm okay. I don't need special treatment.'

She frowned. 'I'm worried about you.'

'Well –' he fiddled with the spoon beside his place mat – 'I'm *more* worried about *you*.' When she didn't say anything, he carried on. 'Look, Emma – I've been a basket case for the last year, and you've had to deal with literally *everything*. I think it's about time I started looking after you.'

'Dad –'

'You treat me as though –' he scratched his beard – 'you're

carrying around a bin bag full of fragile porcelain. I'm not going to break into pieces, Ems – not any more.'

He could see she was chewing relentlessly on her bottom lip – a childhood tic that never went away. He was willing to bet her future husband – wherever and whenever he was – was going to fall for that first.

'I just...' She looked away from him. 'I just don't want to lose you as well, Dad.' He could hear the wobble in her voice as she tried not to cry. 'I don't want to go on without any family left. I want you there on my wedding day, to give me away. I want my kids to know at least one of my parents.'

A tear spilled over and tumbled down her cheek.

Boyd reached out a hand and grabbed hers. 'I'll be there, Emma. I'm sticking around, I promise.'

'You'd better keep that promise.' She wiped her nose and then patted her cheek dry with the heel of her other hand. 'So tell me. Why did they suspend you at work?'

'It's a week of sick leave. That's all,' he said. 'I think a cop with half a bra stuck to the side of his head doesn't make for great optics.'

She snorted a wet laugh.

'It's also a bit of politics,' he went on. 'This is about telling me not to be such an arse.'

'Who said that?'

'No one. I did. It's the whole "copper moves out from the big bad city to little town and thinks he can tell everyone how to do their job" cliché.' He smiled. 'What was that Simon Pegg film?'

'*Hot Fuzz.*'

'Right. It's kind of that. I'm getting reminded that coming down from the Met does not make me Sherlock Holmes or Inspector Morse.'

She nodded. Ozzie swaggered back into the dining room and rested his muzzle on her knee.

'So, look, no more of this feeling sorry for me,' he said

gently. 'I want to see you begin your life. Not hang around with me because you're worried I'm not going to cope without you. All right? Deal?'

'I'll try, Dad.'

He grabbed her other hand, and raised his eyebrows, waggling them at her. 'Just *try*?'

'Okay!' she laughed. 'Deal!'

Chef Mike pinged and the kettle clacked off a moment later. Emma grinned. 'Right! It's puddin' time!'

33

Rather than spend the whole of Monday morning brooding and scrolling through news sites on his phone, Boyd decided to throw himself into the to-do list entitled 'Things about the house that need sorting'. He'd been pushing that list away from the moment they'd started unpacking. It was time to man up. It was too bloody easy these days to sit on the sofa, endlessly swiping upward or trawling nostalgically through Facebook.

Boyd shook his head.

Facebook. That was something he'd not looked at in a long, long while. It was too bloody painful. The constant trickle of condolences had finally dried up, thank God, but Facebook itself was continuing to be an insensitive arse. The 'On this day whatever years ago' photographs took their toll. The pictures of all four of them together – at Alton Towers, Harry Potter World, eating a bucket of deep-fried chicken at a music festival… It was never-ending. There should be a button on Facebook, he thought, that allowed you to say those people are dead, so fuck off with all the memories for a bit please. The opposite of a Like button. A middle finger button, maybe.

Well, there was stuff here in the real world that he could and really should be cracking on with. The house – lovely, grand and incredibly priced though it was – was shabby, sad-looking and in need of some Lawrence Llewelyn-Bowen style make-over.

The first time he'd viewed it with Emma, he'd been amazed at how much he'd be getting for his money. The contrast from their Clapham two-up two-down to this vast mansion had dazzled him. He hadn't needed to request a second viewing. He hadn't even bothered to offer less than the asking price; it had seemed like such a bargain.

Now, having been here for a couple of weeks, the magical spell was beginning to lift. He could see all the little gotchas that the surveyor had dutifully pointed out and that he'd wilfully ignored: the cracked ceiling roses and missing sections of coving, the rotting window frames, the patches of damp. The pointing on the brickwork that was beginning to fail. The roof tiles that would need replacing...

His phone buzzed in his trouser pocket. He fished it out, expecting to see Emma's face on the screen. She'd gone to do the weekly shop and tended to check in with him at least twice to see if there was anything he could think of to add to her list.

It was an unknown caller. Chances were it was another sales-bot calling to see if his was a legitimate phone number.

'Boyd,' he answered.

'What?'

'Boyd,' he repeated. 'Who's this?'

'It's Jo. Jo Bambridge. I was expecting Samantha Okeke to answer.' 'Is this not her number?'

For a moment he had a complete mental blank. Then he suddenly remembered. Okeke must have picked up the wrong cards.

'It's okay, Ms Bambridge. This is DCI Boyd. Did you want to speak specifically to DC Okeke?'

She hesitated. 'Well... she said if anything else occurred to me, if I remembered anything else that might be useful –'

'To call, yes. And have you? Remembered anything?' He grabbed a pen and his notebook.

'I... I just wanted to say that last night I was going through photos on my old phone. I've got thousands –'

Don't we all?

'– and my photos go back, well, quite a few years. I can't bring myself to delete them, you know? So, I was going backwards, to the time before we split up – you know, happier times. God, we looked so happy... smiling, laughing.' She paused and took a deep breath. Boyd hoped she wasn't going to start crying again. 'Anyway, I came across some photos I took in the office the day I walked out. I completely forget they were there on my phone.'

'Photos of the office?' he asked, willing this to turn into something useful.

'Gerald's computer screen. His chat screen. The things they'd been saying to each other... *sending* to each other. I took photos to confront him with, in case he just closed it down or tried to claim I imagined it or... or... misunderstood –'

Boyd interrupted in disbelief. 'You've got actual *readable* images of his chat history with this woman?'

'Yes. Oh, god...' Her voice was wobbling now. 'It was... just so lewd. Disgusting. She was... throwing herself at him. And... oh... God...' She began to sob.

Where was Okeke when you needed her? Boyd was no good at this sort of thing.

'All right, all right,' he said. 'Slow down. Take it easy.'

'I... completely... forgot about them... I suppose I tried to blank it all out...' Her words were slurring. He wondered if she'd been drinking. 'He was...'

'He was what, Jo?'

'He was *desperate* for her.'

Boyd sighed. That couldn't be pleasant for the poor woman to read again after all this time. 'Look, Jo, that must have been horrible to stumble across.'

He could hear her breath hitching down the line. He doubted he was helping that much.

Finally she spoke again. 'I can send you the screenshots, if it helps. But I'd need you to be completely discreet.'

He was fully aware that he ought to tell her to call DC Okeke and send them to her instead. Officially he was on sick leave. He'd be in a whole heap of shit if he continued to investigate. But since when had that ever stopped him?

'How many photos do you have?' he asked, trying not to sound too eager.

'I took three screenshots. Very quickly. One's a bit blurry but the other two are fine.'

'Okay. And you can definitely read what's on his screen?'

She mumbled an affirmative. 'It's just text. Slightly blurry. There's no pictures of her.'

'All right.' He sighed. *What am I doing...* 'Text them to me.'

'You promise you'll be discreet with them?' Jo asked, worried.

'Yes, I promise.'

A pause. 'Thank you, Mr... sorry... PC Boyd.'

'*DCI*,' he corrected her. He'd sweated fifteen years to get those letters in front of his bloody name. But she'd already hung up.

Ozzie was looking up at him, curiously.

'Now,' he explained to the dog, 'that was just a phone call about some sleazy sexting. You're way past that kind of nonsense, aren't you, old son?'

Ozzie opened his mouth, letting his pink tongue roll out of the side.

Boyd smiled. 'Maybe not, then, you randy sod.'

His phone buzzed again. He tapped the screen and opened the message.

Here you are. Please, please be discreet with these.

As promised, she'd sent three images of a computer screen. He tapped and expanded the first one. It showed a spreadsheet open in the background and on the left a chat box with speech bubbles on the left and right trailing upwards. And, yes, Jo Bambridge had been right: it was legible, and it was lewd.

But what caught his eye was the deep pink banner at the top of the chat box, showing the usernames of both people in the chat room. He could see that 'GerryBoy' was one. *Classy.* The other was just a blur.

He opened the second image. The banner was entirely out of shot in this one. He tried the third.

The name GerryBoy was on the left of the banner in blue. In the middle was a red heart logo, and on the right, in Barbie pink, was the name Zophia Kardevev.

'Zophia Kardevev. That,' he said, turning to the ever-attentive Ozzie, 'sounds very much like a Russian name. What do you think, boy?'

Ozzie tilted his head to one side and blinked in agreement.

34

Emma came in the front door, carrying three Tesco bags and one from Homebase.

'You all right, Dad,' she said as he ran up the hallway. 'You look like someone in a big hurry.'

Boyd opened the door to his study, and his jaw dropped. He'd probably only stepped into the room twice since they'd moved in. The last time he'd peered into it, it had been a dumping ground of stacked cardboard boxes, his Ikea computer workstation in pieces on the floor and his slouch chair on castors shoved into a corner, still wrapped in plastic.

Now, everything was all set up.

The workstation had been assembled. His ancient PC was out of its box, the cables and monitor all waiting patiently to be plugged in. The cardboard boxes – *thank you, Ems!* – had mostly gone. There was just one more stack of boxes to be processed, and chances were they contained the Christmas decorations and the plastic tree anyway, all of which could be dumped in the loft until they were needed.

'Whoa!' he exclaimed, turning round to face Emma.

'I sorted your study out days ago,' she said. 'I thought you –'

'This is amazing, Ems! This is amazing! I promise I'll say thank you properly later – I'm really sorry, I just need to do something for work,' he said as he entered the room, leaving her standing, bags in hand, in the hallway.

'Police work?' she called out.

'Yeah. A bit.'

'You want a coffee?'

'Yes please,' he mumbled, already busy with the nest of cables draped across the table.

He busied himself plugging everything in, setting things out on the workstation's modest table surface, and then switched the PC on. He tapped his fingers impatiently as he waited for Windows to slowly stir from its slumber. It gradually dawned on him that there was a new Wi-Fi router he'd have to connect it to, before he could actually get online. *Bloody technology.* Finally his computer woke up, but before it would connect to the world again it decided it needed a thorough update.

'Oh, for fuck's sake,' he muttered as Emma entered with his coffee.

'What's the matter?'

'Microsoft's the matter,' he said, nodding at the blue screen. 'Stupid fucking thing.' He stood up and took the mug from her.

'What are you doing on the computer? Research? Investigating? Is it something you're allowed to tell me?' she asked hopefully.

Technically, no, it wasn't. But then, technically, he should probably have redirected Jo Bambridge to the inquiry team's phone number in the first instance.

'I'm looking for a woman.'

Her brows bounced up in surprise. 'Right... For yourself or for "a friend"?'

He laughed. 'No, not for me, you muppet. One of the victims on the yacht was – well, it looks like she was – a Russian woman. We've only had a first name to work with up until now.'

'And now you have a surname?'

'I'm hoping so.'

Emma pulled her iPhone from the back pocket of her dungarees. 'All right – give it to me.'

'Her name?'

'It's okay, Dad,' she said, 'I won't share it with anyone. Promise!'

He glanced at his computer. The updates bar hadn't moved. 'Kardavev,' he told her, and spelt it out.

'Do you know what she looks like?'

He shook his head. 'We haven't managed to get a single clear shot of her face so far.'

'Well, is she old? Young? Blonde? Dark? White?'

Boyd re-ran the CCTV images in his head. 'Dark hair. Long. White. Slim. Young.' He thought back to what Jo had told him and mentally added *Big tits* to the list. She'd said Zophia was twenty years younger than her. 'Early to mid twenties, at a guess,' he added. 'Probably quite glamorous.'

'And from Russia,' prompted Emma.

'Yes, well, based on her name, I think so.'

'Oka-a-a-ay... glamorous, Russian, young... and over here?' Emma frowned through her glasses as her thumbs got to work. 'I think I know exactly where to go.'

'I've got a gut feeling she's some kind of a scammer. Or maybe just a girl looking for a rich sugar daddy.'

'Aha!' Emma said. 'There's actually a social media platform dedicated to that.'

'A social media site for sugar babies seeking sugar daddies?' Why didn't that surprise him. These days there seemed to be a social media platform for everything.

While Emma tapped away, Boyd looked back at his computer. The monitor was displaying a cheery image of

Douglas fir trees and the snow-dusted Rocky Mountains, on top of which the bloody Windows Update bar had barely advanced.

'There,' she said. She turned her phone round to show him.

He took it from her. The deep pink at the top of the screen was what drew his attention first. The same suggestive, fleshy hue from the screenshots. The site was called AskFor-Sasha.com.

Below the banner were a list of smiling female faces and profiles. All very glamorous selfies that he suspected had been filtered to within an inch of their absurd, almost cartoonish lives.

The name Zophia Kardevev in the search bar had produced two direct hits, plus a seemingly endless list of near-misses.

The first Zophia Kardevev was young, attractive and had long brown hair. He looked at her biography. Christ – it was like looking back in time to the seventies – she gave her vital statistics (36, 24, 34) before anything else. Then her age (twenty-four). After that came her sales pitch.

I AM LOOKING FOR A NICE MAN TO TAKE CARE OF ME. I LIKE BIG DADDIES. NOT MODEL TYPES BUT A REAL-LOOKING MAN. AND NOT YOUNG. I LIKE MY HUSBAND TO BE MATURE, THOUGHTFUL, INTELLIGENT, GENEROUS. SO LET'S TALK ABOUT LOVE!

'Jesus. They're not exactly subtle, are they?' said Boyd.

'Well, it is what it is,' Emma replied. 'They want some rich old saddo to shower them with gifts and in exchange they'll, you know, be their trophy girls.' She shrugged. 'At least it's honest. *This is what I've got to offer and this is what I want* kind of thing.'

True.

'It's a lot less random and expensive than going out to bars or night clubs,' she added. 'And honestly, after Covid, the idea of sweating on a crowded dance floor and getting corny chat-up lines sprayed into your face by some drunken arse isn't that appealing to us girls these days.'

He looked up at her.

'And before you ask, Dad: no, I'm not on Tinder and I'm not on AskForSasha.com either. Well, not yet anyway,' she added with a smirk.

He glared at her, then turned his attention back to the phone. Zophia Number Two was blonde and equally glamorous in a sort of caricature-like way. Her painted brows made her look like Groucho Marx, though.

I WANT A MAN WITH GSOH AND PLENTY OF MEAT ON HIM. I WANT A LOVE BEAR WHO CAN MAKE ME SMILE AND MAKE ME FEEL SAFE. I WILL BE YOURS, IF YOU WILL BE MINE.

'What's a g–'

'Good sense of humour,' Emma said matter-of-factly. 'You'll have to learn what those sort of things mean if you're ever going to get out there again, Dad.'

He laughed sarcastically. 'I'm not going to be "getting out there" any time soon, Ems. That ship has sailed for now.'

'You're forty-six, not eighty-six,' she replied.

'I'm also not ready to put myself out there like a sad old Toby mug sitting in a charity shop window! Neither do I want to go "shopping" for a partner like they're a pair of Nike trainers.'

She smiled. 'Well, hopefully not on this website at any rate.'

'Or Tinder, or... Match.com... or... the others.'

She looked over her glasses at him. 'That's pretty much exhausted your knowledge of dating sites, hasn't it?'

He shrugged. 'It's not something I've felt the need to research yet, my little lambkin.'

'Oh, so you're just going to trust to blind luck, then? Hope that Mrs Perfect will one day bump into you and you'll have one of those rom-com encounters in the canned veg aisle at Tesco?'

'I've already met and married Mrs Perfect. If I ever meet someone again, it's, at best, going to be a Mrs You'll Do.'

She laughed. He returned to scanning the search results . The names of the near-misses were growing more and more approximate. The ages increasing. He wondered if that was coincidental or whether the search results, other than the exact hits, were actually sorted by age, youngest first.

Jesus. It really did feel like the grubbiest place in the virtual world to be loitering around. The kind of site that demanded a history purge and a thorough hand-wash afterwards.

He scrolled back to the top of the list. 'Can you screenshot the first two girls and text them to me?'

She took her phone back. 'Sure. I'll send you their links too.'

Boyd returned to his computer to see the updates bar had managed to budge a couple of inches. Clearly Microsoft Windows would need the whole morning to get re-acquainted with his computer.

'You should, though,' Emma said.

'Should what?'

'Think about it.'

'Think about what?' he asked, deliberately not getting her meaning.

'Putting yourself out there. Maybe using something like Match.com?'

He sighed. 'Look, Em, if it happens, it happens. I'm really not in a hurry to find someone.' He paused. 'Anyway, what about you? You're not getting any younger, chicken.'

'*Pfft!*' she replied. 'Luckily things have moved on a bit since, you know, *ancient times*. It's not like I need to find a man before I'm thirty or I'll be doomed to be a spinster for the rest of my life.'

'Well, no –'

'I'm not in a hurry either, Dad. Although...'

'Although what?'

'That barman down at the Olde Pump House was quite cute.'

'The one who wanted to get a selfie with me?'

'Uh-huh.'

He turned, snorting out a laugh as he did so. 'Good god. What fresh hell is this?'

'I got his number,' she said, looking up at the ceiling. 'Might give him a call sometime. Might not. I'll see.'

He sighed. 'Well, what can I say? God help the poor bugger.'

35

'Is your dad in?'

Emma recognised the uniform – a practical dark grey trouser suit and flat shoes. 'CID?'

DC Okeke nodded. 'I'm on your dad's team.'

'Ah.' Emma narrowed her eyes. 'You must be Samantha.'

Okeke's eyes widened ever so slightly. 'He's mentioned me?'

'Yeah,' said Emma, smiling. 'You're the token female in the department, right?'

Okeke laughed. 'For my sins, yes, I am.'

Emma stepped back and gestured for her to come in. 'He's just in there. In the study.'

As she went to knock on the study door, Boyd simultaneously opened it, mid-yawn, mug in hand, headphones dangling from his good ear and his shirt half untucked. Ozzie emerged and pushed past his slipper-clad feet.

Emma simply smiled and pointed to her right, indicating DC Okeke standing in the hallway.

Boyd hurriedly pulled his headphone out and tucked his shirt in. 'What are you doing here?' he asked.

'It's nice to see you too,' said Okeke, catching Emma's eye

and smiling. 'I'm checking up on you, guv. Sutherland came in this morning and said you were on sick leave.'

'Well... technically, I suppose. Though it might be more accurate to say that Her Madge has put me on the naughty step.'

'Because of the press conference?'

He nodded. 'Among other things. You want a coffee or something?'

Okeke checked her watch. It was half five. 'It's half past beer o'clock – I'll take one of those, if there's a cold one going?'

'Ah, I'm afraid this is a red-wine-and-alcopop house. Can I tempt you to a stale glass from yesterday's bottle?' said Boyd.

Okeke grimaced.

'Or a WiKeD Orange?' offered Emma.

She nodded. 'That sounds better.'

'You want me to pour *you* a glass of stale wine, Dad?' asked Emma, already on her way to the kitchen, Ozzie dutifully following.

Boyd gave that a few seconds of deep consideration before saying. 'Why not?'

He scratched his jaw awkwardly and turned to Okeke. 'You here to talk shop or... point your finger at the naughty boy?'

'Like I said, just here to check up on you, guv. And Minter wanted me to say thanks.'

'Well, he was making a bit of pig's ear out of it, truth be told.'

'Yeah, he knows. We've all been relentlessly *errr*ing and *uhh*ing at him all day.'

Boyd smiled. 'He was really shitting it, poor sod. Anyway, I suppose you better come into my man cave. 'Scuse the mess.'

He led the way into his study and dropped into his slouch chair. The chair wheezed wearily beneath him.

'There's a stool there,' he said, pointing, 'if you want to sit.'

Okeke grabbed a chrome bar stool with a small leather

backrest from the corner of the room. 'The inquiry team are behind you, sir.'

'What do you mean?'

'We think that this feels like a botched kidnapping rather than some migrant encounter.'

'Of course it is. The Chief Stupid's more concerned with keeping Border Force happy than making sure the news is reporting this accurately.'

'It's about political currency,' said Okeke, supressing a smile.

'Huh?'

'A story about bloodthirsty migrants in the Channel works wonders for the government, doesn't it? For Border Force funding, particularly.'

'And for selling toilet-paper tabloids.'

'Exactly. It's... er... ' She glanced at his computer screen and pulled an awkward face. 'Have I caught you at a bad time, guv?'

Boyd followed her gaze. *Shit!* He still had the lurid pink AskforSasha website up. 'Oh, that – no, that's not for me!' he exclaimed, feeling the heat rising in his cheeks. 'That's a bit of research.'

She nodded slowly, pressing her lips together in an attempt to hold back a smile 'Right. If you say so.'

'No, seriously.'

'It's fine, guv.' She nodded, grinning. 'There's no judging going on here.'

He sighed. 'It's Nix casework.'

'No!' She feigned shock. 'Surely not. Being on sick leave, you'd have passed this on –'

Boyd rolled his eyes. 'Yeah, yeah, I was going to. I was just making sure it wasn't some dead-end alley. Didn't want to waste everyone's time, you know?'

Okeke smirked. 'Well, is it?'

'Jo Bambridge called me a couple of hours ago. Turns out

she had my number, not yours. She remembered she took photos of Gerald Nix's screen the day everything blew up and she left him.' He nodded at the columns of thumbnail images of young women. 'Nix was on *this* website chatting up some young lady called Zophia Kardevev. This is what Jo saw while he was out of the office, and she took some photos in case he tried to deny what she'd seen.'

'We've got a full name?'

'If it's real, then, yeah, we finally have a full name.'

Okeke did an air punch. 'Yuss!'

'Well, let's not get too excited. It could well be an alias –' Boyd clicked on her profile – 'but it's more than we had yesterday!'

She leant forward to get a closer look. 'You sure it's *this* woman?'

'Look,' he said, pointing to her profile page. 'No updates from her in over four months. And this one? Her last update was over two years ago. Status: *adopted*.'

'Adopted? Wow.' Okeke shook her head. 'Like they're pets.'

'I know. The whole thing is pretty creepy.'

'I wonder if this is how Trump found Melania?' she joked.

'Christ alive. I really don't want to think about what pictures he might have sent her.'

Boyd heard Ozzie's loud bark through the study wall. He glanced at his watch – six o'clock. From the desperate tone of Ozzie's insistent barks, she was probably prepping his dinner.

'Anyway,' Boyd went on. 'I've been thinking about this Zophia. She could be just some innocent, looking for a sugar daddy – or she could be the key to this whole thing.'

'How do you mean?' asked Okeke.

'I mean, maybe Nix was being played. Suckered into believing she wanted him to –' he looked at her profile again – 'Christ, *adopt* her. Maybe she lured him into some sort of compromising situation and he was suddenly hers to ruthlessly exploit.'

'To what end?'

'To suck him financially dry? Then discard him?'

Emma pushed the door open without warning. She entered with a glass of red for Boyd and two bottles of neon-orange pop-for-grown-ups. He suspected the unannounced entrance was deliberate. Emma – ever hopeful that she might catch the beginnings of something going on with her dad and any female in his life.

Emma was way off the mark if she thought he'd carry on with someone he worked with. Especially someone so much younger. Sam was almost young enough to be his daughter.

Emma gave Okeke a bottle and placed Boyd's wine glass on the workstation desk. She glanced at the screen. 'Relax, Dad's not investing in a Russian mail-order bride, by the way.'

Okeke looked disapprovingly at him. He didn't have to think too hard to guess what that meant: *This is work. It's supposed to be confidential.*

'Thanks, Emma,' he said.

She lingered.

'Thanks, Emma,' he repeated, looking from her to the door.

She huffed and rolled her eyes, momentarily looking twelve again. 'Right. Sorry. Shop talk, huh?'

'Indeed. Feel free to close the door on your way out.'

'How very rude,' she mock-scolded him, flouncing out of the study and pulling the door to behind her.

'There,' said Boyd, when the door clicked shut.

'I like her.' Okeke grinned. 'She's haughty.' Then she nodded at the screen. 'So we have a photo of Nix's girlfriend, and it looks like we may have a name.'

'The photo is the thing to pursue,' said Boyd. 'The name is almost certainly an alias.'

Okeke pursed her lips. 'It's been insta-filtered to death.

She's probably a sixty-year-old fishwife with a mono brow and a moustache.'

Boyd almost spluttered his wine onto the keyboard. 'I'm sure she is.' He wiped his mouth. 'But what won't have changed are her facial details like relative pupil distance, nose-to-lip-line ratios.'

'You're talking about facial recognition software?'

'Uh-huh. It's disturbingly good these days.'

'Even on filtered social media pictures?'

'Particularly on those. They tend to flatten the skin tones and blemishes out that the software doesn't give a crap about anyway. Plus there's the embedded image metadata, which will give up some more information.'

Okeke swigged her bottle. 'English please! I didn't have you down as a digital forensics nerd, guv.'

He pointed at the time on his computer. 'It's gone half five. You may call me Boyd now. Anyway, I'm no digital expert, but I read a book. That's how it works, you know... Knowledge. You read it, you take it in.' He smiled to make that sound a little less smart-arsey.

'You want Minter to log this into the –'

'No,' he replied quickly. 'I want to follow it myself.'

She looked at him warily. 'Why?'

'Because it'll get buried. The higher-ups are nudging this investigation in a decidedly different direction –'

'The migrant story?'

Boyd nodded. He wasn't entirely convinced Border Force *did* have an ongoing investigation into Nix. It could easily have been utter bollocks coming out of Hatcher's mouth. He wouldn't put anything past her. Whatever the truth, she clearly had an interest in steering anyone in Sussex Police well away from looking too closely at Gerald Nix and his affairs, business and otherwise.

'Then how are we going to do this?' Okeke asked.

'I've got an old contact who owes me one,' said Boyd, noting the 'we' and appreciating it. 'Can you keep this to yourself for now?'

She nodded.

'It's not that I don't trust Minter and the others, but it puts them in a shitty situation if they know we're going off-piste and they get asked about it.'

'Sure. Makes sense,' agreed Okeke.

There was a gentle knock on the door.

'All right. Okeke, are you sure about this?' he asked.

She nodded. 'I'm in.'

'Okay, good.' Then Boyd raised his voice: 'Yes. We're done talking shop!'

Emma opened the door and peered in cheekily.

Boyd fixed her with a stern look. 'You're not interrupting anything, Em. Come in.'

His daughter almost managed to disguise the flicker of disappointment on her face. 'You staying for dinner, DC Okeke?'

Okeke smiled. 'Call me Sam. No... my boyfriend's making me supper tonight. But thanks, Emma.'

'Ah, okay,' replied Emma, backing out of the study and closing the door again.

'She's started hassling me to find someone else,' Boyd explained. 'She's worried I'll end up a crusty old bachelor. I expect I'll be signed up to God knows how many dating sites now she's got the idea in her head,' he added mournfully.

Okeke laughed. 'You might enjoy it!'

'Well, you'd better watch out! I think she was eyeing you up as a potential candidate.' He laughed too. 'You dodged a bullet there, mentioning your boyfriend. She'll be off your case now. Very well-played, DC Okeke. Kids, eh? Are they on your to-do list?' he asked, nodding in the direction of the door.

'Me? No, sir. Uh-uh!'

'Sorry, that was a bit forward of me.'

'A career,' she added. 'I much prefer one of those. Though if we get this Nix thing wrong, we're both shooting ourselves in the foot there, aren't we? Anyway –' she took another big swig of her bottle to finish it off – 'the man I'm with is more than enough of a kid for me to deal with.'

36

The next morning, Emma drove him to the hospital's outpatients department to have the Princess Leia Pretzel removed from the side of his head and the stitches examined.

'That's looking fine,' said the nurse.

'I'm going to put on a smaller dressing this time. Just a plaster should do,' the nurse continued.

'Thank fuck for that,' Boyd blurted out in relief.

'Dad!' Emma yelped beside him. 'I'm so sorry,' she said to the nurse. 'He's got a right potty mouth.'

'Don't worry,' the nurse replies, laughing. 'I've heard far worse, my love, far worse.'

'I've had the mickey taken out of me for a week now,' grumbled Boyd. 'I think I've earned a bloody swear word or two.'

'By who, Dad? You've hardly seen anyone but me and Ozzie.'

'The postman, for example,' he retorted. 'He asked if you'd hit me with a frying pan.'

The nurse and Emma chuckled. Rather unsympathetically, he thought grouchily.

'And it's only been five days, Dad. Not a week.'

'Feels like a lot bloody longer,' he muttered.

The nurse gently dabbed the stitches with antiseptic, then laid a plaster over them. 'Well done. It looks no worse than a shaving accident.'

'Seriously?' he said. '*Behind* my ear?'

EMMA DROPPED him off at Hastings train station. She wanted to come along for the ride up to London, but then Ozzie would be trapped in the house all day, so she reluctantly accepted she was going to have to stay at home. Boyd was secretly relieved. He had to see a man about an entirely different dog, and Emma was too nosy by far.

'What time will you want picking up?' she asked.

'I'll text you when the train's approaching Hastings. I can't imagine it'll be that late.'

'Will you want some dinner?' she asked.

'No, you sort yourself out, love. I may just grab a McFatBastard at Charing Cross.'

'Well, if you're sure,' she said, with a not-too-subtle stare at his tummy.

He leant across and a planted a kiss on her cheek. 'I'm sure. Apologise to Ozzie for me, will you?'

'I think I'll take him out later on today anyway, if it's not too wet.'

'All right. See you later, Ems.' He got out of the car and, with a wave, set off towards the station entrance.

IT WAS weird returning to London. They'd only moved away just over a couple of weeks ago and yet it felt like it had been much longer. It was a similar sensation to returning home after a by-the-pool package holiday – the sense that months had passed yet nothing had changed. From sunshine and sangria back to grey skies and grumbling – the greater the contrast, he suspected, the longer the perception of elapsed time.

And Hastings had been a contrast in many ways. The omnipresent squawk of gulls, the constant nagging tug of an offshore breeze and the salt 'n' vinegar smell of chippies along the seafront promenade.

And the slopes. Jesus Christ, those bloody inclines.

Sunil Chandra was already waiting for him at the bar inside the Nags Head by Covent Garden, listening to something on his phone. He was nursing a pint of Guinness that sat on the counter beside him.

Boyd had picked the Nags Head because it usually emptied out completely after lunchtime and, being a London landmark pub, you didn't need to bother with directions. It was the same with the nearby Punch and Judy, down in the Piazza. That had been a favourite of Julia's.

'All right, Boydy,' said Sunil, putting his phone away. 'Get you a pint, bro?'

'I'll take an IPA.'

'Cool.' Sunil craned his neck and looked at the plaster above Boyd's ear. 'What happened there, mate?'

'I got chased by a giant clown with blades for fingers,' Boyd deadpanned. 'You should see the clown, though.'

'Fair enough.' Sunil shrugged, guessing he wasn't going to get a straight answer. He ordered and paid. 'You want to go sit down somewhere?'

Boyd nodded. They found a booth of dark wood panelling and frosted glass, well away from the bar and the dwindling number of regulars finishing their lunchtime pints and checking their watches. The afternoon business at the Nag's Head used to be a steady trickle of curious Japanese tourists or bawdy Americans wanting to try out some 'weird British beers'. But no longer, it seemed.

'How long's it been?' asked Boyd.

Sunil stroked his bushy black beard as if it was a touchstone full of wisdom. 'Two or three years – gotta be at least that, right?'

The data analyst was whippet thin, but his big black beard made his face look round and fat. He wore his dark hair short – *shaved* short – and his thick-rimmed glasses made him look like one of the Proclaimers.

'Yeah. I think you're right,' replied Boyd. '*Tempus fugit* and all that.'

'How've you been, mate?' Sunil asked.

That question came far too easily, thought Boyd. *He doesn't know. Does he?*

'I've been better, Sunny. Been better.' He decided to leave it there, hoping to avoid ten minutes of awkward questions, commiserations and so on. 'How's you?'

'Lots has happened, bro, hasn't it? 2020 was total shit, wasn't it?'

'Not my favourite year, all told,' said Boyd.

'And last year wasn't much better. My department's been downsized. We're all wondering who's next for the chop.'

'Really? I'd have thought digital forensics would be a safe place.'

'Shrinking budgets, bro.' Sunil sipped his Guinness. 'So, I heard on the bongo drums you're living out of the Big Smoke now?'

'All part of the cash dash. I managed to get a good price on my place and bought a mansion, well... half a mansion... on the south coast. It's all right there. I like it.'

'Nice one.' Sunil was far too urban to consider such heresy. His idea of a view was city lights sparkling across the Thames and the reassuring glow of multiple takeaways within easy reach.

They small-talked about property prices. Sunil was planning to move more centrally when the property bubble properly burst. He was hoping to take advantage of some foreign fat-wallet speculator, who'd eagerly overpaid for one of those city-centre investment apartments with their floor-to-ceiling plate-glass windows, and buy the property for a fraction. He was just waiting on that bubble to pop – *Any time now, mate. You just watch.*

Eventually, niceties over, Boyd nudged the conversation towards the reason they were both sitting there this afternoon.

He pulled his phone out. 'Sunny, I've got a face I need you to identify for me.'

'You got a decent picture?' he asked, peering over at Boyd's screen.

'It's a social media profile picture. Filtered to fuck, of course.'

'As long as it's not got a cat's nose and whiskers, we should be all right,' quipped Sunil.

'Quite.' Boyd tapped his phone and pulled up the picture of Zophia.

'Hey, she's cute.' Sunil pulled the phone towards him for a closer look.

'She's probably dead. And quite possibly in a number of pieces.'

Boyd filled him in on the basic background to the case, leaving Nix's name out of it for the time being.

'So you think she was some Carole Baskin type?' asked Sunil.

'Something like that. What's the expression – *Blag, shag, then bag*?' Boyd shuddered.

Sunil took the phone and studied the picture carefully. 'How did you get the photo onto your phone?'

'Copied and saved it. Why?'

'Good, then the EXIF file will still be attached.'

'That the metadata?'

'Yup. It contains stuff like when it was originally taken, where it was taken, and a whole bunch of other things. I'm guessing that'll be helpful to you.'

Boyd nodded. 'Very.'

'And do you have the link to the site you grabbed this from?'

'Sure. But, remember, her name's most likely an alias. It's any other names you can find for her that I'm interested in.'

'If it's one of those niche social media platforms, they're very hackable,' said Sunil. 'I could probably dig around her profile and unearth a lot more information than she would have wanted to make available. Sound good?'

'Yep. I'll text you the link.'

'Okay. I'll throw some facial recognition software at it too – see what that brings up.' Sunil looked at him. 'I'm guessing this one is off the books again?'

'For now, yeah,' said Boyd.

Sunil grinned. 'You do like being a naughty Boyd, don't you?'

'Not particularly.' Boyd shook his head and sighed. 'How long have you been waiting to use that one on me?'

'Since the last time, bro. Thought it up on my way home.'

'Great. Good one, mate. Now, let's see if you can put as much effort into finding out who this Zophia really is.'

Sunil chuckled. 'So what's she done, then? This girl. She kill someone?'

Boyd gave him a flat smile. 'That's more than I'm going to give you. Sorry. So, how quickly can you work on this?'

Sunil sucked in a breath, reminding Boyd of a plumber about to quote for a bathroom. 'Tomorrow. Maybe the day after?'

'And as for the money, Sunny... If you recall, you do actually owe me this one.'

Sunil gave Boyd a long and heavy-lidded stare through the thick lenses of his glasses. 'All right,' he said eventually. 'But if this goes *on* the books...'

'Yes. If it goes on the books, I'll make sure you can bill the force. I promise.'

'Bro, I don't know why you just don't do that in the first place.'

Boyd sighed. 'I've got a feeling about this one. I'd rather know a bit more before I get it out and start waggling it around in front of everyone.'

Sunil made a face. 'Nice image there, bro. Thanks.'

They talked for a while longer, finished their drinks and exchanged, probably empty, promises to not leave it so long until next time. Boyd watched Sunil Chandra head towards the Tube station and decided to give it a few minutes before following suit. There was nothing more annoying and awkward than saying goodbye to someone and then having to say hello all over again on the platform moments later.

Boyd knew Covent Garden very well. He'd been to see many a band at the Marquee Club in his youth, before it closed and relocated. He'd even played a gig there once. Back then he played bass guitar, very badly. He'd been too bloody tall for the stage and its uncomfortably low ceiling, so he'd had to stoop his way through their forty-five-minute set, playing before a piss-poor, mid-week, couldn't-care-less audience of less than twenty.

Still, they were good memories.

He'd first met Julia at the Punch and Judy. And they'd often gone back to the same pub to toast their anniversary and occasionally, drunkenly, to re-enact their clumsy First Encounter. He toyed with the idea of walking over to the Piazza and round the corner to get a quick glimpse of the pub's outside balcony. It was probably not a great idea, he decided. There were way too many memories lurking around there like well-intentioned ghosts.

Best let it go, whispered Julia.

She was right.

As always.

37

'There, what do you think?' asked Emma.

Boyd stood back and looked at the one study wall they'd actually finished. The colour and the special effect on top had been Emma's idea: a base colour of very dark green that had, to his eye, looked almost black in its Dulux tin, with a lighter green dry-sponged on top. It had looked a very bad paint experiment at first, but as she finished the last dark corner he could see, at last, what she'd intended: a wall of dark green leathery marble.

'I love it,' he said. 'Very *Downton Abbey*.'

'I told you to trust me. So, you like it?''

'I do.' He smiled at the wall. She'd done a great job. 'Sherlock Holmes would have been proud of a study wall like that.'

'Shall we crack on then,' said Emma enthusiastically, 'and get the others done?'

It took most of the day to do the base coats and for Emma to work her magic with the sponge. They had a very late lunch, then began work on the skirting boards and the study door with a crisp white silk paint. By the time they were done, the day had gone and Ozzie was marching up and down the hallway, making grumpy harrumphing noises at them both.

'I'd better take him out,' Boyd said. 'Poor sod.'

Since it was already dark and still drizzling outside, he decided that it would have to be a quick walk, down to the bottom of the hill and back. Hopefully enough time for Ozzie to do his business, check his pee-mail inbox and fire off a few replies. There was a well-deserved bottle of red on the dining-room table, with Boyd's name on it.

As he stepped onto the pavement, he remembered something from this afternoon. While they'd been decorating, Emma had said something out of the blue that had really hit him hard.

'Dad, why d'you never talk about Noah. We talk about Mum, but never him. It sometimes feels like he was never with us.'

The truth was that Boyd could hardly bear to think of his little boy; it would have pushed him over the edge. Noah was just four when it happened. He hadn't been a planned baby. Boyd had been thirty-nine when Jules had whispered, 'Oops, honey, I think we did it again,' and patted her tummy. Emma had been sixteen at the time, doing her GCSEs. And she'd adored Noah when he came along, tag-team mothering him with Julia.

Boyd had had only four years with his little boy. Far too much of that time had been taken away by work's late nights and early mornings. What he had left in his mental memorial to Noah were four Christmases, four birthday parties, a few family outings and a couple of poolside holidays. Noah, with his fluffy little peanut-sized head and his big personality. Noah, who – both he and Julia were certain – was going to make his mark on this world somehow. But he never got his chance.

Boyd had tried to ringfence his grief. Half of himself had

been torn away when he'd lost Julia. But having Noah taken away from the world had been an enraging injustice.

Losing Julia had broken his heart.

Noah had broken him entirely.

HALFWAY DOWN THE HILL, his phone buzzed. Boyd pulled it out of his jacket pocket and glanced at the screen. It was Sunil Chandra.

'Hey, Sunny, that was quicker than I was expecting.'

'Boyd...' Sunil sounded a little breathless. 'I've got your girl. And you probably need to back off. Or proceed *very carefully*.'

'Why? Who is she?'

'Her real name's Zophia Salikova.' Sunil spelt her surname and paused, as if expecting a reaction. When none was forthcoming, he continued, 'Her father is Rovshan Salikov?'

Boyd was still none the wiser.

'Okay, so google him,' said Sunil. 'He's ex-KGB, an old buddy of you-know-who. He's been a corrupt city mayor for decades with one greedy hand in the trough and one not so much dipped as right up to his fucking armpit in organised crime.'

'Shit.'

'Absolutely, shit. It's no secret he's been trying to relocate his dirty money to the UK for a while. Some of it's already here and doing its work; he's got a toehold so to speak.'

'What do you mean?'

'I mean, he's *greasing* the wheels, bro. Making heads look the other way.'

Boyd could hear Sunny's unsteady breath. He sounded edgy. Scared. 'You okay, Sunny?'

'If you're getting pushback from above, Boyd... if that's *why* this is off the books and not official, then you need to be super-fucking-careful.'

'You think that –' Boyd didn't finish his sentence. He didn't want to.

'Yes, bro. I do. Be careful. Better still: *drop it.*'

'So this Zophia –'

'She's Rovshan Salikov's youngest daughter. I don't know what she's done, or how she's crossed your path, but, like I said, mate, you should back well away from it.'

'Right.'

'Boyd, it was good to catch up again, bro. Really good. I'll send you over what I've got. But I'm going to step away from this one now.' he paused. 'And I really suggest you do the same.' With that, he hung up.

'Shit,' Boyd muttered again. He stopped walking and turned towards home. Ozzie pulled on the lead – he had other plans.

'Sorry, Ozzie mate, no beach tonight.'

Fifteen minutes later he had a large black coffee, an open packet of chocolate digestives and Google Chrome at the ready.

He tapped 'Zophia Salikov' into the search bar, paused and hit enter.

BOYD OPENED the door before DC Okeke even had a chance to knock.

'I saw your headlights,' he explained, noting her look of surprise as he zipped up his coat.

'Are you okay, sir? You sounded a bit –'

'I need a stiff bloody drink,' he said. 'The Old Pump House will do. I'll fill you in when we get there.' It seemed like a fairly quiet place. They should be able to talk without being overheard.

Okeke made eye contact with Emma over his shoulder. Emma shrugged and mouthed *I have no idea* back at her.

'Well. All right, then,' said Okeke. 'If you insis–'

'Emma?' Boyd turned back to his daughter. 'I'm sorry.'

'What?'

'It's work talk. So it's just us. We won't be long.' He went to leave, then hesitated, turned back to her and kissed her on the forehead. 'I bloody love my study.'

'I know, I'm really glad.'

'And, Emma...'

'Yes?'

He wanted to caution her, to warn her not to answer the door. But she wasn't a child, nor could he give any explanation yet as to why he felt the need to warn her.

'Nothing. Just... stay in.'

'Dad?' She looked concerned now. 'What's up?'

'You're fine. Just stay in.' He squeezed her shoulder and turned to leave.

38

'All right, guv. I've got my sugary drink and my roasted nuts. So, are you going to tell me why you're looking so flustered?'

'I have the girl's proper name now,' said Boyd. 'It's Zophia Salikova. She's the youngest daughter of Rovshan Salikov, a Russian mafia godfather.'

Okeke's eyes rounded. 'Oh, shit!'

'Mr Gerald Nix, it seems, rather foolishly, and I'm pretty sure inadvertently, got himself involved with one of the most brutal criminal families in Russia – well, Russia, but it's part of the old USSR thing. Honestly, Okeke, the stuff I've been reading for the last hour is enough to turn your hair white.' He took a big sip of his gin and tonic. 'The Salikov family are into all the greatest hits – drugs, prostitution, trafficking, slavery. They've got a family tradition of butchering people who get in the way of what they want or pose a threat to them.'

'Oh, shit,' she whispered again.

'And dumb old, dirty old Gerald Nix found himself chatting up *Capo di tutti I capi's* precious little princess.'

'By chance? Surely not.'

'Probably not by chance. I suspect *they* found *him* and got lovely Zophia to groom him and reel him all the way in.'

'But why Nix?'

'Money laundering is my guess,' Boyd said, working with a fifty–fifty mix of information and speculation. 'It seems the Salikovs decided a while back that London would be the best place for their dirty money. Which makes sense. Now we're out of Europe and it's all deregulated, London's the perfect place to toss your dirty laundry, to be mixed around and cleaned up.' He lowered his voice further. 'London's becoming the Wild West when it comes to dirty money. It's all flooding in now.'

'The Thailand of Europe.'

He nodded. 'So, let's look at our Mr Nix. We've got a independent financial advisor with his own practice and licence, who has a speciality in walking money into bogus Guernsey-based shell companies and walking it out again smelling of roses and ready for London. Make no mistake... *she* almost certainly approached *him*.'

'That's not at all creepy.'

'Right.' He continued, 'Now do I have to spell out what I'm thinking... or are you getting my point?'

'Erm, not yet, guv. You're going to have to help me out here.' She glanced around the pub. 'Say it quietly.'

'OK. What I'm about to say is just me freewheeling, okay? It's no more than paranoid shite at this stage but –'

'But?' she echoed.

'Look. I got some pretty heavy pushback on Nix from above. As you know, I was told in no uncertain terms to dress up this case as migrant trafficking gone wrong. Now, I'm not saying the pushback we're getting from up above is directly linked to this, but... you know how these things work, right? Down the golf club, or at the members-only bar... A quiet word here, a *would you mind awfully* there?'

Her eyes suddenly rounded. 'Her Madge?'

He shrugged. 'Maybe. Or someone in Border Force leaning on her. Like I say, I don't know. And I don't have anything to back this up – I shouldn't even be saying it out loud – but it *adds up.*'

'So what levels of money are we talking about?'

'I have no idea. Millions? *Hundreds* of millions? Who knows? Big numbers, for sure.'

Okeke pulled the bag of roasted peanuts open and Boyd grabbed a handful. 'I think Nix was either *willingly* channelling Salikov money into Guernsey via his company, or he was being *coerced* into doing it. Carrot or stick, or both.'

'Jesus.'

'I know, right?' He crunched the nuts in his mouth, hardly tasting them, then washed them down with another swig of gin and tonic. 'You know, I made the mistake of reading up on them, to figure out their MOs. You ever watch *Breaking Bad*?'

She shook her head.

'Sam, these Russians make the Columbians look like learners.'

Okeke sipped her drink more cautiously. 'Guv, there was something I was going to tell you today, before this. But... I dunno –'

'What?'

'Nix has one of those smart CCTV systems. You know the ones that send an alert to your phone and you can talk through it to the DPD guy dropping your parcel off at the front door, or whatever? I managed to contact the company that runs the operations side and get permission to access Nix's camera log.'

'And?' This was good.

'There's nothing much to show. Lots of ten-second clips of cats walking past, the occasional postie delivering spam mail. But there's one entry with a deleted media file.'

'From when?' he asked, wondering if it was of the day he'd

nearly lost his ear. Maybe it had shown the bastard on the recording.

'From the twenty-ninth of November. Two days after the *Magpie* left Sovereign Harbour Marina.'

He frowned. 'So the boat sets sail. Then –'

'Two days later someone enters the house.'

He reached for the peanuts again. 'Who?'

She shrugged. 'I guess that's why the video was deleted, guv.'

'Okay then.' He let out a breath. 'So... who were they? Why were they there? And what were they after?'

'The thing is,' she continued, 'I was talking with the operations people. They said that since the video is stored remotely, rather than, you know, normally on the camera, the only person who can delete it is the account holder.'

'What? Nix?'

'Or someone else who knows the account password.'

It took Boyd a moment to realise who she was talking about. '*Jo Bambridge?*'

She sipped her drink. 'If Nix was out at sea, with his mafia-daughter girlfriend and a plus-one, and presumably busy being murdered... then who else could it be? She's got a motive.'

'Yeah, but I still don't see her arranging a hit.'

Okeke pressed on. 'The third person on the boat could have been some local scrote-for-hire? What about Rigby? Does she know him? They both hated Nix more than enough to join forces.'

Boyd shook his head. 'I don't know. A Jo Bambridge commissioned "hit"? No, I don't buy that. Given the facts, the simpler, fucking scarier answer is that Nix got suckered into helping a mafia family launder their money. The obvious explanation, to me, is that he was either no longer useful to them, or, possibly, he was after a larger commission.'

'Or he wanted to get out?'

Boyd nodded. 'I reckon that's what did it for him. Zophia calls in one of Daddy's heavies to help and they take him out to sea to kill him.'

'What about the man at the house?' prompted Okeke.

'The same bloke, or another one. Maybe he came back to do some cleaning up?'

'Three months later?'

'No. I'm talking much earlier. Two days later. He comes back to clean up any evidence of Zophia having visited. Deletes that CCTV footage. Presumably any earlier footage that might have shown her coming in and leaving with Nix.' He looked at Okeke. 'Presumably this CCTV log must have a load more earlier entries with missing video?'

She shook her head. 'The server refreshes every three months. We're actually right at the end of that window with Nix's account. I believe they were almost due to do a wipe and refresh. The log would have been ditched for good.'

'I'm presuming you've got that halted?'

She nodded.

'Good, well, that's something.' He finished his drink and realised he could do with another. 'Same again?'

'I'm driving. So no thanks. Anyway, *who* do you think jumped you?'

He shrugged. 'Could well be the same man – the mysterious third person – who also deleted the CCTV footage. Maybe they asked him to come back when the boat was found. To double-check there was nothing incriminating left behind?'

'They left Nix's computer,' she pointed out. 'But then we did interrupt him. Jesus,' she whispered. 'I'm not ready for this.' She looked at Boyd. 'If the Chief Su–'

He raised a finger to stop her. 'Let's *think* it, by all means, but let's not *say* her name.'

'Like Voldemort?'

'Yes,' he said with a wry smile. 'The point is, there may

come a day in the future where you'll have to swear under oath and relay *some of* the contents of this conversation. So, let's be careful, all right?'

He could see her hand trembling ever so slightly.

'Relax, Sam... it's just theory at this stage. Okay? Just a theory. One with many unanswered questions. And one we're probably best off keeping to ourselves for now. Right?'

Okeke nodded and finished her drink. 'I think so. Though if this looks like it's going somewhere we'll have to let someone know. Sutherland?'

'Agreed,' he said.

They looked at each other.

'I should probably get home,' she said, standing up. 'I can give you a lift back up the hill if you –'

Boyd shook his head. 'No, I think I'm going to walk back. Blow off some cobwebs. Get some air.'

'Okay.' She turned to go, then hesitated. 'Can't we at least share some of this with Minter? It'd be good to have him on our side.'

Boyd made a face and shook his head again. 'Not yet.' It wasn't that he distrusted the man, not at all. Detective Sergeant Minter seemed like a steady, trustworthy officer. 'We've already put our own careers on the line,' he continued, 'and I'm not ready to put anyone else in that position. Not unless we absolutely have to. So, let's keep it between us for now, okay?'

Okeke looked as though she was going to argue, but finally nodded. 'All right.'

'Go on, then – bugger off,' he said, waving her away. 'I'm off to the gents.'

By the time he came back out, she was gone. He ordered another drink to settle his spiked adrenalin. He was glad he hadn't gone into the more grisly details of the Salikov family with Okeke. There were things he'd read that he wished he could unread. He picked up his drink and downed it in one.

It was nine when Emma finally cracked and phoned to see if he was okay.

'Yup. I'm coming back now,' replied Boyd, slurring a little more than he would have liked.

'You want me to come get you?' she asked, sounding worried.

'Nah, I'll walk off the booze. It'll do me good.'

He hung up. It was getting busier in the pub and, anyway, he'd done enough wistful staring at the fireplace for one night.

He pulled his coat on and stepped out into the cold night.

The crisp air was a sharp contrast to the fuggy warmth of Ye Olde Pump House and sobered him up a little almost immediately. He turned left at the end of George Street onto the old town's narrow High Street and Old London Road, which wound inland (and up that bloody hill) towards Ashburnham Road.

He was getting to know the place-marker buildings in the old town now. The Blue Dolphin Fish Bar, the Jenny Lind Inn, the various antique and knick-knack shops, the up-and-down pavement on the left, and that little gingerbread house at the end of the High Street.

He was nearing the junction for Torfield Close when he noticed, belatedly, that a figure in a grey hoodie appeared to be watching him. The figure was standing on the front green of All Saints Church, on the other side of the main roads, and was definitely staring in Boyd's direction. Something was tugging at his memory, but in his semi-drunken state he couldn't place it.

Boyd changed course, walked past a rockery and a sculpture of a lifeboat towards the church's front green. 'Hey?' he called out.

The figure in the grey hoodie slowly, and very obviously,

patted the gravestone it was standing beside, then turned away and disappeared into the church's wild-looking graveyard.

Boyd stopped in his tracks, beneath a street lamp. It probably wasn't the smartest thing in the world to do – to follow some dodgy-looking hoodie into an overgrown graveyard. He hadn't, he recalled, had the best of luck with dodgy strangers recently. And he wasn't exactly match-fit after several double G&Ts.

He stood there for a moment to see if the figure would emerge again. If it did, he decided, and if it tried anything, he was going to call it in. He'd have a patrol car swing by and check there were no scrotes, local or otherwise, up to no good back there in the trees and bushes.

The figure didn't emerge and Boyd was on the point of convincing himself it might not have been there in the first place. Not that being somewhat pissed made a person hallucinate, but it did make you interpret things differently.

He shook his head and was about to carry on his way up the hill, when he spotted something on top of the gravestone the figure had touched. Something pale. He hadn't been patting it – Boyd was going with 'he' for now – he'd been placing something on it. Something he obviously wanted Boyd to see.

Boyd's internal debate between caution and curiosity was short-lived.

He walked up to the front gate, up the steps and onto the grass, keeping a wary eye on the overgrown rear of the church, just in case Mr Hoodie decided to make a reappearance.

As he approached the grave, the pale object became clearer.

It was a piece of paper, held down by a large stone.

He picked it up carefully, by one corner – imagining Sully staring over his shoulders. *Mind the fingerprints, you clumsy muppet.*

Gently he unfolded the paper and stared at what had been written on it in an untidy, impatient scrawl.

detective Goodnight
CHaser Alone!
0231221 900

39

B oyd woke up to Ozzie licking his face. Which would have been a charming demonstration of canine adoration were it not for the fact that his breath had the most horrendous, fishy odour.

'Get off!' he grumbled, pushing him away.

He opened his eyes and saw it was gone eight thirty. Emma was usually up before eight, and her regular routine began with feeding Ozzie his breakfast and letting him out for a morning poo. Arse about tit really, Boyd thought. You'd think he'd be desperate to go out and do his business after a long night, but that's the way the routine seemed to have been decided by Ozzie. Food first. Always.

'Emma?' he called out.

There was no answer. It was silent.

Normally by now the radio would have been on in the kitchen. Emma normally tuned into LBC so she'd have something to grumble and tut at.

Feeling the first niggle of concern, he sat up, swung both legs over the side of the bed and slid his feet into his slippers. 'Emma?' he called again.

He crossed the large and largely empty bedroom and pulled the door open. Across the landing he could see Emma's bedroom door was wide open and she wasn't there.

That odd encounter last night in the graveyard and the message left on headstone, presumably for him, had given him an uneasy hungover sleep and he'd woken up feeling not entirely sure if it had all been real.

Ozzie padded past him.

'Ozzie... stop!' he snapped.

The dog blithely ignored him, scrambled clumsily down the bare stairs and clicked-clacked down the hallway into the dining room.

Boyd followed him halfway down the stairs. 'Emma?'

There was still no reply from her. He tried to brush away the sense of unease creeping over him. He remembered now: the cryptic note had been real, that figure in the hoodie too... and Zophia Salikova.

Someone *had* been watching him last night.

Waiting for him. Making sure he got that note. And why? He was pretty sure it wasn't from the Russians. From what he'd been reading yesterday, the Russian mafia, particularly the Salikov family weren't big on serving coded notes as warnings. Their advisories, at least according to the Russian press, usually came in the form of a severed appendage or a missing person.

'Emma?' he called out softly. He heard the first tremor of panic reach his voice and it scared him.

Relax. The Russian mafia isn't interested in a lowly cop's daughter, you muppet.

He heard movement coming from the kitchen.

Slight rustling movements. Like the ones he'd heard back in Nix's house.

He ran the rest of the way down the stairs as his daughter appeared in the dining-room doorway, headphones hissing in her ears, a bowl of muesli in one hand and the cryptic note from last night in the other.

She caught sight of him and jumped a little. She pulled her headphones off. 'Oh, you're up finally.'

He allowed himself a barely concealed sigh of relief. 'Yeah. Ozzie woke me.'

She raised her eyebrows. 'Sore head?'

Now that the growing sense of dread had suddenly evaporated, the full joy of a morning- after headache was crashing in. 'Uh-huh,' he muttered sheepishly.

Emma waved the note at him. 'I've been trying to make sense of this note you were given down at the pub.'

His memory of last night was gradually reassembling into a coherent order. Yes, he'd come back last night and had told her about the note. And, no, he hadn't mentioned the creepier elements of the story – the watchful hoodie or the fact that he'd been a little drunk and stupid enough to be lured into a grave-yard by some suspicious-looking stranger who could easily have been after grabbing his wallet – or worse.

He vaguely recalled he'd made it sound as though some bloke with a pint in one hand had waggled it at him on his way out of the door. More vaguely he remembered coming back and attacking the second half of an opened bottle of Malbec, which had been begging to be finished. And, yes... he had shown the scribbled note to Emma and asked whether it made any sense to her.

'It reads like your nickname is Detective Goodnight, and the note says you're 'chosen alone'. Or... it could be signed by someone called Chosen Alone?' She looked up at him and pulled a face. 'Errr... this is not at all weird and stalker-ish, Dad.'

He followed her as she went into the lounge, placed her cereal bowl on the coffee table and sat down on the sofa.

'And that number at the bottom can't be a phone number.

There aren't enough digits.' She looked up at him. 'Is this something we need to worry about, Dad?'

He slumped down heavily beside her. The short and sensible answer was: maybe. Rule Number One in the Detective's Handbook was to build, and keep, a firewall between your job and your personal life. Which was why, social media was devoid of images of police officers hanging out at the pub after work.

He became aware that she was still looking at him, waiting for an answer. The longer he waited before saying no, the more her bullshit-meter was going to start pinging. And if this wasn't some random snarky hoodie 'just 'avin' a larf', then it could be a warning.

He sighed, realising he'd reached a decision.

'Emma, I'm going to do something that would be a sackable offence if it reached work. I'm going to tell you what I know about the case I'm working on. Can I trust you to keep this completely to yourself?'

She nodded calmly, though he could sense a hint of eagerness in her face. 'Sure. If it means you keeping your job.'

'I mean it, Emma. This is serious,' he cautioned her.

'Who am I going to tell, Dad?' She shrugged. 'I don't know anyone.'

She made a good point. So he told her. Most of it. The important bits, certainly not the incredibly scary shit he'd read. Emma really didn't need to know what the Russian criminal world did to people it didn't like. He gave her the early evening news 'Not-very-nice Russian crime family moves dodgy money to the UK' version.

Emma, all the same, had paled. 'Oh, shit, Dad. This is heavy stuff.'

'Well, quite,' he replied. 'There is some degree of heavy shit involved.'

'You need to tell your bosses!'

'Ah, about that...' He got up. His head was pounding. Why hadn't he gone home when Okeke left? 'I really need a strong coffee, Ems – gimme a minute.'

He returned to the lounge with a coffee for them both and tried to explain why he'd effectively gone against all orders and ended up somewhat off-piste with the inquiry. 'Which, by the way, is also a very sackable offence.' *What a bloody mess.*

'Shit, Dad. Have you at least talked to Sam about this?' she asked.

He nodded. 'She knows I've been doing my own sniffing around.'

'But does she know about the *mafia*?"

'Yes. That's what we were discussing last night.'

'Jesus, Dad.' Emma put her head in her hands.

'The note, on the other hand, she doesn't know about. Yet.'

'This is not good,' she said, looking up. 'This is not good. Dad? Are we in danger?'

'Emma, no, I'm sure we're fine. The note's either a joke –'

She interrupted, 'Or it's not!'

'Or,' he continued, 'more likely it's an informer who wants to talk confidentially.' He looked at her. 'Love, this stuff happens all the time in CID. It's routine, honestly. I just think it wouldn't hurt us all to take a bit more care when we're out and about. Just until we know what we're dealing with.'

She didn't look convinced.

He looked at his watch. It was gone nine. Okeke would be in the office now. If Boyd called her and asked her to meet him, she'd have to log in with Minter and give a reason for the trip. Boyd pulled out his phone and dialled Minter's desk number.

He heard a click, followed by Minter's unmistakeable Welsh lilt. 'DS Minter.'

'It's Boyd.'

'Ah... hey, how're you doing, boss? Feeling better, I hope.'

'Not bad. Not bad. How's the investigation going?' he asked.

'Flack's been drafted in and he's getting up to speed on the action log. Truth be told, he's getting on my tits already, sir. When're you coming back?'

'Monday, but I suspect he'll get to keep the case when I return. Look, is DC Okeke there?'

'Yup. You want to speak?'

'Yeah please.'

He heard Minter call her over and a moment later Okeke's voice: 'Guv?'

'We need to talk,' he said quietly. 'Can you find a reason to come over to mine?'

SHE PULLED up outside his house half an hour later.

'What did you tell him?' Boyd asked as he let her in.

'I said I dropped around last night to check on you and left my warrant card.'

'He didn't bollock you?'

She shrugged. 'He's misplaced his before. So, what's happened?'

Boyd handed her the note. 'Walking back home last night, there was a man watching me. He left this note for me to find.'

Emma frowned. 'I thought you said it was in the pub?'

Okeke looked from Boyd to Emma, then glanced at the note. 'What is this? Some sort of warning?'

'Maybe. I was thinking it sounds more like an informant.'

She looked at it again. '*Detective. Goodnight. Chosen. Alone.* Or is that *Chose*? As in a misspelling of *choose*?'

He peered at it. 'Or the word *Close*?'

Okeke nodded. 'Yes, it could be that.'

'Close? Close to what?' asked Emma. 'And who's "alone". You?'

'I'm more worried by "Detective Goodnight",' said Boyd only half-jokingly.

'And what's that number?' Okeke counted the digits. 'It's not enough figures to make a phone number.'

Emma shrugged. 'Unless whoever wrote it made a mistake. Left one out, maybe?'

'Wait.' Boyd frowned as he studied the numbers again.

0218221900

'Is it a date? A date and a time?' he asked.

Emma shook her head. 'The second pair of numbers should be between one and twelve for months.'

'Unless it's written US style,' said Okeke. 'Month, date, year.'

'Then could that "1900" be 7 p.m.,' suggested Emma.

'The "02" is February. The next two numbers: the eighteenth. Which would be *tomorrow* at seven in the evening,' said Boyd. He looked at the two women and slowly smiled. 'I thought it was an informant. It's a rendezvous.'

'But where?' asked Emma

'That's a location,' Okeke said. 'The first three words. Then it says "alone" as in *come alone*.'

Emma frowned. 'How's that a location?'

'What Three Words,' she said. 'It's a co-ordinate system that uses language as an identifier.' She pulled out her phone. 'There's a website. Hang on...'

After a minute or so of tapping, she set her phone down on the dining table and they all peered at it. Boyd could see a webpage that resembled Google Maps. Okeke checked the note again then carefully entered *detective.goodnight.closer* into the search box at the top.

'Oh, that's not it,' she said, staring at the screen. She pinched the screen to zoom out.

'Where is that?' asked Emma.

'It's a forest in Norway, apparently.'

'Maybe the words aren't correct,' said Boyd. He looked at the piece of paper again.

'I really don't understand how this works,' said Emma.

Okeke pointed at the screen. 'It's a system that divides the world into a three-by-three-metre grid and then assigns each of those grid squares a unique three-word address.'

'Try *chose*,' said Boyd.

That put them in a random lake in northern Norway.

'*Chosen*?' he said hopefully.

The screen froze for a second before whizzing across to another location, finally settling and zooming in on the south coast of England.

Okeke sucked in a deep breath. 'Shit.'

'What?' Boyd and Emma asked in unison.

She looked from one to the other. 'That's Winchelsea.'

'Where's that?' Boyd asked.

'Near Rye,' said Okeke. She looked at him. 'It's only a few miles away from Nix's house.'

'Shit,' he said. 'Shitty-shit-shit. That's it. It's got to be.'

'It is a rendezvous, then,' said Emma. She grabbed her dad's wrist. 'Which you're not going to go to, right? You're going to call it in and let your team do the work.'

'Just... let's think a minute,' he said, putting a hand over hers. 'So it's a meeting. Tomorrow, at seven, at whatever this place is,' he said, staring at the peg on the screen. *Clever.* Whoever had selected the location must have been amused at the poetic coincidence of *detective* in the three-word address.

He tapped the screen to switch to satellite view and zoomed out a little, trying to get an idea of this location. He saw dozens of grubby white rectangles gathered in clusters around a meandering dirt track.

'That's a trailer campsite,' said Okeke. She shook her head and pressed her lips together. 'It's out of season. It'll be completely deserted.' She looked at Boyd. 'You don't want to go there, guv. Not on your own.'

'You're absolutely right I don't want to go on my own,' he replied, looking meaningfully at her.

'Dad, don't go!' Emma begged.

He continued to look at Okeke. 'It was honestly one skinny-looking kid.'

'You want me as backup, guv?'

'Yeah. If you wouldn't mind.'

'Dad, no!'

He reached out and grabbed Emma's hand. 'It's okay. Look, Em. This is just someone who has some information, that's all. It could be a friend, family, maybe even a neighbour of Nix's. Somebody who saw the news and wants to help... but discreetly.' He glanced quickly at Okeke. 'It could even be Jo Bambridge.'

'Who's she?'

'His ex-wife.' Boyd looked Emma in the eye. 'It's certainly no Russian mobster, trust me.'

She pulled back from him. 'Well, I really think you should call this in.'

'Emma, this is part of the job. We cultivate informers. We meet them, sometimes in places like this. If a bunch of patrol cars and uniformed officer turn up, we'll get nothing. The note says *alone*.'

'Dad, I'm scared.'

He squeezed her hand reassuringly. 'No one *does in* a Detective Chief Inspector to keep things discreet, Ems. That's the dumbest thing ever. You hurt an officer and all of a sudden you're dealing with the whole police force.'

Okeke nodded. 'Your dad's right,' she said. 'This happens all the time.'

'But the *Russians*?' Emma said, spreading her arms wide.

A whole counterargument in one word.

'This is just intelligence gathering, Emma. That's all it is. Like Okeke said, it's what we do. The only reason I showed you the note and let *you* know about this is –' he sighed – 'is because I was a little pissed last night.'

'You nearly got killed last week.'

'Emma, I hurt my ear. And if I thought I was preparing to meet that particular twat again, I certainly wouldn't be going in alone. Trust me.'

She didn't look convinced.

'Look... I suspect the person who wants to meet me is trying very hard to avoid the person who did this,' he said, pointing to his stitches. 'Which sort of puts us on the same side. That being said...' He turned to Okeke. 'I don't s'pose there's any chance you could smuggle out a stab vest, some pepper spray and a taser? Just to be on the safe side.'

40

'**G**uv, this is my other half, Jay.'

The man Okeke was sitting with got up from the bench and, for once, Boyd found someone standing at his own eye-level.

'Jay,' he said, grasping Boyd's hand unnecessarily firmly.

'Uh, hello. I'm Boyd,' said Boyd, resisting the urge to massage his throbbing hand.

'You're Sam's boss,' said Jay. Which, Boyd noted, was more a statement than a question.

'That I am,' he agreed.

Jay sat back down.

'Uh, Okeke?' Boyd muttered under his breath, 'I don't recall saying bring a plus-one.' He looked back at her boyfriend. 'No offence there, Jay.'

'None taken.'

'I asked him to help and, thankfully, he said yes,' she replied. 'Anyway –' she nodded at Emma, standing beside him with Ozzie – 'I don't recall us saying this was a "bring your daughter and dog" meeting, either.' She smiled at Emma. 'No offence.'

'None taken.' Emma smiled back. 'And he didn't get much of a choice, to be fair.'

Boyd shook his head. 'Where does Minter think you are?'

'At home.' Okeke smirked. 'I took a sickie.'

'Good thinking.' He nodded approvingly.

They were outside the Dolphin Inn, a small pub that looked as though it might have once been some harbourmaster's modest home. It looked out across the narrow strip of Rock-a-Nore Road at the labyrinth of fisherman's hanging huts, all dark lumber, shutters and no windows. It was Okeke's suggestion to meet here as it was the other end of Hastings to the police station and far enough away from the pier that they weren't going to bump into any of the rest of their team.

Boyd looked up at a gang of steely-eyed gulls perched along the top of the huts; he was sure one was ready to swoop over and assault him. 'Shall we go inside and grab a beer?' he asked, moving towards the door of the pub.

Just like Ye Olde Pump House, the Dolphin Inn had a cosy, twilight ambience even during the day. Tiny lead-lined windows let in the meagre light of the grey day; the rest of the light seemed to come from the flickering flames of an inviting log fire and an overexcited slot machine that was blinking and flashing, as though it was about to have a heart attack.

The pub was virtually empty. There was an old man muttering to himself over a pint and a newspaper, and an old woman – possibly his wife – feeding coins into the slot machine and tugging repeatedly on its lever.

Jay offered to get the drinks and Boyd watched as he weaved through the empty tables and chairs towards the bar.

'I appreciate you bringing some extra muscle,' Boyd said to Okeke as Jay leaned against the bar, 'a *lot* of extra muscle, but –'

'I've told him nothing that's sensitive to the case, guv. Just that you're meeting an informer in a place that could be a bit dodgy and we need someone to watch your back and look scary.'

'Thank you for doing that,' said Emma.

Okeke nodded. 'It was the sensible thing to do. I think your old man's been knocked around enough already.'

'Yeah, all right, thanks.' Boyd nodded, secretly a little relieved. Jay looked like he ate scrawny Russian thugs for breakfast. 'So he's not curious at all as to why we're not just using other plain clothes officers?'

'I explained this was off the books, guv.'

'And he didn't think that odd?' Boyd asked.

Okeke smiled. 'He thought it sounded rather cool, actually.'

'What does Jay do when he's not playing cops and robbers?' asked Emma.

'He's a furniture restorer by day and a bouncer at night,' Okeke replied.

Boyd nodded. That explained the muscles and the general Jason Statham-like appearance. He turned to look at Okeke. 'Did you manage to sneak some kit out?'

She nodded. 'Stab vest, telescopic baton and a pepper spray. No taser, I'm afraid.'

Boyd wasn't surprised. While most forces were planning on rolling out tasers as standard issue for uniformed officers, budget restraints meant they were still in relatively short supply and issued to named and trained officers only.

'Jay's got a replica handgun, though,' said Okeke. 'You want him to bring it?'

Boyd's first instinct was to say no. Producing a gun during any tense situation didn't tend to help matters much. But then... with the Russians possibly lurking around it might not be such a bad idea. He'd rather they had something gun-like to pull out if things did suddenly go tits up.

He nodded. 'Yeah, just in case. Anyway, I've looked over the campsite on Google Maps,' he said. He pulled out his phone and lay it on the table for Okeke to see.

'The three-word meet location is pretty central to the camp. It's in an open space near a small copse of trees and overlooking what looks like a small artificial lake. There are dozens and dozens of trailers that have line of sight on this spot. I'm guessing it's the campsite's equivalent to a town square or something. So, our informant picked a place he could clearly see from any number of these trailers. He's going to be watching to make sure I'm there alone before coming out, that's for sure.'

Boyd pointed at the satellite image. 'The entrance to the camp is down here by the bottom corner of the lake. There's a lane that runs off Nook Road, then along the southwest side of the lake. And this looks to me like the entrance to the campsite. I'll drive up this lane, park at the entrance barrier and get out. I'd say it's about sixty yards to the spot where I have to stand... alone.'

Jay returned with a tray of drinks and some crisps. 'They're not taking food orders until twelve,' he told them.

'It's okay – I'm not that hungry,' said Boyd. He'd eaten a big breakfast. Beneath the table, Ozzie sighed at the disappointing news and curled up into a dog-doughnut around one of the table legs.

Jay handed out the Cokes and passed the vodka orange to Emma, then sat down. His eyes lit up at the sight of the map on Boyd's phone. 'Planning the mission, eh?'

'Basically, I meet someone there,' said Boyd, pointing. 'I'm going to park my car over there. And you're going to just lie low in the car, Jay. I'll have a concealed stab vest on me, a radio handset, pepper spray and a baton under my coat, so I'm going to be fine. But, if you hear me call for help, turn the car lights on and hit Sam's rape alarm. Make a shitload of noise. Then come running.'

'What about me, guv?' asked Okeke.

'You stay –'

'You don't get me involved, then tell me to stay out,' warned Okeke. She glanced at her boyfriend. 'Jay might look the part, but he's not hands-on-arrest trained.'

'Hey, babe,' interjected Jay. 'I can look aft–'

She put a hand on his arm to stop him. 'I'm coming, guv.'

'Me too,' said Emma.

Stupidly, Boyd hadn't thought this far ahead. Of course Emma was going to insist on coming, and, short of cuffing her to the house, there wasn't much he could do to stop her.

'Okay,' he said, sighing. 'But you're going to be further back,' he said in his best non-negotiable tone. 'You'll be parked up a little further away. Let's say further up on ... what's that say there...' He squinted at the image on his phone. 'The Ridge?'

He could see a few houses with sea views and cars parked outside them. Judging by the Google satellite image, the ground beside the Ridge was fairly flat and marshy, which would afford them a clear line of sight to the lane leading up to the campsite entrance.

'You'll be able to see my car. If the headlights go on, that's Jay coming for me. Okeke, you do a code zero on your radio handset.'

'Got it.'

'And,' he added, wagging a finger, 'you both stay back and wait for the cavalry to arrive.'

'Right. Just like you did, Boyd,' said Okeke, 'at Nix's place...'

'Hmmm.' Absently he reached up to his left ear. 'Well, wasn't that a teachable moment for us all.'

'Dad, no. If you're in trouble –'

'We'll stay put,' said Okeke firmly. She looked at Emma. 'And we'll call for backup.'

'How long will this take?' asked Jay. 'Only, I'm on the door of Cuzzin's at ten tonight.'

'I don't know,' said Boyd. 'I doubt it's going to be a long conversation. But if it looks like it's going that way, then I'm going to give him a ChatterBox password and we can resume talking online.'

'You know about that?' said Emma, surprised.

The social media platform had launched only last year – basically a cooler version of WhatsApp. Not being Facebook-owned and subject to relentless data-mining, the kids loved it.

Crooks loved it too.

'I'm forty-six, not eighty-six,' he reminded her. He turned back to Okeke and Jay. 'So, to recap: I'm expecting this should be a quick chat. And, to be entirely clear, none of that reactive stuff – the headlights, Jay coming, the code zero – happens *unless I call out for help*, got that? Otherwise, whoever it is that wants a chat with me will probably bolt for the hills and never be heard from again.'

They nodded.

'Good. Right, then – we just need to arrange somewhere quiet and discreet to meet at six this evening. I'd suggest some-where a couple of miles away,' he said, reaching out for the crisps.

41

'There they are!' Emma pointed.

He saw them standing in the layby, caught in the glare of his headlights – Okeke and her boyfriend were at the rear of a white Bedford van. Both of them smoking.

Didn't know she smoked. Being an ex-smoker himself, his nose was as good as a blood hound's when it came to picking up the acrid, delightful tang of a curl of fresh fag smoke. He'd not detected so much as a whiff on her so far, at work or anywhere else.

Could be nerves, then.

'I think her boyfriend's taking this very seriously,' said Emma.

Boyd pulled up behind the van. He could see they'd both dressed in sensibly dark clothing. But Jay had gone the extra mile and daubed camo make-up across his face. Boyd noticed he had a black balaclava clasped in one gloved hand as well. He suspected Jay might have watched a few too many Guy Ritchie movies.

He switched off his lights, got out and greeted them. 'Jay, thanks again, by the way, for helping us out.'

'No sweat, guv.'

'*Boyd* is fine, mate. Your girlfriend only calls me guv, because she *has* to.'

'Right.' Jay smiled. 'Got it. I brought the shoo'er.' He dropped the middle T in *shooter* Statham-style.

Boyd suppressed a smile. Then he took the fake handgun and hefted the weight of it. It certainly looked, felt and weighed real. He tucked it into the waistband at the back of his jeans, so that the grip wouldn't be visible.

Sam opened the back of the van and reached in. She came out holding a standard-issue tac vest. 'Some muppet left this over the back of the chair in the canteen. So I nabbed it.'

'You went in to work today?' Boyd asked.

She nodded and said, 'After the pub. I told Minter I was feeling better.' She shrugged. 'I realised a partial day off means it's not logged as a sick day.' She looked at him. 'I'm not losing a sick day for this, guv.'

'Right, well, in future I'll be watching out for that, Okeke,' said Boyd, amused.

'It's all on there,' she said. 'Walkie-talkie, baton, pepper.'

Boyd took off his coat and reached for the heavy vest. 'It's been about ten years since I last wore one of these,' he grunted as he shoved his arms through the loops and shucked his shoulders in to get it to sit right across his broad frame. 'Here,' he said, handing her the walkie-talkie, 'you take this and let's hope we don't need it or we'll both be out of a job.'

Jay pulled a baseball bat out of the back of the van. 'And I've got this, just in case.' He swung it experimentally a couple of times.

Boyd nodded appreciatively. If he had to cry for help and this crazy-looking bat-wielding monster came charging out of the darkness, he was pretty sure that would scare away anything with a pulse and an ounce of common sense.

Even Russians?

Maybe not Russians. *Hopefully* not Russians. It could just as likely be some local scrote with a bit of intel about Rigby or Nix. Perhaps some other crook who'd had his nest egg 'misplaced' by Gerald and wanted to anonymously grass him up.

'The bat suits you,' said Boyd, pulling on his coat over the vest.

Jay grinned. 'Hey, thanks, boss.'

Emma joined them. She had Boyd's phone in her hand. 'You forgot this, Dad.'

His mind was full of the different ways the next hour could go. Despite laying it on thick that this was no biggie – *just some intelligence-gathering theatre* – he was having to hide his jangling nerves from his daughter. Yet another reason why he wished Emma hadn't come along tonight.

'Okeke, I need to talk shop with you for a moment.' He looked at Emma and Jay. 'Alone.'

Jay nodded. 'Righto, I'll uh... I'll go and stand over here.'

'You too, Emma,' said Boyd. 'Go and keep Jay company.'

They walked a little further along the layby.

Okeke waited until they were several metres away and turned to Boyd. 'How are you feeling, guv? Nervous?' she asked.

'A bit. A lot happier you brought your boyfriend along, to be fair.'

'He does look the part,' she said. 'But he's as soft as a puppy really. Be gentle with him.'

'What's the word at work? Has anyone mentioned anything I need to know about?'

'It looks definite that Flack's going to keep the case when you get back on Monday. He's been going over the action log with Minter so he can brief the press next week,' she said.

'And what about Her Madge? Sutherland?' he asked.

'I haven't seen Her Madge come down from her penthouse

in the last few days. I suppose she's content with the way things are going now. Sutherland's stuck his head in a few times, but that's about it.'

'So, no one's missing me?' said Boyd, actually managing to sound a little hurt.

'You're still just the new boy,' she said, then smiled. 'Sully asked after you. I think *he* likes you.'

'Good. Well, at least someone has good taste.' He checked his watch. It was twenty to seven. The pin on Google Maps indicated that the meeting point was about five minutes' drive away.

'Right,' said Boyd. 'So Jay's with me in my car. Emma's in the van with you. You clear on where *you're* parking?'

'Yes. Relax, guv,' she said. 'You look nervous.'

'A little, yeah. I'd be an idiot not to be,' he admitted.

Okeke nodded and glanced over at Emma and Jay. They were chatting and laughing about something. 'Boyd, who do you *really* think's waiting for you?'

He huffed a breath and blew it out slowly. 'Hopefully just someone wanting to rat on Rigby. But...'

'But?'

'It could be a warning.'

'A Russian one?'

He shrugged. 'My worst-case scenario? A couple of utterly charming ex-KGB knuckle-draggers with a few words of wisdom about me sodding off and leaving well alone.'

'And what are you going to say?'

Boyd pulled a contrite face. 'Yes. Absolutely, sir. No problem. Have a good evening and Salisbury Cathedral is *that* way.'

She laughed.

'No, I'm serious. If that's what this is... the force doesn't pay me enough to be Eliot Ness.'

She frowned. 'Eliot Ness?'

'You really don't do movies, do you?'

'Not the old ones, guv, no.'

'Or history,' he muttered. He sucked in another deep breath and tried to steady his nerves.

'If it *is* that,' said Okeke. 'If it *is* Russians... or Russians, or whoever, where does that leave us?'

'It leaves us minding our business, Okeke.' He paused for a moment, then added, 'We're not going to change the world, are we? We're just coppers, here to deal with the small stuff.' He glanced again at his daughter. 'And I don't intend to end up as fish bait like Nix.'

Okeke bit her bottom lip. 'It's a shitty feeling, Boyd. It's really shitty.'

'What is?'

'The thought – the suspicion – that Her Madge is somehow involved.'

'I don't think she's involved directly,' he said. 'Not for a moment. I'd say she's back-peddling this case under instructions from someone further up.'

'From who?'

He shrugged. 'There's not much more in the way of uniformed ranks above her. Someone in the Home Office, perhaps?'

'Jesus.'

'Could be,' he quipped.

She laughed.

He watched Jay stub out his cigarette, wishing, even though he hadn't sparked up in nearly five years, that he could have one right now.

'Okay,' he sighed. 'I guess we'd better saddle up.'

◆

BOYD DROVE ALONG THE SINGLE-LANE, tarmac track that was the Ridge. To their right, the ground dropped away into darkness and a salt marsh below. To their left was a row of very expensive-looking homes that, during the day, had an unobstructed view of the marsh, the beach and the sea beyond.

'So you do this kind of undercover operation much then?' asked Jay.

'Not really. CID work is mostly office work. Maybe a quick outing to a crime scene every now and then, but it's actually mostly paper shuffling. Crime-based Sudoku.'

'Oh.' Jay sounded disappointed. 'It's just... you see shows like *Line of Duty* and stuff, and it's all action, action, action. *Silent Witness* is another one.'

'They're forensic pathologists.'

'Yeah, well, sort of crime doctors, right?

Boyd smiled. *Crime doctors* – that was a good name for them.

'Well, even *they* get to chase down and tackle bad guys,' said Jay.

Boyd grunted. 'Forensics folks see even less daylight than we do.'

'So, what you're saying is the TV stuff is mostly bollocks, then?'

'If only detective work was so exciting and glamorous,' said Boyd. 'I suspect a night-club bouncer sees more action.'

Jay laughed and rocked in his chair, his knees banging on the bottom of the glove compartment. 'It's just tough-guy acting, really. If you get a difficult idiot, you just gotta give 'em some Bouncer Face.'

Boyd nodded. 'It's all about fronting it out?'

'Yeah, exactly. It's all front.'

They passed the last house, leaving open muddy, marshy ground to their left. Boyd checked the satnav and saw they were pretty much there. Just a hundred yards to go, then a left-hand turn.

'Best shuffle down now,' said Boyd.

Jay fidgeted in his seat. 'There's no room. How do I push the seat back?'

Boyd reached under Jay's seat and jerked the bar. Jay's chair slid back. 'Ah, right.'

'Get as low as you can,' said Boyd.

His headlights picked out a tatty-looking sign.

Sea Breeze Campsite

A newer sign had been erected right beside it.

CLOSED – For property details contact H. Macy & Sons.

'Here we go, then.'

He turned left onto the dirt track and immediately his Captur began complaining about the ruts. The rocking, bobbing headlight beams picked out the smooth surface of the lake through the trees to his right, and a fleeting dappled reflection glinted back.

If they had to drive away from this meeting, fast, there might not be time to turn the car round. He'd realised he'd be frantically reversing up this muddy rutted lane.

My Captur's going to hate me.

Suddenly out of the darkness the entrance to the campsite emerged. He slowed down and stopped just before it.

Jay, hunched down in his seat and unable to see a thing, whispered, 'What is it? We there?'

'There's a metal gate. Just got to open it.'

Boyd climbed out, aware that he and his car were probably already being watched. He pushed the gate all the way inwards so that it didn't swing back and close. Then he climbed back into the car.

He pulled out his phone out and dialled Okeke. 'I'm at the camp's entrance now.'

'Okay.'

'I'm going to leave this call open so you can listen in to what's going on.'

'Good idea, guv.'

He pocketed his phone, then drove slowly forward, with the lake to his right and a muddy field to his left. His headlights picked out a second gate. This one was already open. Further ahead, grubby trailer windows dimly reflected his beams.

'All right,' he said, parking beside the open gate. 'This is it. I'm parking you here.'

'Good luck, mate,' whispered Jay.

'Thanks.'

Boyd turned the engine off, followed by the headlights. He picked up a torch from the side pocket of his door and flicked it on, then stepped out into the cold night.

He panned his torch left to right, picking out a hut just past the gate, which presumably was once a reception for visitors, and another small hut beside it that looked as though it could have been a general shop. In front of that there were a few weather-beaten picnic tables with wooden benches, and beyond those were the waiting trailers.

He made his way forward, through the open gate and past the abandoned buildings.

Should I announce myself or stay quiet? he wondered briefly, before deciding to go for it.

'DCI BOYD!' he called out. 'YOU WANTED TO TALK TO ME?'

His voice bounced faintly back off the side of a nearby trailer. It was quiet except for the clatter of restless loose rubbish stirred by the gentle sea breeze.

'SO? COME ON, THEN! I'M HERE!'

There was no reply. He checked his watch. It was four

minutes to seven. Early, but, for Christ's sake, only *just* early. *Seriously? You're actually going to make me wait until bang on seven?*

'Okay, then,' he muttered to himself. 'I guess I'll wait.'

He carried on walking slowly until he was standing in the middle of the open area – on the three metre by three metre patch of weed-tufted ground identified by those three random words: *detective.goodnight.chosen.*

He blew a cloud of breath out into the beam of his torch. *It's fucking freezing out here. Hurry up.*

Boyd switched his torch off. He'd made himself known. He wasn't going to be a surprise to anybody lingering in one of those trailers.

It was pitch-black. Not even a sliver of moonlight to add to the haunting creepiness of this forlorn-looking meeting spot.

He waited patiently, knowing full well that Okeke and Emma were undoubtedly listening in, hearing his laboured breath and the occasional muttered *For fuck's sake.*

Then, a few moments later, he spotted the faintest flicker of amber light. It disappeared. He kept his eyes on the same point, trying not to lose his place. Just as suddenly the faint flickering illumination returned in the form of the soft and steady glow of a candle, sitting on the windowsill inside one of the trailers.

Here we go. Showtime.

He heard a door swing open and clatter against something. By the faint light of the candle, he could make out the silhouette of a slight figure slowly, cautiously, approaching him.

It looked familiar. The hoodie. The same short, narrow frame. Boyd had thought it was a he, but now he wasn't so certain. Surely it wasn't actually Jo...?

'It's the same guy that left the note,' Boyd muttered in the direction of his phone, then, more loudly: 'I'm going to turn my torch on! All right?'

A voice came out of the darkness. 'No... please don't.'

No accent. Not Russian, then. Thank fuck.

And definitely male.

Closer now, the figure came to a halt.

'I need help,' he said. The voice sounded weak, fragile, trembling. 'My name is Gerald Nix.'

42

'Shit!' Okeke gasped.

Emma looked at her. She was about to say something, but Okeke quickly raised a finger to her lips.

Whispering softly, Okeke gestured at the phone on the dashboard. 'He's meant to be dead!' Emma seemed confused, so Okeke continued, 'His blood was found on the boat. I mean lots of it. *Shit-shit-shit!*'

Emma looked at her.

'Well, I can't see how we can keep this off the books now. *Shit.*' Then Okeke raised her finger and pointed to the phone again.

'It's cold out here.' Boyd's voice.

'I... I've been living over in that... trailer –' Nix's voice – 'for months...'

'You want to go talk in there?' Boyd again.

No answer. Perhaps Nix had nodded.

'All right,' said Boyd. 'Come on...'

NIX STEPPED into the trailer first, then turned and waited for Boyd to join him. 'It's all right... I'm not going to attack you,' he said quickly. 'I... I just need your help.'

Boyd nodded. 'Okay. But kill me and I may decide not to,' he quipped, in an attempt to ease the tension.

Nix ignored this and gestured for Boyd to enter. 'Please... just come in. Come in.'

Inside, Boyd noted the layout of the trailer was pretty standard– a lounge-cum-galley to his left, a flimsy door ahead into what he guessed was a tiny wet room and toilet, and another door to the right into the bedroom. What he wasn't expecting though was the smell. The stench reminded him of a last-day festival toilet – not that he'd been to one in over twenty years, but the memory of that particular odour lingered long after the names of the bands he'd gone to see.

Nix could see the face he was pulling by the faint light of the flickering candle. 'The flush doesn't work. There's no running water or power to these things. So... you have to make do.' He shrugged miserably.

Boyd could see empty tin cans piled up in the galley sink and the side was stacked with take-away wrappers and fast-food cartons, plastic bottles of drinking water and pop.

'Don't tell me you've been camping out here since November.'

'Not in this trailer. But in the camp, yes.' Nix nodded. 'I changed trailer several times. The smell eventually gets overwhelming.'

Eventually? It was pretty overwhelming already.

'Please... sit.' Nix pointed at the bench sofa to the left. A sleeping bag was strewn across it, socks and pants spilling out and cascading onto the floor.

Boyd shoved the mess aside and sat down. He looked once more around the cramped and squalid interior. 'So, my first question is: Gerald Nix... what the hell are you doing alive?'

Nix let out a single snort, halfway between a laugh and a sob. 'Hiding.'

'Hiding from who?' Boyd asked.

Nix was silent.

'Okay. So why don't we start with this. How are you *alive*? Your blood was all over your yacht.'

Nix slumped down on the sofa and looked up at Boyd. '*Some* of it was.'

He carefully rolled the left sleeve of his hoodie up to the elbow to reveal yellowing bandages wrapped round his forearm. Either side of the bandages was discoloured, darkened skin. Even by the light of one solitary, guttering candle, Boyd could see it was a wound that had gone septic beneath the dressing.

'I got cut, quite badly...' Nix took a deep breath, then let it out slowly, shakily. 'Most of the blood on the boat was theirs'.'

'Who?'

'Zophia,' he replied.

'Your AskForSasha girlfriend?'

Nix looked surprised.

'It's what we do at the CID, Nix. We *detect* stuff. Who was the other one?'

'She said the man was her uncle.'

'Russian too?'

A look of relief washed over Nix's face. 'Yes. So you know about Zophia?'

Boyd nodded, then asked, 'She *is* dead then?'

Nix hesitated.

'Come on, Nix – just tell me what happened.' Boyd could see the man was balanced on a knife edge – all darting eyes and facial tics. He decided to try more softly-softly. 'Gerald, tell me why I'm here. You invited me after all.'

'I'm f-fucking frightened.' Nix's voice was fluttering on the edge of tears.

'You want protection?' Boyd asked.

Nix nodded.

'From who?'

Unheard words formed on Nix's lips. He couldn't say it. He was too scared.

'The Salikovs?' Boyd prompted.

Nix nodded, then began to cry – a long hissing, wet sound as his lips curled and his unshaven cheeks quivered. He looked a lot less like Bill Gates now than he had in that photo, proudly holding his certificate. He was, Boyd thought, more like Shaggy from *Scooby Doo*.

'They're going to find me,' he mewled, snot and tears mingling on his chin. 'They won't give up. Ever. They've sent people over here to find me.'

'You know that for a fact?' Boyd asked, unconsciously touching his left ear.

'Of course they have! His daughter's dead. And it's all my fault!'

More tears. Boyd needed to speed this up. He needed to get them both out of here and take Nix to the station to be interviewed properly.

'Rovshan Salikov?'

Nix nodded again. 'Yeah, her father. The big man. I-I met him once. Just once.'

'When you went over to Russia?'

'Yeah. He – ' Nix's voice rose hysterically – 'He's Saddam Hussain-crazy. Batshit crazy. She told me... after she came back to England. After she moved in, she told me what he... what he does...'

Boyd nodded. 'I've read some of the Russian articles on him.'

'H-he wanted to move h-here. He wanted my h-help.'

'Right. So that's what they had you doing? Laundering their money?'

'Yeah. Just a little bit at first. Then... then... more and –'

'Gerald, I think we should get you into police custody. You'll be safer there, mate.'

'I won't!' he snapped. 'Not if he knows where I am!'

Boyd leant forward and tried to look friendly and reassuring. 'The nick of a police division HQ, Gerald, is just about the safest place you can be –'

'*You don't understand!* I brought their fucking money *in!*'

'What do you mean?' Boyd asked, momentarily confused.

'Into the country! Hundreds of millions!' Nix whispered. 'And I know where it all is. I know everything. Don't you fucking get it? The fucking police won't stop them getting to me.' Nix reached a grubby hand across the trailer table and grasped Boyd's wrist. 'Please. Don't take me in. They'll find me.'

THE NISSAN JUKE rolled slowly down the country road.

It was a hired car from an Avis outlet at Heathrow airport. A common enough make and a very forgettable silvery grey colour. Inside, two men sat silently, one driving, one staring at his small glowing phone screen.

'*Povernut' nalevo,*' said the passenger.

The driver grunted. 'Your English. Practise it.'

'Left. Here.'

'Better.'

The Juke turned left at the T-junction, and headed along a single-lane road. It rolled on past nice homes with broad seaview windows. The man in the passenger's seat got momentary snapshot glimpses of family lives: two children yammering at each other at a kitchen table, an old couple on a couch watching the television, a German shepherd standing guard at the window barking ferociously yet unheard at the car that glided by like a shark in the shallows.

'Who's that?' Okeke muttered. Her eyes fixed on the approaching glare of headlights in the wing mirror.

They'd passed one or two cars parked along the Ridge – overspill from small gravel driveways occupied by caravans, boat trailers and fix-up projects that were never going to be finished. Okeke fervently hoped that the car belonged to someone who lived here and would pull in soon.

Emma squinted at the rear-view mirror. The headlights grew large, filled the mirror, then passed them by. She exchanged a look of concern with Okeke.

They watched in tense silence as the twin lights dwindled, occasionally flaring as the vehicle's brakes were tapped and released.

'It's not stopping,' said Emma, heart hammering.

Okeke's phone was still connected to Boyd's, the men's voices and rustling from Boyd's coat pocket playing out on the dashboard.

'Your phone,' she said urgently to Emma.

'What?'

'I need to use your phone.'

Emma pulled it out, unlocked it and passed it to her. Okeke dialled a number. It answered quickly.

'Jay, it's me,' she said quietly.

'Hey, babycakes,' he whispered. 'You missing me alrea–'

'Not now, Jay. A car's just gone past us; it's heading your way.'

'Okay. So what do you want me to do?'

Her eyes were still on the tiny pinpricks of red. If they veered to the left, then it had to be turning into the road beside the lake, heading up towards the campsite.

'Hold on... Hold on... It's slowed down. It may just be parking up.'

'THE SALIKOVS,' said Nix. 'If they f-find me... if they get hold of me... they won't just kill me. You d-do understand that, right?'

Boyd had a pretty good idea of what would happen to Nix if they managed to get their hands on him. They'd take their time with him, for sure.

'Listen to me,' said Boyd. 'I'm not going to let them find you. All right? I'm going to get you somewhere safe, somewhere we can talk properly.'

'Not the p-police –'

'I've got a couple of friends with me who –'

Nix's eyes bulged.

'No! Listen! Trusted friends. People I trust. We're going to get you out of here, take you to safety and get you cleaned up and get you something to eat.'

'Okay, okay, okay.' Nix rocked back and forth in his seat. 'Then what?'

'Then we'll work out next steps. I –'

Nix laughed, shaking his head. '*Next steps?* There are no next fucking steps! I'm going to b-be hiding for the r-rest of my fucking life! They always get what they want, Boyd. You want to know how?'

'How?' Boyd asked, in what he hoped was a calming voice.

'*Money, money, money,*' sang Nix. A tuneless, haunted whimpering rendition of the old Abba song. 'We're all corrupt these days. We're all rotten to the core. And thing is, you have no choice. You *have* to take the money; you don't say no. Not to these p-people. You just don't say –'

'And that's what happened to you?' cut in Boyd. 'You couldn't say no?'

Nix stopped. His lips pressed together, then finally he nodded. 'It was Zophia. I-I thought she was stunning. I mean...

oh God.' He clamped his eyes shut and pulled his knees up into a pitiful self-hug. 'Why did I even think –'

Boyd answered for him. 'You were flattered. She made you feel young again.'

'Yes! Yes! I... I just... I was... She made me feel like, fuck, like ... *James Bond.*' Boyd could see the glint of his wide eyes reflecting the candlelight. 'She pulled me in... then...' He licked his lips and took a breath. 'Then it was... *A little favour, Gerry. Just a little favour. Please. For my family,*' he said, mimicking a breathy little girl's voice. '*Father has money he wants to invest. You are clever at this, yes?*' Nix palmed his forehead several times, thumping himself for his stupidity. 'I didn't know who they were at the time. I didn't think.'

Or maybe you didn't want to know? Boyd had the feeling Nix's common sense had departed the moment this young woman had appeared, leaving his quivering libido to do all the decision-making for him.

'I should've guessed! I told her I wouldn't do it any more and she said it would be okay.' Nix's rocking was becoming more agitated.

They needed to move.

'Look, Gerald. We're going to get you somewhere secure and –'

Nix stopped rocking and looked at him. 'I killed them, Boyd,' he blurted. 'I killed them both!'

43

Doing her best to ignore the drama coming from the phone on the dashboard, Okeke tried to make out what was going on up ahead.

The car had pulled over and stopped. It appeared to be waiting.

'I don't like the look of that,' she whispered to Emma.

Through the red glow of the brake lights, Okeke could see clouds of exhaust drifting away. The engine was still running.

'It could just be visitors, I suppose, said Emma. 'It's Friday night.'

Okeke turned to her. 'Then why are they just sitting there?'

'Talking?' muttered Emma. 'Making out?' she added hopefully.

'Come on, come on,' hissed Okeke, staring at the back of the car. 'Get out or bugger off.' It had been there for nearly a minute now.

'Sam?' It was Jay's voice. Her call was still open to him. 'What's going on there, baby?'

'It's still sitting there,' she whispered.

'What are my orders?'

Okeke smiled briefly. Her boyfriend was clearly getting a big kick out of the whole covert operation thing. 'Just sit tight for now, love – but be ready!'

'Roger that.'

~

'WE WERE out in the middle of the Channel when it happened,' said Nix. 'She said she wanted us to sail to France for the weekend. To impress her 'uncle' with my boat? She said we could talk to him about getting out of the business.'

'And that didn't make you at all suspicious?' Boyd asked, hoping that Okeke was getting this.

Nix shook with mirthless laughter. 'It should have, shouldn't it? I just wanted to trust her.' He laughed again. 'Fuck it. I *loved* her. Crazy head-over-heels shit, you know? She was gorgeous, way out of my league. I would have done anything she asked.'

'So go on. What happened?'

'They both went down below. I was at the helm.' Nix was absently tugging at the bristly tufts on his chin. 'I heard them talking. It sounded like Russian. Then they both came back out...' Nix had a haunted look on his face as he spoke. His eyes were wide and glassy, not just telling Boyd the tale but actually *reliving* it. 'I just knew. I put it together as soon as I saw them. I actually *knew* it was coming. Better late than never, eh? But what the fuck was I supposed to do? Jump? Run? I –' He took a deep breath to steady himself.

'It's okay,' said Boyd. 'Take your time.'

'Her "uncle" had come up the steps into the cockpit with a big fucking knife in his hand. He was actually fucking smiling at me!'

'Okay,' said Boyd calmly. 'So then?'

'I jibbed and cast off.'

'What's that mean?' Boyd asked, confused.

'I turned the boat round and released the mainsheet. The beam swung round and knocked him down. I think it knocked him out for a second. I... it all happened so fucking fast!' Nix paused and took in a deep, steadying breath. 'He dropped the knife. I picked it up. And...'

'And what?'

'I stabbed him.' Nix gnawed on his grimy nails as he replayed the moment. 'Not just once. Fuck! Boyd... he wouldn't die! He wouldn't fucking die, no matter how many times I...!' Nix looked at the dirty bandages around his arm. 'He was biting me. I mean, right through my skin, like a bloody dog! And I just didn't know what to do, so I kept stabbing and stabbing and stabbing!'

Jesus Christ. 'Okay,' Boyd said, trying to keep his horror from showing on his face. 'So what about Zophia? What was she doing?'

Nix didn't answer.

'Did she run from you?'

Nix shook his head and clamped his lips tightly shut.

'Gerald! Come on. What happened next? Did she run? Did she hide?'

Nix looked at him, and then, like a little boy all out of lies, he nodded. 'In the forecabin,' he whispered.

'You killed her down there?'

He nodded again. 'I h-had to Boyd. I... She was going to kill me. I had to do it. If I let her live, if I took her back home and let her go... What the fuck do you think would have happened to me?'

His voice was growing sharp and ragged. The rocking was becoming exaggerated and frantic. Boyd decided he'd heard enough. The rest of this story had been told by Sully through the crime scene report. It was time to go.

He placed what he hoped was a reassuring hand on Nix's shoulder. 'It's all right, mate. It's all right. Come on – let's get you somewhere safe.'

'She played me like an idiot. Betrayed me... Fucking made me her little bitch. I was... I was just a bloody poodle. Pathetic.' Nix looked up at Boyd. 'They saw me coming. They played me from the very fucking beginning.'

'It's over. Okay, Gerald? She's gone.'

Nix's breathing deepened. He dipped his head. 'I feel sick.'

'You need to puke?'

Nix was doubled over now, his head between his knees.

'You do what you got to do,' said Boyd. He inched backwards slightly, not wanting to catch any splash. 'Take your time.'

But Nix didn't puke. He remained doubled over as he continued. 'I was panicked. I didn't know if bodies float or sink. I didn't... So I just... just in case they did, I cut the heads and hands off.'

Shit. Emma's hearing this. Instinctively Boyd reached into his coat pocket and fumbled for the phone's power button. He had his confession now. Okeke had heard it. The rest, the dismemberment, could wait for later.

Okeke grabbed her phone and was about to call Boyd back, when she thought better of it. The phone had been rustling. It was clearly pocketed. She was pretty sure he'd cut the call on purpose.

'What's happened?' said Emma and Jay in unison.

'He's got what he wanted,' she said. 'We've got our confession.' Okeke picked up Emma's phone. 'It looks like we may be all done here, Jay. Sit tight until Boyd comes back out.'

'Copy that, gorgeous.'

She ended the call with Jay and handed Emma her phone.

'So what do we now?' Emma asked.

'Your dad's probably going to read Nix his rights, cuff him and walk him over to the car. Then we'll call in the boots to formally caution, arrest and process him. Jay will take you home in the van, and your dad and I will hope and pray that the good outweighs the bad and we get to keep our bloody jobs!'

Emma sighed with relief. 'Thank God.'

Okeke suddenly froze. 'Shit!'

'What? said Emma, following her gaze.

Okeke was looking at the car up ahead. Both doors opened simultaneously, the interior lights casting a momentary soft glow onto the rutted and cracked tarmac road. Okeke caught a fleeting illuminated glimpse of both figures. There were two men. Both of them carrying something that glinted dully in the light.

'Shit! They're getting out.' She snatched Emma's phone back. 'Pin!'

'Huh?'

'What's your fucking PIN!'

'Three-two-four-one!' Emma blurted out in a panicked voice.

Okeke unlocked Emma's phone and hit redial.

'I was in the boat for a day and a night. Twenty-four hours. Just floating. Watching the blood dry. I didn't know what to do, where to go.'

'But you came back,' said Boyd. 'Right?'

Nix nodded.

So that had been Nix on the CCTV, then. Okeke had said there'd been a CCTV activation event at Nix's house two days after the boat had gone out. 'You made your way back home? But how? The *Magpie* was found drifting.'

'I was panicking. I didn't know what to do. I sailed back to England. I was fucking terrified some Border Force boat was going to intercept me... but I stopped when I got close enough...'

'Close enough?'

'To shore.'

'Jesus, Nix. You swam to shore? In *November*?' The water would have been freezing.

'No. In a blow-up dinghy. I paddled. I didn't swim. But... before... before I abandoned *Magpie*... I couldn't think what else to fucking do!'

'You tried to scupper her?'

He nodded. 'I put a hole in the front. Turned the boat round. Put the engine on. Locked the helm and let her head out into the Channel.'

'And you hoped she'd sink. You hoped everyone would think *all three* of you were dead.'

Nix let out a snotty, edgy bark of a laugh. 'I'd just killed Zophia. Rovshan Salikov's daughter! What the hell was I going to do? Hand myself in?'

He had a point. Whether he could make a self-defence argument and make bail or not – he'd be a sitting duck. Going missing alongside the other two was probably his only option. If someone as rich and powerful as Jeffrey Epstein was an easy target in prison, some unknown nobody like Gerald Nix would be a piece of cake.

'I tried to make it look like we'd all died,' Nix continued. 'I came back to my house. Got some clothes, as much money as I had in the house... I left my car, because... I'm meant to be dead, right? Dead. So... this.' He gestured around him. 'I've been like this ever since. Hiding here.'

'Why not go to friends? Family?'

'I don't have any. No one I trust. Anyway, I was out of options. I saw you on the TV. I got a bus into Hastings and I followed you. It was me in the graveyard.'

'Well, I worked that out. I'm here, aren't I?' Boyd said. 'What else did you do? Did you find out where I live? Did you watch my house?'

Nix nodded. 'I saw you walking your dog.'

Fuck. If this idiot could find him, then he doubted it would be a problem for the Russian mafia. Boyd looked at the clutter of rubbish around the trailer and shook his head. 'This is no way to live.'

Nix nodded. 'I'm out of cash now,' he said. 'There's none left. I don't know who else to turn to! I. Am. Fucking. Terrified. Boyd, please – you've got to help me.'

THE PHONE VIBRATED on the seat beside Jay. He picked it up and answered, 'Hey there, Babyca –'

'There's two men coming down the track,' Okeke said urgently. 'Towards you! I think they're armed! Alert Boyd and get the *hell out of there*! NOW!'

Jay didn't need telling twice. He hung up. *Shit just got real.*

He leant over the gear stick and turned the ignition. The Captur sputtered to life and the headlights winked on. He recalled Boyd's instruction. Fire up the car. Make a shit-ton of noise.

He hit the button on Sam's rape alarm.

PWEEEEEEEEEEEEEEEEEE!

'SHIT!'

In the car's small interior, it felt like the high-pitched siren was actually piercing his brain. He opened the passenger-side door and clambered out with the shrieking alarm still in his hand.

'BOYD!'

44

'FUCK!' Boyd nearly shat himself.

'*What? What's happening?*' Nix had leapt back at the sudden screaming alarm;

'It's okay,' said Boyd quickly, trying to control his nerves. 'It's a signal. Someone's coming. We have to move *now*.'

He looked out through the rear window of the trailer and saw that his car's headlights were on and spilling light across the open area, casting long shadows from the picnic table and benches.

'We've got company. Talking time's over, Gerald... You're coming in with me.'

'Ohgodohgod!' Nix leapt to his feet. 'They'll kill you too!' he whimpered, wild-eyed.

'Listen to me.' Boyd tried standing up, but his thighs caught the small fixed table and he had to sit down again and shuffle along. 'Gerald! For now the safest place is the police station, okay? We'll get you –'

'NO! You can't!' Nix yelled. 'They'll get to me!' He backed away from Boyd, down towards the trailer's front door.

'Don't be a fucking idiot!' snapped Boyd, successfully on his feet at the second attempt.

Nix reached for a holdall, packed and ready to grab, from beside the door. The trailer door was already open.

'You led them to me!' he screamed. 'You've fucking killed me!'

He shot out of the door and into the night.

'NIX!' Boyd reached the doorway and caught sight of Nix disappearing into the labyrinth of rusty trailers.

A moment later he heard the heavy slap of approaching trainers and Jay's silhouette appeared before him.

Jay switched off the rape alarm. 'Uh, Boyd – Sam say's we've got company on the road coming up. Two men. With weapons.'

'Shit!' Boyd instinctively reached for the police baton under his coat, unclipped it and flicked it out – retained muscle memory from those long-ago uniformed days. 'How close? Where are they?'

'Coming down the lakeside track towards the entrance.'

Probably *running* down the track by now.

Boyd's car was about fifty yards away, invitingly close with the doors open, puffing out a cloud of exhaust at the rear that looked like baited dragon's breath in the glare of the brake lights.

Car or Nix?

Fuck it. Car.

He jumped down the entrance steps and started sprinting towards the waiting vehicle.

'Let's go!'

~

'WHAT DO WE DO?' Emma's voice was shaking.

'I'm already doing it,' Okeke replied. She had her finger depressed on the panic button of her radio handset. A code zero would be going out on all police frequencies along with a GPS signal.

'Try not to worry, Emma. Help's on its way.' She started up the van. 'But we have to get a bit closer.'

'Oh, God. I... I'm not sure...'

'You can get out and stay here if you want,' offered Okeke.

The option nudged Emma off the fence. Emma nodded so vigorously her glasses lifted off the bridge of her nose. 'Do it. Go, go!'

Okeke turned the key, and Jay's transit van rattled noisily to life. She threw it into gear and swung out into the lane, kicking up a spray of crumbled tarmac and wind-borne sand.

Boyd grabbed the edge of the open driver-side door when the rear window suddenly shattered, showering him with granules.

'FUCK ME!' yelped Jay as he hurried around the front to shield behind the passenger-side door. 'What was that?'

'A gun, you muppet!'

The windscreen suddenly exploded too.

Warning shots. Two of them. The next explosion would almost certainly be his head. Or Jay's.

'STOP!' a heavily accented voice barked out of the darkness.

Boyd dropped the baton, stood up and raised his hands. Jay saw and quickly followed suit. They held their pose, both panting out clouds of breath, waiting to see what would come next.

'Are we gonna be shot?' said Jay.

'Shut up,' Boyd hissed.

Finally, emerging from the gloom into the crimson pool of the car's rear lights, two men approached.

As they neared, Boyd could see that they were both holding silencer-tipped handguns. They advanced quickly and confidently. No caution, no wary approach – just two hard-faced men who had absolutely no doubt that the situation was theirs to control.

They separated, one coming towards Boyd, the other walking around the car towards Jay.

Boyd found himself staring down the silencer's barrel at the face beyond it: pockmarked skin and grey eyes, a crew cut of silvered hair. A slim, scrawny even, old man who was a foot shorter than him, all twitching tendons and varicose veins.

'Hello, Boyd,' he said in a thick accent.

'Do I know you?' Boyd asked, meeting his eyes and trying not to look away.

The old man's smile broadened, showing his teeth – all metal fillings, tobacco stains and gaps. He tapped the side of his head with his free hand. 'Ear,' he said.

'Ahh.' Boyd nodded. 'That was you.'

The man grinned again as he looked around. 'Nix. Where is?'

Boyd jerked his head over his shoulder. 'Gone.' He wasn't ready to be a hero, but he wasn't going to be a total pushover either. 'He left. Minutes ago.'

'Where?'

Boyd tipped his head in the opposite direction to the one he'd seen Nix take off.

The old man turned to his younger colleague. '*Poyti! On v lagere!*'

The other man pushed past Jay and hurried forward into the glare of the headlights, through the open gate and into the campsite.

'You speak English?' said Boyd.

'Yes, good,' replied the old man. 'Fluent.'

'The cavalry's on its way.'

The man cocked his head and frowned.

Not that fluent, then.

Boyd pointed back down the track. 'Police are coming. Lots.'

'Ah, *politsiya*.' He shrugged like it wasn't that big of a deal. 'Not worry.'

'They'll be here, mate. Any second now,' continued Boyd. He was struggling to keep his voice even and calm. Captive–captor psychology 101 – *sound* like you have leverage or a deal to offer. 'You really don't want to shoot a British cop dead. Trust me. You'll have the whole force after you.'

'Shhh,' said the old man gently. 'I decide.' Then he pursed his lips and began tilting his head from side to side, looking from Boyd to Jay, almost as though he was running through a silent eeny, meeny, miny, moe.

'Mate. You're making a big mistake,' Boyd said, trying to catch Jay's eye. They'd have to move soon if they were going to get out of this, while it was two against one.

Shushed him again and smiled. 'I choose now.'

With that, he swung his aim to the right and fired over the top of the car.

PHUT! The silencer reduced the shot to something that sounded like an abrupt comedy sneeze.

Boyd took what would undoubtedly be his *only* chance.

He ducked down and charged forward, bulldozing into the small man and knocking him off his feet. They were both now sprawled on the ground, tangled up with each other. Boyd's hands were frantically trying to get a purchase on his gun hand before –

PHUT!

The shot whistled past his ear, off into the night somewhere. Even though there was a small glow of red light from the rear of the car, Boyd was doing this blind, relying on touch. His hand followed what felt like an arm, then grabbed the wrist – fucking well hoping to God it was the correct bloody one.

PHUT!

Shit! He felt a puff of air beside his other ear this time.

Another inch to the left and the shot would have been right in his eye.

The Russian writhed around, trying to tear his wrist free of Boyd's desperate grip. Boyd felt the man's weight shift, then a sharp elbow came out of nowhere and smacked him in the cheek. It knocked him almost senseless, but he hung on, his left hand creeping over his right until it, suddenly, touched the hot metal of the gun.

'Thank fuck,' he grunted.

The sharp elbow hit again, mashing Boyd's lips against his teeth. The squirming ball of intertwined men rolled over to the side of the lane like dung beetles clinging tightly to each other. All of a sudden, Boyd found his face was pushed up hard against the side of the Russian's head, one fleshy cauliflower ear temptingly within range of his teeth. *An ear for an ear you, fucking bastard.*

He sank his teeth into the flesh and ground down hard into crackling cartilage.

The older man barked out in pain and swung his arm up, aiming for Boyd's face again.

The first swing was a glancing blow. Boyd hung on. He could feel his front teeth beginning to meet each other through the flesh. His mouth was filling with warm blood.

The Russian managed to jerk his gun hand free. He swung it up hard so that the pistol grip slammed into Boyd's temple. Stunned, Boyd came loose with a chunk of ear in his mouth.

The old man – so goddamned fast and agile for his age – twisted round sharply. Something cracked into Boyd's forehead. Right between his eyes.

Boyd flopped backwards to the ground. His hearing was gone. There was just the dull roar of blood in transit. He was lying flat on his back and looking upwards at swirls of dust caught in a headlight's beam, dancing like cigarette smoke.

Boyd was dully aware that he must be dying.

The impact was undoubtedly a bullet. He didn't need to feel around the back for some jagged exit wound to confirm that.

He felt drunk and dizzy – light-headed, like he'd felt the last time he'd tried a joint. That was decades ago now. He could feel warm blood rolling down from his forehead, past his temple and tickling his good ear as it found a groove and began to pool there.

Sorry, Emma, was all he could think right now. *Sorry, Emma.*

The Russian appeared in his narrowing cone of vision, looming over him. The ugly little bastard was actually nodding appreciatively down at him, as if to say, *Good effort, comrade.* He raised his gun arm, lined up the end of the silencer at Boyd's eyes, ready for a second and final tap.

A baseball bat swung gracefully, *beautifully*, into view.

The Russian disappeared.

A moment later Jay's face appeared over him. He was a picture of adrenalin-fired exhilaration – wide-eyed and grinning like a winning *Strictly* finalist. His mouth started moving. It looked like, *You all right, mate? You all right?* But all Boyd could hear was that steady traffic roar of his own rushing blood.

'Grab. The. Gun,' Boyd managed to say, his voice sounding like someone had thrown a thick wet blanket over a shitty little PA speaker on the other side of a submerged room.

Jay disappeared from view, then returned, holding the gun by the long barrel of the silencer. He winced at the heat and promptly dropped it.

Boyd scrabbled for it blindly in the dusty ground beside him. His finger brushed it, doubled back, and he grasped it before Crazy-Bloody-Ivan could return from wherever he'd gone.

Well, I guess I'm not dying, Boyd reasoned, his head still spinning. He struggled onto his elbows to get a look around at the current situation.

The Russian was on his back, legs crooked and splayed like

a spatchcock chicken ready for the oven. But not dead, and definitely not out. He was cradling his head in his arms, his legs rocking from side to side.

Jay got his hands under Boyd's armpits and began to lift him up.

'Just get me in the fucking car and drive!' Boyd shouted.

Jay nodded, hefted him into the passenger seat, then dived into the open door on the driver's side.

'Go! Go! Go!' Boyd yelled.

Jay threw the car into reverse and kicked up a cloud of grit and sand into the twin headlight beams.

Boyd realised, just in time, he still had one leg hanging outside the car, the toe of his shoe scraping along the ground. 'Fucking wait!'

Jay slammed the brakes on and Boyd smacked painfully against the door frame – half in and half out of the car. Boyd writhed frantically and somehow managed to get himself fully in the car. 'Now go!' he screamed, pulling the passenger-side door closed.

As the car bumped and lurched wildly, Boyd fumbled for a seat belt. The sprawled form of the Russian, now joined by his younger colleague, receded as the reversing car jolted chaotically over the muddy ruts in the lane.

Then the younger man raised his arm.

Followed by several silent flickers of muzzle flash.

Sparks pinged off the edge of the windscreen.

Shrieking, Jay raised an arm to protect his face. The car bounced and rocked and skidded as it continued its erratic retreat.

But all this was like a silent action movie to Boyd. He was *still* hearing nothing but that damned roaring in both ears, and he was frantically blinking to keep a steady trickle of blood out of his eyes. Blackness was edging in, narrowing his field of vision.

That was annoying. Because he really, really, *really* needed to see how this was all going to play out. He especially needed to see Emma.

That was all that mattered to him now.

Not Nix. Not himself. Not this case.

Just Emma.

45

Ahead of him, a receding procession of red tail lights and blinking hazards. The PC on traffic duty recognises Boyd and seems to instantly pale at the sight of him.

'Uh... up ahead, s-sir,' the PC stutters, pointing. 'But –'

Boyd pushes past him, but the young copper grabs his arm.

'Sir, I don't think it's a good –'

'FUCK OFF!' Boyd snarls, shaking off his grasp and shoving the young man aside. He can see the flash of blue lights, the yellow stripes of the ambulance, a solitary twist of smoke rising into the grey, overcast sky.

It was a very average Tuesday, mid-morning, not even rush hour, not even raining. He got to work a couple of hours ago, enough time to gossip a bit in the canteen, make a coffee and make a start on some paperwork.

Then the call.

He got here in less than seven minutes – courtesy of blues-and-twos all the way. Got as close as the patrol car could get. And now he's running towards that spiral of smoke, treading granules of glass spread far and wide across the motorway tarmac.

The smoke's coming from their car.

Only it doesn't look like a car any more. It looks more like a big compressed ball of KitKat foil.

Two articulated trucks flank it, wheeled back to allow the first responders enough elbow room to reach it.

He races past a first responder who's trying to stop him, trying to prevent him from seeing what no husband and father should ever have to witness. He deftly dodges traffic police, firemen, paramedics.

And then he arrives.

He's seeing heads shaking. He's hearing words quietly exchanged.

Then one of the paramedics is beside him. 'I'm sorry, sir.'

He remains hopeful. 'She's still alive?'

A pause. 'Your wife is. While everything's kept in place. But it won't be for much longer.'

'Kept in place?' That doesn't make sense to him.

'We've given her ketamine. She's not in pain,' is all he hears before he ducks down and peers inside the compressed wreck of their car. A glance to the right. Noah's gone from the bridge of his nose up. Just gone. There's hardly any blood on his pale cheeks. It doesn't seem real. Somebody's put a sheet over the mess above. In his chubby little hands he's still holding an action figure. It's an Avenger – the blue one with the round shield.

Julia, though, is alive – just as the man said.

She's pinned into her seat by a jagged sheet of plastic dashboard. It's gone right through her waist, into the back rest, cutting her almost completely in half. The dashboard is holding everything in.

She sees him and smiles with relief.

'Hey, Jules,' he whispers.

'Noah?' She looks at him, hope in her eyes.

He's going to have to lie. He wants her to go knowing her boy's just fine.

'He's okay, honey.' He manages a weak smile. 'He's going to have a corker of a bruise tomorrow, though.'

She wheezes with relief.

He grabs her hand and squeezes it. 'They're going to get you out next.' Then he quips, to make her smile: 'Tell me you renewed the insurance?'

She smiles and rolls her eyes.

He looks down. There's so much blood. She must have seen it. She must know this doesn't end well.

Like him, she's pretending it's all fine.

Like him, she's avoiding heart-breaking final words.

How stupid of them.

Her eyes roll again, but it isn't forbearance this time. This is the close-down.

He leans forward, 'Jules. I love you,' he whispers in her ear. Then he kisses her. 'I love you.'

He feels her squeeze him back, to let him know she's heard. To let him know she loves him too.

Then she's gone.

46

'Dad?'

Boyd opened his eyes to see Emma leaning over him, stroking his head. He could hear a bustle of activity beyond the green curtain that had been drawn around him and his daughter.

'We're in A&E,' she said.

'What?'

'We came in earlier. For some stitches. Don't you remember?'

No, actually he didn't. The last thing he'd had in his head was Julia.

'What time is it?' he asked, disorientated.

She checked her watch. 'Half past two... in the morning.'

Boyd reached up – more bandages around his head. He felt oddly misplaced, hovering in a timeline he couldn't quite make sense of. Were they back in London? His head was pounding with the most dreadful ache that synced perfectly with the thudding sound of his heartbeat. A hangover from hell, plus he was wearing a turban-like wrapping of bandages around his head. He must have gone on another bender and either been knocked down or face-planted into the pavement.

Oh, what a stupid mess you are, Boydy.

'Dad!' Emma's voice again.

'Hey,' he said groggily. 'Sorry, love. I think I might've got pissed again.'

She frowned. 'What the hell are you talking about?'

Maybe not a bender, then.

He suddenly remembered gulls. And chips. His timeline was hopelessly confused.

He had a flashback of an old man with a crew cut and shit teeth, grinning at him. *I will choose now.*

Scenes reshuffled in his mind's eye. Hastings. Nix. The campsite.

The Russians.

'Shit.' He tried to sit up. 'Where's Okeke? Where's Jason?'

Emma put a hand on his shoulder reassuringly. 'She's at home, Dad. Jay's at... Well, I guess he's finished work and back at home too now.'

The confusion was sorting itself out. Events slotted back into their correct order.

Julia and Noah had died nearly three years ago.

Boyd turned to his daughter. 'What happened?'

'The doctor said you suffered a concussion,' she replied. 'They wanted you to stay in for a few hours so they could keep an eye on you.'

'No. I mean, after the campsite.'

She lifted a finger to her lips to indicate his voice was getting a tad too loud. 'You don't remember?'

He shook his head, which only made him groan. 'The last thing I recall is Jason doing a Vin Diesel impersonation behind the wheel.'

'You mean Jay?'

Oh, that's right. Jay. He'd reminded Boyd of Jason Statham. 'He was driving us backwards.'

'And nearly crashed right into us,' Emma added.

'You came to get us?'

She nodded.

He was suddenly furious, 'For fuck's –'

She gently shushed him; he was getting louder again.

'We got away. No one was hurt.' She pursed her lips. 'Apart from you.'

'What about Nix? What happened to him?'

She shook her head. 'Something at the campsite.'

'What?'

The curtain suddenly swished aside and balding male nurse stuck his head in. 'How're you feeling?'

'Groggy.'

'I'm not surprised. Any whiplash pains in your neck or spine, Mr Boyd?'

Boyd frowned. Emma answered for him. 'No, he's fine.' She looked back at her father. 'It wasn't that big a prang in the car, was it, Dad?'

Ahhh... Okay. He was up to speed. 'No. I'm thirsty, though.'

'No problem. I'll get you some water.' Then he was gone.

'I see what you did there,' he wheezed.

'That was *your* story, Dad,' she replied. 'You said to say we had a prang in the car.'

He didn't remember saying that. So not completely fine yet, then. 'You were telling me... something's happened?'

'There was a big fire. At that campsite.'

'*What?*'

She nodded. 'It was on *BBC South East*. Dozens and dozens of those trailers on fire.'

'What about –' He lowered his voice. 'What about the Russians? What about Nix?'

She shook her head and shrugged.

'Where's Okeke?'

'You asked me that already, Dad. She's at home.'

'Where's Ozzie?'

Emma smiled. 'Aww, so you *do* love him. He's at home, obviously. But I rang him and he said to send you a lick!'

Boyd smiled. 'Okay. All good. Everyone's good. Great.'

He closed his eyes, let his head sink back into the pillow and allowed himself to drift into a fitful sleep.

AT 7 A.M. when the A&E shift changed over, a doctor came in to give Boyd a quick examination. 'That's a nasty bang on your forehead,' he said, teasing the dressing aside to look at the stitches between his brows. 'Airbag?' he asked.

Boyd decided it would be imprudent to tell him it had been the barrel of some Russian hitman's gun. He shrugged. 'Maybe the steering wheel.'

'You'll need to return to outpatients to have those stitches removed in a few days,' he said.

Boyd wasn't sure if he was talking about the ear stitches or if there were new ones hidden beneath his bandage-turban. He didn't like to ask.

Emma called a local taxi company and by eight they were back outside their house.

'Poor, poor Ozzie,' muttered Emma as she fumbled in her bag for the front-door key. 'He's been stuck indoors since yesterday teatime.'

'Great,' said Boyd. 'There'll be protest craps all over the place.'

'Well, don't get angry at him. It's not his fault.' She peered through the letterbox. 'Ozzie?'

That should surely have drawn him clattering along the

hallway floor to the front door. But there was no sound. She straightened up and carried on rummaging in her bag.

Boyd ducked down and tried the same thing. 'Ozzie boy! You there?'

No response.

'Ah!' said Emma. She produced the jangling keys, jammed one into the lock and turned it.

The door creaked open.

'Ozzie?' she tried again.

Boyd suddenly felt a twinge of concern. 'Stay right there, Em.' He took a few steps forward and pushed the study door inwards. 'Ozzie?' he called tentatively.

He wasn't there. There was no poo on the floor either.

Boyd took another couple of steps down the hall, then stuck his head into the lounge.

No sign of the dog.

'Ozzie?' he said more loudly, hoping it might provoke the bleary-eyed idiot to trot out of the dining room. He quickly checked both dining room and kitchen. With a growing sense of dread, he called up the stairs.

'Ozzie! We're home!'

They both heard it.

A single gentle thump from above. The hallway ceiling creaked as something moved slowly across the floor of the front bedroom.

Shit. The thought had been there at the back of his mind since they'd left the hospital. *If they found Nix, they can find me.*

And of course *they* weren't just a couple of local scrotes. They were pros. Quite possibly ex-KGB/GRU – at least the older one might have been.

The ceiling creaked again, then, finally, between the bannister support struts above he saw Ozzie's twitching wet nostrils poking through.

Thank God.

'Ozzie?'

He seemed reluctant to come down.

'Come on, mate.'

Ozzie let out a solitary whimper in response.

'Dad? Is he okay?'

'Yeah. He's fine, love,' Boyd answered as he started up the stairs, not entirely sure what the problem was. At the top he rounded the balustrade and approached the dog.

Ozzie's tail thudded against the floor. He was giving Boyd serious side-eyes, not quite able to look him in the face.

'What is it, mate?' Boyd asked gently.

Ozzie doubled down on the side-eyes. He licked his lips. His tail thumped. Both of them stress responses, Emma had informed Boyd days ago. Both signs of a deeply troubled, possibly traumatized animal.

Boyd had a premonition that there'd be something waiting for him in the front bedroom. A message. A warning.

We know where you live.

He pushed the door of his bedroom inwards.

'Oh, shit.'

He was right. The message was loud and clear.

Ozzie had left a protest crap, balanced like a piece of installation art, right in the middle of one of his pillows.

47

Okeke and Jay arrived shortly after with McMuffins and hash browns for breakfast.

As they sat around the dining table, nursing mugs of tea and passing the bottle of ketchup, Okeke updated them all on last night's news about the campsite fire.

'It was the Russians. About a third of the trailers were burned down. Jay took you and Emma to the hospital and I waited in the van. When backup arrived, I told them I'd been driving past, seen the flames and heard gunshots. They're saying it was probably arson. They think a butane canister might have been set off and that was the gunshot I thought I'd heard.' She rolled her eyes. 'Because of the steady wind fanning the flames and the close proximity of the caravans, they just caught fire and went up one after the other.'

'My God,' said Emma.

'Apparently it took five fire crews to put it all out,' said Jay.

Boyd grimaced. 'Any bodies?'

Okeke nodded slowly. 'They found one. They're going through the site and searching in case there are any more. At the moment they're saying it's probably a homeless person.'

Boyd very much wanted to believe it was one of the hitmen, but he suspected not. 'So probably Nix.' He shook his head. 'They must have found him.'

'Jesus,' whispered Jay. 'What do you reckon they did to him?'

Boyd glared across at him, shutting him down and shooting a quick glance at his daughter. Luckily Emma missed it; she was busy feeding Ozzie her hash brown. 'Not much, Jay, given the time they had. But they did what they came to do. They found him and executed him. Job done.'

Emma looked up. 'They murdered him?' She looked ashen.

Boyd nodded. 'That's what this was all about. Punishing him and shutting him up. It's all over, Ems. I suspect they've been watching me, in case Nix reached out to me.' Boyd shook his head. 'So basically I did exactly what they wanted me to do. I led them straight to him.'

'But what does that mean for us?' Emma asked.

'Nothing,' Boyd said. 'It means they've got a chunk of their money over here now and they've silenced the man who helped them do that. They'll buy some nice London property, several racehorses and a few cabinet ministers; they'll join polite society and live happily ever after.'

Okeke nodded. 'That sounds about right.'

'It is what it is,' Boyd added. 'Sometimes the bad guys win.'

'What about you, Dad? They were following you, and you and Jay half killed one of them!'

'If it was important to them to have me dead, I'd be dead already.' He could see his daughter's mind was spinning through unsettling scenarios.

'It's over, Ems. I promise. They got Nix. Papa Salikov got his revenge and saved face, and tidied up a loose end. It's done.'

'You think they'll try and find someone else to carry on laundering their money?' asked Okeke.

'I'm sure they already have. It's no different to smuggling

drugs; you need alternative routes – built-in redundancies in case one avenue gets shut down. Nix told me he'd wanted out. Well, I guess he got his wish.'

'Jesus,' whispered Emma.

She looked from him to Okeke. 'Dad?' she asked. 'How are you going to square this with work?'

Boyd looked at Okeke, trying to read her expression. 'I think we should keep this to ourselves,' he said eventually.

His colleague looked relieved. 'Too right! I've not worked my arse off to have my career go tits up now!'

Jay huffed. 'God, this really is like TV.'

Okeke shut him up with a glare. 'I'll say I'd found the tac vest in the canteen and just hadn't had time to sign it back in. They already think it was kids who started the fire.'

'I don't think Her Madge will want anything investigating that takes away from her migrant theory,' Boyd added.

Emma looked shocked. 'So neither of you are going to tell *anyone*?'

They looked at each other. 'This is something we both need to agree on, Okeke,' Boyd said.

'They came for Nix,' she said. 'I don't think they'd think twice about coming for us. We're just the little people, guv. Let's not be *inconvenient* little people, eh?'

'You're right,' Boyd said. 'It's shit, but I'll be honest – this is just a job for me now. I'm working it until I get to retire, that's all. I'm not a crusader.'

Feigning ignorance. That was the smart choice.

Okeke nodded. 'Okay.'

Boyd looked at Emma. 'I should never have let you get involved,' he said.

'Dad.' She raised her hands. 'I'm not involved. I know nothing. I –' she shook her head – 'I don't know what you're talking about.'

'Good,' he said. 'Well, let's keep it that way.'

48

The post-Sunday lunch walk seemed to have become a firm part of his weekly routine. The long route from East Hill down to the Rock-a-Nore cove, then along the beach towards the pier and back home. It was a good two-hour-walk during which Boyd could decompress, unpack his thoughts and file them tidily away.

And he had a lot to pick over. A week had passed and so far there had been no consequences. The investigation into the fire at Sea Breeze Campsite had been passed from the police to the fire service. The fire itself and the body found in the trailer had become the tragic story. Local kids with nothing better to do, and a body so badly burned that there was no possibility of identification. A local councillor had talked about lessons needing to be learned, how more needed to be done to engage the local teenagers. And that led to a discussion about the many closed-down campsites along the south coast. That they shouldn't be allowed to fall to rack and ruin, and should instead be put to good use or cleared out, and not left to become festering fire hazards.

Boyd had dialled in an extra week of sick leave and received a Get Well Soon card from the CID team.

Even Hatcher had signed it.

He realised he wasn't ready to lose his job or be put out to pasture. He needed the make-busy. He needed to be back in a noisy office, dealing with mundane crimes, filing local criminal intelligence tidbits and rubbing along with other human beings.

Emma had been quite right that there was life after loss. She hadn't put it as succinctly as that, but that had been her guiding instinct through it all. And, to be honest, getting Ozzie had been another good idea of hers. Not a puppy – everybody went for puppies – but another old-ish bugger, like himself, who deserved to have a second crack at life.

Speaking of Ozzie... Boyd looked around. 'Oz?'

He'd absentmindedly unclipped the lead from Ozzie's harness so that he could go carry out some investigative door-to-doors among the overturned hulls of the fishing boats and the bric-a-brac of discarded tackle.

'Ozzie!' he called again.

The dog casually emerged from behind a boat, making his way towards Boyd with an *I'll come when I'm done* expression on his face.

Then a figure emerged from the side of the hull, taking Boyd by surprise.

It was a slight figure with a hood up, its face hidden in shadow.

The hooded figure approached, holding something out towards him. It was small, black, sack-like.

The hood was pushed back; it was that woman who'd busted him over poo-gate a week ago.

At arm's length, she held the small bag by the knot she'd tied at the top. 'It's even more gross when it's not your own dog's,' she said, pulling a face.

He took it from her apologetically. 'Thank you. I lost sight of him. I'm really sorry about that,' he said, with what he hoped was a disarming smile.

'So you should be,' she scolded him, but not unkindly. 'Kids play here, remember. I told you last time.'

He nodded. 'Right. Yes, I'll be more mindful.'

She narrowed her eyes. 'You're that policeman, aren't you? The one they had to bleep out?'

Christ.

'I saw you on Facebook. Somebody uploaded a video.' She smiled. 'I don't know what you said, but it was quite funny watching the expressions on the faces of the officers behind you.'

'It wasn't that bad a word,' he said. 'I just –'

She raised hand. 'I don't need to know, thanks.'

'Right. Sorry.'

'You're a local celebrity,' she said, chuckling. Then her face straightened. 'Oh.'

She nodded past him. 'Look out.'

'What?'

She pointed. 'He's crapping again.'

49

Chief Superintendent Margaret Hatcher looked up from her laptop screen.

'Ah, take a seat, Boyd.'

'Thank you, ma'am.'

He sat down and waited for her to finish pecking out an email. He heard the soft *woosh* as she sent it on its way.

'So, here we are, then,' she said as she lowered the laptop's lid and pushed it to one side. 'How are you feeling now? Better, I hope.'

'Yes, much better,' Boyd replied. 'Ready to get back to work.'

'Good. You really have had an unfortunate start here, haven't you? All those lumps and bumps to your head?'

He sighed. 'Luckily I have a pretty thick skull.'

She nodded and smiled. 'Yes, I think you probably do.' She sat back in her chair. 'Maybe there was too much confusion in the Nix case. A little too much to throw at you straight away after so much time off.'

'Maybe,' he replied. There was a tone to her voice that he couldn't unpick. 'It was a bit of a messy case, ma'am.'

She narrowed her eyes. 'Indeed,' she replied slowly. 'Very messy.'

What was going on here? He had the distinct impression that they were talking about one thing but pulling faces about another.

'You've been updated by DCI Flack?' she asked.

Boyd nodded. 'Yes, ma'am. It was a migrant-trafficking incident that went wrong. Just like you said.'

She shot him a tight smile. 'Border Force say Nix's finances have been forensically examined. It seems he was struggling with quite a few rather nasty gambling debts. And dealing with some very unpleasant types.'

Is she fishing? Is she testing to see if I'm going to query anything? He couldn't tell. He decided that playing dumb remained his best option. 'Right.'

'CPS reckon Rigby will get at least three years inside for assaulting you, Boyd. And probably another couple for the counterfeit drugs business he was running.'

'Good. That's a good result.'

'Well, anyway.' Her lips tightened into a perfunctory smile. 'I don't suppose we'll ever really know what happened out there in the Channel, will we?'

'No, ma'am.'

'So, it's time to start over and put this one behind us. Do you feel ready to start over, DCI Boyd?'

He was damned if he was going to give her a *Yes, ma'am* to that. Instead, he let his brows arch upwards. They sat like that for a solid ten seconds: Boyd with his raised brows, Her Madge challenging him with a direct stare over the rim of her half-moon lenses.

'You know, Boyd,' she said eventually, 'this country's an island once again. We're on our own now. We really do all need to pull together.'

She let that hang in the air for a moment, almost daring him to comment.

Finally he nodded. *Keep your enemies close...*

'Well, good,' she said. 'It's good to have you back on board, Boyd.' She gestured towards the door. 'Now, off you fuck.'

50

Boyd's first week back had been uneventful. In fact, exactly what he'd been hoping for a fortnight ago – an easy settling period with nothing more taxing than HR paperwork and a few bite-size cases involving simple checks on the computer system, and a couple of no-comment interviews thrown in.

On Friday lunchtime he decided to wander down to the pier and grab a bag of chips and a coffee at the café. He met Okeke and Minter waiting in the queue and they exchanged some idle banter about the previous night's crime log.

A septuagenarian idiot with a rusty old Saxon sword and a Union Jack shawl had been terrorising Warrior Square over at St Leonards, waggling his sword around and threatening the alcoholics and drug addicts in the gardens. Fortunately there hadn't been any injuries, just a lot of colourful language peppered with a barrage of old-school racism.

When he arrived back home that evening, Boyd found a note from Emma on the dining-room table.

Got asked out on a date!!

With that guy in the Olde Pump House. The one who wanted the selfie!

Your dinner's in Chef Mike. It's yesterday's roast leftovers.

Ozzie's been fed, walked and pooped.

Be back later.

Love, Ems xx

He smiled. He remembered the floppy-haired doofus down at Ye Olde Pump House. He seemed harmless enough. At least he wasn't covered in tattoos and piercings.

The doorbell rang, and Ozzie responded with a series of barks that echoed through the hallway.

Boyd shut Ozzie in the dining room – he was getting pretty territorial and feisty when it came to *his home* – and switched on the hallway light. Through the frosted glass of the front door, he could just make out the red jacket of a DPD courier. The man waved, pointed down and disappeared.

Boyd opened the door to find a small parcel on the doorstep. 'Cheers mate!' he shouted as the courier climbed back into his van and drove off.

He bent down and picked up the parcel, pretty sure he hadn't ordered anything recently. It must be for Emma, he decided. He'd been too busy adding the finishing touches to his study, putting up shelves and setting out his DVD collection. Not in alphabetical order – that would be too sad – but just tidy-looking.

He looked at the label. The parcel was addressed to him: W. Boyd.

Maybe he *had* ordered something. It was all too easily done with one-click buys these days.

He closed the front door behind him and went back to the dining room. He grabbed a pair of scissors from the cutlery drawer, sliced open the packing tape and opened the lid of the plain brown cardboard box.

Inside was a note atop a bed of polystyrene packing chips. He unfolded it to reveal a very short, hastily scribbled message.

Boyd -
Nix – no more. Stay away. Stay silence.
:)

He felt his skin go cold, goosebumps covering his arms, and his stomach flipped over. He spotted a dark dot of blood on one of the packing chips and then another. Like stars in the sky, once you notice one, you see them all.

He stared at the small cardboard box in front of him, unwilling to dig into the packing chips to see what was waiting at the bottom for him... yet knowing it had to be done.

He carefully started picking them out and then saw what it was the Russians had sent as a parting gift.

'Oh, shit...'

THE END

DCI BOYD RETURNS IN…

Old BONES, NEW BONES available to pre-order here

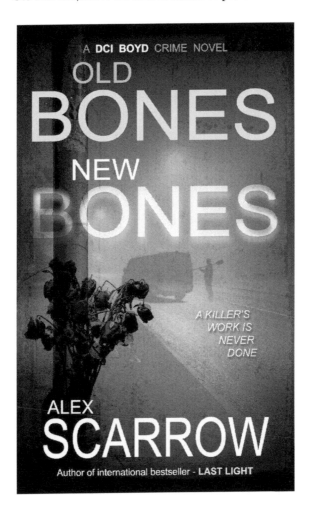

ACKNOWLEDGMENTS

A big round of applause for the following folks, some of whom know they're in Team Boyd, and some who don't.

First of all, to Debbie Scarrow, my better half and outsourced brain. I come up with ideas that one might laughingly call a 'story', but Debbie bashes them into something far better – a plot.

Wendy Shakespeare for her excellent copy-editing and advice in turning this story into a proper grown-up book. She spares my blushes many times over.

Maureen Webb, Samantha Leatherland and Lesley Lloyd for their help, advice and their eagle-eyed proofreading of the ARC.

I'd like to thank the admins and members of the Facebook group UK Crime Book Club. They are an incredibly lovely and very knowledgeable bunch of people to whom I have frequently turned for advice. Special shout-out to Kath Middleton (group admin) who allowed me to gate-crash the group and ask scattershot questions in all directions.

I'd also like to thank the Crime Collective. You know who you are.

And finally, my heartfelt thanks go to Spaniel Aid UK – for allowing us to adopt our adorable boy Ozzie in 2017. He's as much our dog as he is DCI Boyd's dog.

If you would like to know more about Spaniel Aid UK and the work they do please visit their website. www.spanielaid. co.uk

ALSO BY ALEX SCARROW

LAST LIGHT

AFTERLIGHT

OCTOBER SKIES

THE CANDLEMAN

A THOUSAND SUNS

The TimeRiders series (in reading order)

TIMERIDERS

TIMERIDERS: DAY OF THE PREDATOR

TIMERIDERS: THE DOOMSDAY CODE

TIMERIDERS: THE ETERNAL WAR

TIMERIDERS: THE CITY OF SHADOWS

TIMERIDERS: THE PIRATE KINGS

TIMERIDERS: THE MAYAN PROPHECY

TIMERIDERS: THE INFINITY CAGE

The Plague Land series: Plague Land

PLAGUE NATION

PLAGUE WORLD

The Ellie Quin series

THE LEGEND OF ELLIE QUIN

THE WORLD ACCORDING TO ELLIE QUIN

ABOUT THE AUTHOR

Over the last sixteen years, award-winning author Alex Scarrow has published seventeen novels with Penguin Random House, Orion and Pan Macmillan. A number of these have been optioned for film/TV development, including his best-selling *Last Light*.

When he is not busy writing and painting, Alex spends most of his time trying to keep Ozzie away from the food bin. He lives in the wilds of East Anglia with his wife Deborah and four, permanently muddy, dogs.

Ozzie came to live with him in January 2017. He was adopted from Spaniel Aid UK and was believed to be seven at the time. Ozzie loves food, his mum, food, his ball, food, walks and more food...

He dreams of unrestricted access to the food bin.

For up-to-date information on the DCI BOYD series, visit: www.alexscarrow.com

Printed in Great Britain
by Amazon